I0546582

HUNTRESS UNLEASHED

HEART OF THE HUNTRESS
BOOK 7

TERRY SPEAR

PUBLISHED BY:

Wilde Ink Publishing

Huntress Unleashed

Copyright © 2024 by Terry Spear

Cover Copyright by

All rights reserved. No part of this book may be reproduced or transmitted in any form or by any means, electronic or mechanical, including photocopying, recording, or by any information storage and retrieval system, without written permission from the author, except for the inclusion of brief quotations in a review.

Discover more about Terry Spear at:

http://www.terryspear.com/

Print ISBN: 978-1-63311-101-1

Ebook ISBN: 978-1-63311-100-4

To lovely Laura Apodaca Gonzalez who has been waiting patiently for two years for me to write Book 7 of the Heart of the Huntress series. This one is dedicated to you.

HUNTRESS UNLEASHED SYNOPSIS

Dane hunts down rogue vampires and is on a mission when he is ambushed and pays the price. Jacqueline Anderson also hunts rogue vampires, loses to a vampire, and fights her attraction to the hunter when she has her own demons to battle. For the two of them, they've lost friends and gained new ones, but they're ready to right some wrongs while they're being targeted by hunters who should be on their side.

It's kill or be killed. Jacqueline is determined not to fall for Dane while he's head over heels over her and ready to take this further. But they also have to take care of the threat that's aimed just at them and others like them and learn just who set him up to be ambushed in the first place. Time is running out before those who want them dead manage to get their way.

PROLOGUE

On edge after having another disagreement with Wendy, his fiancée, over finances, Dane Edmonton arrived at the popular Wilding Club, a vampire club, late that night in a Dallas, Texas suburb where Lucilla, a rogue vampire, often visited. He watched the establishment, waiting for her to leave. He was sitting in his black pickup, the rain coming down hard on the windshield as he conducted surveillance of the red brick building, disco lights flashing through the windows. Vampires and blood bonds were mostly going inside. Occasionally, a couple of people would leave the club.

The police had verified that Lucilla was killing homeless men, and as a hunter assigned to the case, it was Dane's job to eliminate her. She was known to often have a couple of male vampires with her, but his informant, only known as Green—a blood bond that Lucilla sometimes fed off—had said she was leaving the Wilding Club—going downtown alone again tonight, just before midnight. When she went alone, it meant she was hunting prey.

The blood bond also was an informant to four other hunters—Van Olson, Moose Warner, and cousins, Flynn and Felix Freeburg

—but Green swore he always shared information with Dane first, when he knew a rogue vampire needed to be taken down.

Yet, Green had seemed more nervous than usual. Maybe the vampiress had learned he was an informant, and he was afraid she would kill him. Dane could certainly understand Green's concern.

Then Dane saw Lucilla leave the vampire club and head downtown alone in her black Nissan coupe. He knew he had his chance to eliminate her without any interference from her friends. She was evil to the core and until a hunter terminated her, she would continue to prey on the innocent.

Most vampires paid for a blood bond's blood, a mutually acceptable arrangement between humans and vampires, but she liked to hunt for potential victims too.

Dane assumed she was going to target someone downtown where her other victims had been, and he had to stop her before she murdered anyone else. He parked his black pickup down the street from where she cut her car's engine. She was wearing a long flowing black gown as if she was going to a formal ball, but it made him think of a large black raven, fluttering its wings when it went to kill a small mammal. In her case, a male who lived on the streets.

The police department had hired him to eliminate her, paying the usual bounty that hunters received for taking down menacing rogue vampires. Humans within the police department couldn't successfully deal with the bad vampires, normally. Though there were some Van Helsing human hunter types who took on the missions and risked their necks in this life-or-death business. They didn't have the superior strength that hunters and vampires had, so they were truly at a disadvantage. But they wanted the money and loved to live dangerously. More power to them, Dane figured.

Some hunters did serve as homicide detectives in some police departments. But most police departments hired hunters to do their dirty work because most hunters didn't want to do anything but work for bounties. As homicide detectives, they would have to work other kinds of cases, not just rogue vampire-related ones.

Lucilla spoke with a woman sitting next to a grocery cart stacked full of her treasured possessions. If she attempted to kill the woman, she would be changing her MO. She had only killed men in the past. Any age, race, it didn't matter. She didn't discriminate, except that she didn't target women.

Dane was following her, his sword out, keeping to the shadows, making sure she didn't hear or see him approaching. The vampire's hearing was as good as a hunter's, and hunters were just as stealthy as a vampire. And they had the same kind of strength, healing up quickly from injuries suffered.

She had to know she would be on a list for termination. Unless she was so arrogant that she thought no one knew who was killing the homeless men.

Then she slipped into a dilapidated building, and he hurried after her, afraid he was going to lose her. As soon as he did, two male vampires hiding in the darkness attacked Dane. Damn, he hadn't expected that.

Worried that he would alert Lucilla that he was after her, he swung his sword at one of the vampires, and the other cut him in the shoulder. *Hell.* He ignored that vampire because the one in front of him was defending himself and wasn't as good a fighter. Dane suspected he might have been more newly turned. Dane quickly penetrated the vampire's heart and swung around to fight the other vampire who was just trying to strike him again. Dane slammed his sword into the vampire's sword, sweeping it away, nearly making the dark-haired vampire lose it. The vampire quickly lost his composure, his jaw dropped, his blue eyes wide. What did he think? Just because he cut the hunter once, he would win the battle?

The vampire tried to recover, but he couldn't swing his sword around fast enough before Dane attacked and killed him with a sword to the heart. Both vampires had dropped to the ground when they were mortally wounded and remained in the same physical state as when they were alive—so they were more newly turned. Ancient vampires would turn to dust when they died.

But where was Lucilla? That's when two more male vampires came after Dane and Lucilla made her appearance. She had blood on her mouth and Dane was certain she'd found her victim. She didn't look surprised to see him and he figured she'd lured him here to his death. The male vampires attacked, and he was fighting from one to the other when she suddenly was behind Dane and bit him on the right side of the neck. For a moment in time, he wondered if his informant had known that this was a setup.

He expected Lucilla to drain him dry like she did with her victims, though he was trying to shake her loose, while swinging his sword at the male attackers. Yet they *weren't* going in for a kill. No, they were working with Lucilla to keep him under control. He sliced at one of the vampires, cutting his arm, and he howled. His dark brown eyes turned nearly black, and he tried to cut Dane this time, even if it wasn't what Lucilla wanted. Then to Dane's horror, he was afraid she meant to just turn him. He was trying to fight back, his vision blurring, his strength waning when she released him and he sank to his knees, trying to rally his strength, knowing if he didn't, he was going to die. He smelled her blood then as she bit into her arm and the males held Dane's arms while she pressed her bloody wound against Dane's mouth. He shook his head, trying to get away from her, knowing that if he tasted her blood, the mutual exchange would have been made.

One of the vampires reached over and pulled his chin down and Dane tasted Lucilla's blood. "You're here because a hunter you know made it happen and so did someone close to you."

"Who?" He had to know which hunter would set him up. And who was close to him who would do this horrible deed. Green? His informant?

Dane was doomed. He couldn't kill her. She had turned him. And now he was going to be a hunter turned, owing allegiance to the vampiress. He would rather have died in the battle between good and evil this night.

Worse, she wouldn't tell him who the hunter or the other person was who had sabotaged his career, his life, and turned his world inside out.

JACQUELINE ANDERSON HAD THOUGHT the mission she was going on would be easy. The vampire was known to eliminate blood bonds he had recruited after they riled him. She often didn't know why the vampire who she was hired to eliminate went rogue or targeted some type of person. But in his case, the trigger seemed to be when the blood bond refused to do anything for Moulson, and then in his eyes, they became disposable. Once they had become one of his blood bonds, he owned them.

He often recruited blood bonds at a human club, so she'd been staking it out for nights until she finally saw him. He left the building at two in the morning, wearing black boots, a black satin shirt, and blue jeans, leading two new potential blood bonds outside on the rainy Dallas night that spring. The two men looked like they were in their mid-twenties, wearing jeans, sneakers, and T-shirts. She didn't know when Moulson would snap and kill the blood bonds, so she didn't want to leave him with them for any length of time and discover he'd left more victims in his wake.

He got into his van and the potential blood bonds hesitated. Not a good idea when faced with a short-fused vampire. Then they reluctantly got in.

She started her car but didn't follow Moulson. She knew where his house was located, and he always went there after he visited a club. Before he arrived at his Spanish style estate, she was waiting curbside at a house down the street. She saw his van drive past her vehicle, a black sedan, and then he parked inside the garage. The two humans and the vampire left the van. He told them to enter the house. He was hostile, probably still annoyed because they hadn't gotten into the van right away near the club. Anything would set him off.

These guys were already in trouble.

Jacqueline got out of her car while the three of them went into the house, the garage door still open. She rushed toward the open garage and slipped inside and hid behind the van when the door leading into the garage opened, and someone pushed the button to close the garage door.

She studied the shoes of the wearer. White sneakers. It was one of the humans. As soon as he shut the door to the house—glad it didn't squeak—she moved quickly to that door and listened. She heard voices deeper in the house, and with her sword out, she quietly opened the door. Thankfully, it wasn't locked though she had a lockpick she could have used too but it might have alerted the vampire that she was trying to gain entry into the house.

She entered the house and saw that the short hallway was clear. She carefully closed the door to the garage. A laundry room was off to the left, the door open to it, and then the hall opened to another hallway. The voices were off to the right. Before she could make a move to eliminate Moulson, a knock at the front door made her heart skip a bit.

Now what? Please be a pizza delivery, not another vampire. She never knew how blood bonds would react either. They usually left the fight to the vampires and the hunters, but sometimes they were so loyal—or brainwashed, they would fight on the vampire's behalf.

She ducked into the laundry room off the short hall as she heard footfalls—one person—heading for the door. She so wanted to peek to see who it was—Moulson or one of the blood bonds—but she was afraid she would be caught at it.

Still, if the person at the door was another vampire, she could be in trouble. One could be hard enough to take down on her own.

She made the decision, good or bad, and checked to see who it was. It was Moulson. But she couldn't trust that the person at the door was someone like an innocuous delivery guy and not a vampire. She quickly moved to take Moulson out, praying that the blood bonds wouldn't come to his aid. She couldn't look and see how they were reacting, but at least they were quiet and didn't alert the vampire. Maybe they didn't really want to be his blood bonds after all.

Moulson whipped around when he spied her move in behind him. It was too much to ask for that she could just swing her sword and take his head. She tried, but he leapt at her with a vampire's flying leap and hit her with such an impact that he knocked her flat on her back on the marble tile floor. Not a good position to be in for a hunter who was fighting a powerful vampire. She couldn't use her sword in such close quarters and instead, she yanked a dagger out of its sheath and cut into his chest. But she didn't reach the vampire's heart. *Damn it.*

He screamed in pain and anger. "Open the front door," Moulson said to the humans, but neither moved from wherever they stood, maybe afraid if she killed the vampire, she would take them out next.

When Moulson turned his head to growl at the humans again to make them do his bidding, he made a fatal mistake. She stabbed the vampire in the heart, and he looked shocked right before he disintegrated on top of her. An ancient vampire, arrogantly believing the huntress he'd taken down was done for the count.

Then the front door burst open and a man—who looked like Moulson—saw Jacqueline getting off the floor, throwing aside Moulson's clothed, wizened body. He appeared aghast. *Oh, no.* This man looked like Moulson's twin brother. Even though she didn't know he had one. And she hadn't been hired to kill him, though if he attacked her, she had every right to defend herself because she had been in the right where Moulson was concerned.

Like Moulson, this guy swooped in, and it appeared that he was planning on using the same maneuver, plowing her down and forcing her onto her back. But she quickly sidestepped him and being ambidextrous, she swung her sword with her right hand, cutting him in the arm, her dagger still ready in her left hand and she cut into his chest, but nothing fatal. It only made him angrier.

The two humans—appearing to think this was the time to make their escape before whoever was the victor decided their fate— dashed for the front door, still standing wide open. They stumbled over each other, trying to get around Jacqueline and the vampire, hoping to avoid the fight. But as she moved back to get her stance to thrust her sword at the vampire and strike his heart this time, they bumped into her and threw her off balance completely. It was time enough to give the vampire the advantage. He grabbed her shoulders and rammed her against the wall, then bit into her shoulder before she could stab him with her dagger.

"No...no...no...no...no." She tried to pull free from the vampire's vicious bite. She attempted to stab him in the heart with her dagger while he was drinking her blood, but she was losing too much blood, and she was afraid she would pass out soon.

The next thing she knew, she was on the floor, coming to, tasting blood in her mouth—his blood—and she knew that the exchange had been made. She was no longer just a huntress, but one of them. A vampire. Worse, she couldn't kill the one who made her no matter how much she wanted to. And then he smirked at her and vanished.

1

A week later
In the pouring rain, Jacqueline Anderson stalked across the cracked asphalt parking lot to a red brick building where Hunters turned by Vampires Group Therapy was meeting in Dallas, Texas—not that she wanted to go to it at all. No other vehicles were there yet, and she was hoping no one was coming. She had a list of five rogue vampires to eliminate, and she felt this was a total waste of time.

The brick building looked like it had seen better days, the asphalt shingle roof sagging, moss and ivy growing all over the red brick walls, the door needing to be sanded and revarnished. Inside, one of the rooms was serving as the meeting place for the therapy group. She wouldn't be here if it wasn't for her parents and brother forcing her to do this. They were hunters still and they believed after she was bitten and turned, she was living on the edge—taking risks she could ill afford, going after rogues without a hunter partner to back her up, working all hours of the day and night and not taking time to rest. She was a ticking timebomb some hunters said. Rogue vampires had given her the tag that she was the huntress unleashed. Which truthfully, she didn't mind at all. Though it could make her more of a rogue vampire target.

She considered the look of the building again. She'd learned Anne Struthers had purchased it after she was turned a month ago —the building standing idle after the ring of rogue vampires who had owned it had been terminated thirty years ago and no one had wanted to own the building since, some saying it was cursed.

Jacqueline didn't believe in curses or ghosts, like she suspected Anne didn't, and opened the door and headed inside, brushing wet strands of hair off her cheek. She headed down the hall past empty rooms. She stepped into room five and observed the mostly bare walls, a clock hanging on one, but only shadows remained where framed pictures had been removed. Plastic chairs had been hastily thrown together in a circle, so it appeared. It looked like a place for members of an Alcoholic Anonymous group to meet, except that this was a meeting place—first meeting ever for a group of hunters who hunted rogue vampires down for the murderous killing of innocents or turning innocents into vampires so they would be at their beck and call. But these hunters had been turned by such rogue vampires and were now considered hunters turned.

Jacqueline smelled stale coffee, nothing freshly brewing in the coffee pot on a table against one wall. It looked like it had seen better days—grimy, a can of coffee, and a half-crushed box of filters sitting next to it. At least the coffee can wasn't rusty.

She pulled off her rain jacket on the bleak March day where the sunlight hadn't shown in four days and wind and rain had sent the temperatures dropping. She wondered what the vampires had used this building for before they were terminated, and the place fell into disrepair.

And where everyone was! She had to be early—always. She glanced at the clock, and it said she was two hours late. She glanced at her watch and sighed. The clock on the wall was wrong. *Natu-*

rally. She hung her rain jacket on the back of one of the chairs and then did stretches in the form of sword practice.

She heard the main door shut that she'd walked through a little earlier and stiffened. She really didn't want to be here, exposing her feelings to a bunch of strangers. But they would be like her, wouldn't they? Their worlds turned upside down because they had viciously been attacked by a rogue vampire and turned.

She listened to the footfalls of the person walking down the hall, like a good hunter always did—on edge, watching for someone to initiate an attack. She couldn't tell if it was a man or a woman. If they ended up with hunter turned vampire sponsors, they better be of the same sex. Unless the hunter was gay and then they had to have a sponsor of the opposite sex. That was to keep the therapy on a professional level and for it not to turn into a sexual relationship. At least she hoped it was like AA meetings in that regard.

Not that she'd attended them for herself, but she'd had a human friend who'd needed them for her own sobriety and had told her what the protocol had been.

A woman walked into the room looking wetter and more haggard than Jacqueline even. She was about thirty, her curly blond hair hanging over her shoulders, wet, spots of water on her raincoat. She was wearing nice slacks, boots, and when she pulled off her coat, a sweater featuring a butterfly. "Sorry. I'm Anne Struthers. I set this group up and didn't mean to be late. Six others are coming, but one is having trouble finding a sitter for her baby girl. One is on a job on Sixteenth Street"—which meant she or he was probably tracking a rogue vampire—"and said he would be here if he finished the job before the meeting was over. The others, I'm not sure about. I wasn't able to get a hold of them to confirm they were coming."

"You organized this?"

"Yeah. You know how it is for things like this. It's all so new.

We're the first group like it in all of Texas. It might be a while before we get real active participation. I'm excited about it. Though I can see how most might feel reluctant to share their stories. At least at first. So what do you want to do? Have a one-on-one meeting between us and if others show up late, they can join in? Or should we skip it and try for next week when more can come?"

In truth, Jacqueline was ready to keep her story to herself. Most likely no one could think her story was all that traumatic. She did like Anne though. She was outgoing and organized. Jacqueline admired her for it. And she felt she owed it to Anne for setting up the meeting in the first place. Maybe Jacqueline would feel better if she spoke with someone who was like her now.

"We can have the meeting, just you and I." Then it wouldn't be a wasted trip out here. The five vampires that she needed to track down were on the other side of town so she wasn't even close to where she needed to be. And she needed to do it before they learned she was the one hired to take them down. At least they were individuals, not working together in their criminal enterprises.

"Sure, great. Let's take a seat then. Okay, so unless you want to talk, I'll go first," Anne said.

"Yeah, sure, go ahead." With just the two of them there, Jacqueline felt more comfortable with the notion of sharing how she was feeling about all the changes in her life. But then she wondered about the huntress and her baby. "Oh, what's the situation with the woman with the baby? Had the mother been turned while she was pregnant? Is the baby a mix of hunter and vampire, or just a hunter, if born before the mother was turned?"

"Doreen's baby was born before she was turned. The baby is nearly a year old. So the baby is a hunter, not a vampire mix."

"Wow, that's scary."

"Yeah. She said when her daughter is an adult, it would be her choice if she wanted to be turned or remain a hunter."

"Oh, sure." Jacqueline just couldn't imagine a situation like that. "What about the baby's daddy?"

"He's out of the picture."

Maybe if he hadn't been "out of the picture," the huntress wouldn't have been turned.

Jacqueline and Anne took seats opposite each other, but then heard footfalls headed their way.

Jacqueline let out her breath in annoyance. Just when she was feeling like she could do this, when she normally wasn't afraid of anything, more participants would be listening in.

"Looks like some more folks found us," Anne said, sounding cheerful.

A woman was saying to the other person, "Well, I know what *you've* been doing."

A man laughed. He had a lovely, deep laugh that sent a whisper of a thrill up Jacqueline's spine, which annoyed her. Hadn't she gone through enough of an ordeal with her ex-fiancé? She wasn't about to show any interest in a man after that had happened. She had enough to deal with now that she was a vampire and a hunter.

The young woman came bouncing through the doorway first and smiled. She was a pretty brunette, dark brown eyes, tall, model-like, in good shape, perfect for fighting vampires. "Oh, good, we're not too late. I'm glad I didn't skip the meeting since just the two of you showed up. I'm Stacey."

"Welcome, Stacey. I'm Anne."

"I'm Jacqueline." She couldn't help that she didn't sound enthusiastic to greet the newcomer.

Then a dark-haired man of about thirty walked in with a limp, wearing a shredded shirt, where he'd been clawed—most likely by a rogue vampire—blood on his black button-down collared shirt, but the man's cuts appeared like they had mostly healed. "Sorry, I didn't have time to change. I'm Dane." He had a wet rain jacket slung over his shoulder, wearing cargo pants and boots meant to fight in.

"You could just remove the bloody shirt, if anyone's bothered by the blood," Stacey said, giving him a sexy smile.

He cast her one back.

"It would be fine with me," Anne said, winking at him.

Jacqueline hoped he wouldn't hear her heart beating triple time at the sight of him. He was gorgeous. All six-foot, one of him. He appeared to already have an admirer in Stacey, and Anne was smiling just as brightly at him. He appeared to be alpha to the max.

"What about you?" he asked Jacqueline.

"It's your call." But Jacqueline didn't smile or wink at him. She gave him more of an evil eye, annoyed he would even ask her as if she cared one way or another. She wasn't interested in getting to know him beyond these meetings and maybe not even here.

"Who did you fight, and did you take him or her down?" Stacey asked.

This wasn't supposed to be a "show and tell" about taking down rogue vampires!

"Astrophel, and yeah, he's terminated," Dane said.

Jacqueline's jaw dropped. That was one of the men *she* was after! Hunters were hired to take down rogue vampires and she didn't think a ton of other hunters were searching for him. Though she was exaggerating, but still...

Dane noticed Jacqueline's reaction right away. "Uh, were you after him too?"

"Yeah. He was on my list."

Dane nodded. "I was told there were four hunters hired to take him down because he was so...slippery and difficult to eliminate."

She wasn't told that other hunters had been tasked to take Astrophel down. From now on, she would ask to make sure that there weren't a ton of other hunters trying to eliminate the same person. It was a waste of her time. Then she got a notice on her phone, and she checked it. The police force who had hired her notified her Astrophel was dead and they no longer needed her services. *Great.* She shoved her phone back in her pocket.

"Well, that's great that you terminated him," Stacey said, all smiles.

"Yeah, he was bad news." Dane ran his hand through his wet hair.

"Okay, so we had four others who contacted me that they were coming. But they might not be showing up," Anne said, "so we'll get on with the meeting. Unless someone else wants to start, I'll go first."

"Sure, that sounds good," Stacey said.

Dane agreed and glanced at Jacqueline, but she had already agreed that Anne was going first, and she didn't feel she needed to do it again.

Anne said, "Okay, so like all of you, I was turned by a rogue vampire. Before I could kill him, he bit me and forced me to drink his blood. I was his to control. A hunter friend killed him thankfully, and I was free of the vampire's will. Not only did I have issues with myself for being too slow in killing him, I hated the changes in me—the need for blood, that I was one of them and no longer strictly a hunter—I also hated the looks of sympathy from friends and family, who felt sorry for what I had become."

"But don't you love being able to vanish like vampires do? To be able to fly and leap into the air to fight? I love being able to do that," Stacey said.

Then why was Stacey here if she was so happy with her life? This was a place to talk about their ordeals with dealing with this, not the wonders of being vampires. Jacqueline wanted to shake her head but caught herself before she did.

"I have to admit I enjoy the new feats I have. It has helped me to take down rogue vampires," Anne said.

Jacqueline was ready to leave.

"What about anyone else? Does anyone want to tell us your story of how you were turned or the effect it has had on you?" Anne asked.

Stacey held up her hand as if she had to ask the teacher permission. "I do. Okay, so I was making out with this guy, and I didn't even know he was a vampire."

Jacqueline rolled her eyes, and wouldn't you know, Dane caught her at it. He gave her a smidgeon of a smile.

Then Stacey said, "Anyway when he showed his fangs, I knew it was too late. I had my folded sword with my clothes on the floor beside the bed—"

Way too much information...

"But I couldn't reach it. I was furious when he bit me when I had thought he was just human. Then, as everyone knows, I couldn't end his miserable life because he'd turned me. I ended up finally getting away from him. He knew he could let me go and call me to him anytime he wanted. But my brother came for him and ended him. Then I was free of the vampire's control."

"How do you feel about being turned?" Anne asked.

Other than great things, Jacqueline thought.

"Well, no one understands me. I mean my hunter friends and family," Stacey said. "But what do they know?"

Anne nodded. "Do you want to go next, Jacqueline?"

Jacqueline motioned to Dane. "He can go next."

"I was turned by a female rogue vampire."

Oh, God, like Stacey was making love to a male vampire rogue, except he was fooling around with a female? Jacqueline *didn't* want to hear about it.

"Yeah. I believed she was alone. In fact, a blood bond had told me she always went after homeless men alone, which made us believe she didn't want any witnesses. But truly, I believe I was set up."

"By the blood bond? Maybe the vampiress knew you were

targeting her. Or maybe a hunter had it in for you?" Jacqueline asked, then chastised herself for wanting to know. But if she had been set up by either, they would be on her assassination list.

Dane smiled at her, but this time his smile had taken on a slightly sinister tone. "I'm still trying to learn the truth. Anyway, the vampiress had four male vampires with her. I wasn't prepared to have to fight that many. I'm ashamed to say she got the best of me and turned me. But I was lucky my three brothers had been looking for me, were close by, and they came to my aid and killed the vampiress and the other two vampires. Not that my brothers didn't have some choice words to say to me about going to fight the rogue vampire on my own," Dane said.

Okay, so at least he was humble enough to tell his story and he hadn't been making love to a rogue vampire when he was turned.

Everyone looked at Jacqueline, waiting for her to tell her story. She didn't want to share, but she took a deep breath and let it out. "I was turned during a fight with a vampire where I lost control, like others have said here. My fiancé was furious with me when he learned I was turned. He dumped me and started dating my best friend, a huntress I had known since we were five. My parents are sad about it and can't deal with it. I can't be around them. They... make me uncomfortable. I make them just as uncomfortable. My brother hasn't spoken to me since it happened except for telling me, along with my parents, to get some therapy. And my hunter friends that I've known for years no longer want to be around me. Yeah, sure, some of the vampire skills are handy to have, but it has changed everything for me. And not in a great way." There, she said it. She wasn't going to sugarcoat the way she felt.

DANE WAS IMPRESSED with Jacqueline for having shared her story. He could see how reluctant she'd been to do so. Him? He figured it was the only way to heal from the trauma and the whole change-to-their-lives aspect. He was fortunate his brothers were behind him all the way. Of course, they were angry with him for going off alone to fight, but he'd had his reasons. Still, he felt a hunter might have even been responsible for setting him up, if Lucilla hadn't lied to him about it. He still couldn't believe someone close to him could have been involved in his downfall either. He needed proof though. Which is why he didn't mention at the meeting any names or that a hunter and someone close to him might be responsible. It would be irresponsible to out any hunter who might not have been involved in any kind of shenanigans. He hadn't even mentioned it to his brothers who would be sure to take down a hunter or two if they believed their actions had led Dane to have his current vampiric condition.

He couldn't believe Stacey had sex with a guy she thought was human and turned out to be a rogue vampire though. That was one for the books. At least Anne and Jacqueline had both opened up more about how they truly felt about being hunters turned vampires. He wasn't really able to do that yet. Maybe in the future.

He had wanted to change out of his bloody shirt before he came into the meeting, but he hadn't had a spare one with him and if he'd returned home to do so, he wouldn't have made it back in time for the meeting. As it was, he was a quarter of an hour late. Besides, he figured whoever was there would be used to seeing someone after a fight with vampires. He really thought some other men would be here too, so he felt a little uncomfortable that he was the only male here who had been turned. Maybe in the future, they would have more men in the meeting. Though being with all the ladies had been a boost to his ego when he'd kind of needed it.

He still couldn't quite figure out Jacqueline. She was a gorgeous redhead with penetrating blue eyes. She looked like she could fight most any rogue vampire without any problem.

Anne and Stacey were intrigued with him. Jacqueline seemed

to be immune to him—in a way—like she was trying really hard to not show she was interested in him. Maybe. Perhaps he was seeing things into it that were not truly there.

That was one of the problems he was having with being both a hunter and a vampire. He couldn't quite figure out his place in the world, so he was glad that some of the women who were in the same boat as him seemed to think he was all right. Like Jacqueline, he'd been engaged to be married and that went out the door as soon as his fiancée learned he had been turned. She might have come back to him in time when she realized he hadn't changed all that much, but her parents were dead set on him never showing up on their doorstep again. Period. And she was close to her parents, so it was a foregone conclusion marrying her wasn't a viable option any longer.

"Well, if no one has anything else to add," Anne said, "we'll meet the same time next week, and I'll be sure to bring a new coffee pot, coffee, and filters. Oh, and I've shared everyone's emails and phone numbers with everyone else so we can do group chats or individual chats if anyone is in need of an understanding ear." Anne was a pretty woman who was in great shape and probably could take most of the rogue vampires out that she had to fight. She was a vibrant brunette with dark chocolate eyes, and he was glad she had organized the group.

"Thanks," Dane said.

Stacey and Jacqueline also thanked her, and then Stacey rose from her seat, waiting for Dane to stand and walk out with her. Dane stood, but he wasn't leaving yet. He knew Stacey was hoping to make a deeper connection with him. She was a lovely dark-haired woman with soft green bedroom eyes, but he wasn't biting.

Jacqueline was still sitting, and he suspected she wanted them to leave before she did so she could avoid talking to them. Finally, Jacqueline let out her breath and said, "Night, all. See you next week." She rose from her chair suddenly and stalked off.

"Until next week," Dane said, and found himself inexplicably trying to catch up to Jacqueline.

Stacey hurried after him, and Anne closed the door to the meeting room and followed the rest of them out. Jacqueline suddenly vanished, surprising him.

"Don't you hate it when they do that?" Stacey asked, catching up to Dane and taking hold of his arm.

He was not into women who forced themselves on him. Though, as he left the building and saw Jacqueline driving off in a black sedan, he wasn't used to women fleeing from him either. He smiled. He had every intention of getting to know her better. She was a challenge and a puzzle, and he loved managing both.

"So do you have anything going on tonight?" Stacey asked him as he pulled his arm free of her hand.

"Yeah, sleep. I've been busy the last few days and if I'm going to continue doing my job, I've got to get some rest." Would he have said that to Jacqueline had she asked him the same question? No way in hell. He would have had a cup of coffee with her, though he guessed that wouldn't have been a great option the way he was dressed right now.

"Oh, yeah, me too. But you know you can call me or email me, text me, whatever, any time," Stacey said.

Anne locked the door behind her to the building and said, "We need to do group emails, no dating between males and females. Unless one of you is gay and then you can share chats and the like. But no romantic involvements while we're trying to sort out our feelings."

Stacey looked at Dane as if she was hoping he would tell Anne that he wouldn't go along with it.

He smiled. "Yeah, Anne's right. If a guy joins the group, I can meet up with him to discuss how I'm feeling and vice versa. Unless he's gay and then Stacey can talk to him."

Stacey shrugged, then got into her chartreuse-colored, Flower Power VW Bug. She smiled and waved at him and drove off.

Anne just smiled and got into her Jeep. "See you next week."

"Unless I'm fighting evil, I'll be here." He got into his black pickup and followed them off the parking lot, thinking maybe this therapy group wouldn't be such a bad thing after all. Of course, as soon as he was in his vehicle, he swore his brothers knew it and one of his middle brothers Ryan called him right away.

"So, how did it go?"

"Better than I expected. It's kind of too early to tell."

"How many showed up?" Ryan asked.

"There were only four of us. The other three were women." All three were damned attractive too and none of them appeared to have any mates.

"Bummer," Ryan said, sounding facetious.

Dane knew he was thinking he had all the luck. But really, all of them had issues, so it wasn't like they were all there to get together for fun. Well, maybe Stacey was. Anne seemed to have a good head on her shoulders. All four of them seemed to be about the same age. But Jacqueline was the one who really intrigued him. *Go figure.*

2

J acqueline settled down on the couch with her cat, Princess of Maine. As soon as Princess curled up on her lap, waiting for attention, Jacqueline started brushing her beautiful, fluffy tortoiseshell coat. She was a Maine Coon cat and definitely looked and acted like a Princess at all times. She was quiet and affectionate, loved to sit in windows, and sleep on Jacqueline's bed with her, something her ex-fiancé, Van, had problems with so it was just as well that things hadn't worked out between them.

Jacqueline turned on the TV and started to watch the *Matchmaker for Millionaires* reality TV series. It was all made up, of course. Imagine her being on that show—a millionairess in her own right who was looking for Mr. Right, only he had to be...what, exactly? She had no intention of dating a vampire. And hunters were out. They didn't trust her because she was one of the vampires now. And hooking up with a hunter who had just as many issues as she did over having been turned wasn't going to happen.

She thought of Dane and about how Stacey was holding onto him when they had left the building. He hadn't disengaged from her, so Jacqueline figured they were going to hook up.

She sighed. Who cared? They had to find their way through this somehow and if that's what it took, so be it. At the next meeting, Dane and Stacey might be the most well-adjusted people there. Who knew?

Brushing a purring Princess on her lap while Jacqueline watched the show, she considered the women the male millionaire had been interested in. What he wanted was a blond, who was well-built, not after his money, and she had to be intelligent. The other millionaire was a woman who wanted a young, hot guy, funny, and smart, who could take her sense of humor. Both of the millionaires were in their mid-forties. Both wanted a partner who was in their twenties. Of course. Beautiful, sexy, and young—but for a meaningful, well-thought out, long-term marriage? *Not.*

"Not for us, Princess, eh? We know just how this will turn out. The man and woman will have a date with their respective partners and will find they are just gold diggers who will put on the cutesy charm and it's all just meaningless and proves the matchmaker's advice was right and they should have dated someone else and would have broken the pattern of dating whoever was wrong for them." Jacqueline glanced down at Princess. "And you're sound asleep. We sure dodged a bullet with the last guy in our life, believe me. Well, you especially did. He had insisted you wouldn't sleep in our bed once we were married. Then again, what would he have done if a vampire had turned me while we were married? Insta-divorce for sure." She changed the channel to one about vampires. "Nope, don't want to see this." Even though the vampires weren't like the real ones, her current situation made her shy away from anything to do with them unless they were on her terminal list.

She turned the channel to a story about finding love in the wild. Couples would compete against other couples to see if they could find the right man or woman for them. It looked promising. Instead of blind love where they didn't see each other and learned about each other's wants and dreams, with this new show, the couples would be working together through stressful adventures in the wild

—riding horses through the mountains on narrow, cliffside trails, and across rivers, pulling cantankerous donkeys carrying their crates filled with some kind of puzzle pieces, diving, swimming, rope climbing, rappelling, all of which most had never done. They might even end up falling in love. It was worth checking it out.

There were ten men and ten women to begin with and they had to choose someone of the opposite sex to complete the challenges. She really liked most of them, but she was amused to see how they navigated different obstacles and were still speaking to each other, working together to solve puzzles—at least some of them were. Some weren't and they definitely weren't meant to be together with all the bickering they were doing, mad at each other, blaming each other for not being successful. Then after they completed the rigorous challenge, they could keep their partners or change things up a bit, based on the order they came in during the challenge. She loved seeing the dynamics between the couples. Especially the five that were really doing well together and showed a genuine interest in each other.

She glanced at the clock. It was nearly midnight. Time to get back to reality and go to work. "I'll be home in a little bit." She hoped. She never knew how long the job would take her or if she would get it done when she headed for the location where she thought the vampire would be.

Princess got off her lap, leapt to the floor, and sauntered to the bedroom in her carefree way, like a little princess as if she knew Jacqueline would join her in bed when she returned and so she was going to be ready for her. Then Jacqueline got a call on her phone and looked at the caller ID. *Dane Edmondson.*

The guy from the meeting? What did *he* want?

"Hey, is this Jacqueline from the therapy meeting?"

"Uh, yeah, if you need a sponsor, it has to be a male."

"No. I was calling because I'm going out on a job." He paused.

So? What did she have to do with it? She waited for him to say.

"I just wanted to make sure I wasn't going after someone on your list."

Now that surprised her. "Who are you going after?" she asked, wanting to make sure of the same thing then.

"Axel."

"No, damn it. How many hunters have been assigned this mission?"

"Just two. I guess you and me if you are also after him."

She didn't say anything. She was so annoyed. Not with Dane obviously, but with the police who had hired her.

"Okay, it sounds like you're being hired by the same police agency. Let's see if we have any more of the same names."

"How are you learning there are other hunters who are actively searching for the rogues?" she asked.

"I asked. I've had that happen to me before. I was headed to the location where the rogue vampire was known to go, had surveyed the whole area, learned when he would be there, and when I arrived at the place, I found a hunter had just killed him. Then a few minutes later, I got a notification that the rogue was eliminated by a hunter. I thought it was just a chance happening until they told me that two other people also had the mission. From then on, I ask so I know what I'm up against. I also discover when the posting first came out and when the other hunters were given the job. They don't give me the names of the hunters."

"Great." She didn't say it in a cheerful way, more annoyed than anything.

"So if you're willing to share, who are the rogues on your list?"

She let out her breath. "Besides Axel? Maggard, Quillon, and Paine."

"Yep, we have the same list. I also have Mabon."

"Good. I don't have that one. You can take care of Mabon."

Dane laughed.

She smiled. She didn't think he would be agreeable, but she figured she would just toss that out there.

"I have another suggestion."

She was sure she wouldn't like it. She didn't share kills and bounties with other hunters, if that's what Dane was going to propose. Not even with her ex-fiancé. Neither of them worked well together on hunts. They'd tried it twice, but he had preferred hunting with his own brothers instead. He felt his brothers were stronger and faster than her, so they made a better team.

"Okay, how about we go together and take down the vampires who have the most hunters after them? Then we can both get credit, share the money, and go after the next one at twice the pace."

She didn't want to work with him, since she didn't know his style of fighting or hunting. What if he and she couldn't work in sync like her ex claimed he and she couldn't? What if they lost the rogue because they were getting in each other's way? Worse, what if either of them ended up getting killed because of it?

"Uh, you don't like the idea. We could try it on this one assignment and see how it goes. I don't want to mention it, but we both were hunting alone when we were turned, right?"

She didn't want to be reminded of that. And she really didn't want to try this with him. She could see him being just like her ex and then she would really be angry about it. "Did you ever hunt with your fiancée?"

"Yeah, but it didn't work out."

"What makes you think working with me would?"

"We both have new abilities we're not totally used to, which is the reason I was a bit...well, scratched up before I ended up at the meeting. I mean, really, what could go wrong?"

"One of us or both of us could end up dead?"

～

WHAT WAS the likely chance that Dane would have all the same rogue vampires on his termination list that Jacqueline had except for the one? He was glad he had touched base with her. He really wanted to try working with the huntress so they could at least share in the take downs and maybe even protect each other. He was certainly willing to give it a try. But he didn't believe Jacqueline was going to be receptive to the idea no matter what he said. Still, he figured he would try to prove to her that he wasn't out to get all her hard-earned bounties.

"Well, think on it. In the meantime, I'll take care of Mabon, and you eliminate whoever you're targeting next. We can revisit this talk when it comes to the other names, if you would like." He really felt it would be a way of trying to reach the rogues before the other hunters could do it.

"Did you know the hunter who took down the rogue before you arrived on the one case?"

He was surprised she was still talking to him and hadn't already shut him down. "Olson."

"Van Olson?" She sounded more than surprised.

"Yeah, I take it you know him."

"I don't understand why they're doing this. I mean, assigning so many hunters to eliminate the same rogues."

"I know. It's something new they're doing so I was really surprised too and more than a little annoyed," he said. "They could have at least told us."

"I agree." She was quiet for a moment. "Oh, and yeah, I know Van. He's my ex-fiancé."

Dane didn't really know what to say to that. He suspected from her comment that she probably wasn't on the best of terms with him.

"Okay," she finally said.

Dane hesitated to respond, then he said, "Okay?" Had she

wanted to take down her rogue and he would go after Mabon, and they would consider working together on a different mission?

"I'm after Axel. Meet me at..." Again, she paused.

"We could go together," he suggested. "That way we would be more of a unified force, arrive together, and take him on at the same time."

"You didn't work well with your ex, you said," she reminded him.

"Wendy canceled on me three times when I was about to go on a mission. And the one time she went with me, she held back and never really did any fighting. I was more worried about protecting her at that point and knew she was more of a hindrance than an asset. What about you? Did you ever hunt with your ex?"

Lengthy pause. Jacqueline cleared her throat. "Yeah. He preferred to hunt with his brothers. So, I mean it might not make any difference if we work together. We might not be suited to do it."

"We'll do great. If you want, I can pick you up at your place. I think it would be safer to be together, and after we take him down, we'll go after Mabon."

He tapped his foot on the floor, hoping to get an agreement out of her. He just hoped they could work well together, and they were able to take down the perps and come out unscathed.

"All right. My place." She gave him her address.

"Lakeview Estates." He smiled. He lived in her neighborhood. "I'll be right over."

It was a posh place to live where a mix of humans and hunters had taken up residence. No vampires, that he knew of, so he was hoping he wouldn't have any trouble with anyone who took exception to a vampire suddenly living among them. And now there were two of them. That at least they knew about. Maybe more had been turned but they were keeping it a secret. What did he know?

He jumped into his pickup truck and headed over to her house that was just a few streets north of his place and parked in her driveway. Before he could get out of his truck to knock on her door, she was headed outside wearing a black leather jacket, black leather pants, and thigh high black leather boots. Her jacket was zipped up part way, revealing her black tunic underneath. Her beautiful red hair flowed as she walked, and he swore he was mesmerized by her beauty. She had high cheek bones and a sultry mouth, and her catlike eyes were narrowed a bit. She looked like a huntress who meant business.

"How did you get into my gated community without me giving you the passcode? Oh, you know someone living here and already knew the code."

"I live several streets behind you."

Her jaw dropped. Then she smiled. "There goes the neighborhood."

"Oh?"

"Yeah, two vampires in a mostly hunter neighborhood? I'm sure some wouldn't be happy about it."

He was relieved she wasn't making a jab at him for some other reason and really didn't like him. "I was thinking the same thing. I miss not being able to go to one of the hunter clubs. I'm not sure we would be welcome at a vampire club either."

"I know. I guess we could go to a human club."

He glanced at her, surprised she would say so.

She quickly added, "I mean, you know, like if you wanted to go to a club, you could go to a human one and nobody would know that you were a hunter or a vampire."

"Ah." He had thought she was saying she would go out with him to a club, and he was about ready to jump at the offer, if she had, so he was glad he'd used restraint. "Everyone at the meeting mentioned how family or a friend had killed the vampire who had turned them, but you. So what happened?" He hoped the vampire wasn't still living or she could easily be influenced.

"Did I mention that my hunter friends dumped me after I was turned?"

"Yeah, hell. So you're telling me the vampire that turned you is still alive?"

"Yeah. His name is Heskel, the twin of Moulson and when I dug further into his background, I learned he was the same as his brother as far as disposing of blood bonds that they got tired of. They were sharing them. But his twin brother had taken all the blame and was put on a termination list. Heskel hadn't been."

"Even so, he would be on a terminal list for turning you. He didn't have to attack you. You hadn't attacked him."

"True. I expected it for revenge, but because of his action to take me down without me being able to call a truce, I didn't have any choice."

"Exactly. Has anybody gone after the vampire?"

"He's on a termination list now, and the police said they would inform me when a hunter eliminated him, but he's still out there as far as I know."

Dane didn't say anything for a while and then he finally said, "We have to take him down."

"Yeah, but I can't."

"Right. But if I don't do it on my own, I'll solicit the rest of our therapy group members to help me take care of him."

She frowned at him. "I...I don't know. I mean, we only just met them. I don't even know if the other two huntresses are still hunting."

"Hey, we take down bad guys. If the ladies aren't game or don't feel they can do it, I'll ask my brothers."

She let out her breath in relief and suddenly brushed away a couple of tears. "Thanks." Her voice was choked with emotion.

He reached over and took her hand and squeezed. "I've got your back."

"That means a lot to me. Thank you."

"Has he tried to contact you? Force you to do anything yet?"

"No, but I figure it's only a matter of time."

That's what he was worried about. And being a rogue, he could very well force her to kill someone and then *she* would be on a terminal list.

3

"Here we are," Dane said, pulling into the parking lot of one of the city's libraries. He was glad Jacqueline had located a place that Axel went to regularly. Axel often had lots of people at his house, so if they could get him after he left the library, they would have a better chance at taking him down without any collateral damage. "So what is he doing in there?"

"Reading?"

Dane smiled at Jacqueline. She gave him a smart-ass smirk back. He chuckled. "I probably shouldn't ask but do you know *what* he is reading?"

"He reads everything he can get his hands on regarding swordsmanship and how to use a sword. He trains out with other vampires on his acreage. Once I got his name, because he had turned six humans against their will, I started researching him and watching the house from the acreage around his properties. A lot of woods surround the place so it was easy to observe from there without being seen. The vampires practice fighting in the evenings, blood bonds come and go, and then the vampires leave. Often, Axel goes with a few of the vampires and they're out the rest of the night. Sometimes he doesn't return at all.

"But then I found he goes to the library from nine to ten before they close on Wednesday and Friday nights regularly. I've been watching his movements for three weeks. It's important to make sure that you know as much as you can about the rogue before you take him or her down, unless they're about to murder someone and then it's time to step in and eliminate him."

"I agree," Dane said. "I'm always diligent too on trying to figure out their routines and who they're with and when. Recluses are often easier to take down. That's what Mabon is. I've watched him for about three weeks also. He rarely has anyone over to his house except for blood bonds, no vampires, and he is a vampire that is considered a hitman—an assassin for hire. As far as the police could determine, he has assassinated ten people and had been hired to do so by the victims' partners."

"Brutal. I hope the partners are up on charges for the scheme of a murder by hire."

"They are. The police just couldn't go after Mabon safely so I got the call to take him down."

"How many hunters have been assigned to take down Mabon?"

"Just me, as far as I know."

They saw Axel leave the library dressed all in black, wearing a long black leather trench coat as if trying to embrace the whole vampire persona—as books and movies portrayed them to be—when in truth, they often dressed just like any ordinary citizen so they would blend in with the general population.

Hunters didn't like taking a vampire down in a public place unless the rogue had targeted someone, and they needed to rescue the person before he or she became a victim.

"Oh, oh, he's not going to his car," Jacqueline said.

"Right, he's on his way down the path through the woods right there."

"And there's a thirtyish-year-old woman, wearing blue jeans and a floral shirt walking on the path into the woods. She's carrying a book. He appears to be headed straight for her," Jacqueline said.

Dane watched the scenario, and he agreed it could be that the vampire had found his mark. "Come on. We have work to do." Dane got out of his truck but before he could walk toward the woods, Jacqueline left the truck and vanished. "Holy shit." He was already behind the eight ball on this. Vanishing as a vampire and reappearing somewhere else wasn't something he'd practiced at much. It appeared Jacqueline had this down. He hoped he didn't screw this up. He vanished and reappeared on the walkway, but Jacqueline rushed out of the woods, seized his arm, and pulled him into them to cloak them from view. He was usually a hell of a lot stealthier than this, but he just wasn't used to teleporting like a vampire would. But he couldn't have run on the path to catch up to Jacqueline either and he hadn't wanted her to have to fight the vampire on her own. One fatal stab on the vampire's part and she could be dead.

"They're up ahead on the path. He hasn't approached her yet. She's headed for that bench, I think," Jacqueline whispered.

Jacqueline might be right that Axel could be after the woman. It was isolated right here and no one else was around to witness anything.

They moved closer to where the woman was sitting on the bench, reading the book she had in her hand. Axel had walked past the bench, not even glancing at her as though he wasn't interested in her.

Dane figured it was a bust, but Jacqueline and he were watching the vampire, making sure he wasn't just pretending he didn't have anything sinister in mind. Rogue vampires could be deviously sneaky.

Then the vampire suddenly turned and with a flying leap he was at the woman's throat. Just as quickly, Jacqueline grabbed his shoulders from behind and threw him onto his back into the holly shrubs. The woman ran off toward the safety of the library screaming and Dane rushed in to kill the vampire. Jacquelin had the same idea and the two of them used their swords on him, hitting his heart at the same time. Axel disintegrated into a wizened body, leaving his clothes perfectly intact.

Dane said to Jacqueline, "Do you want to call the police?"

"Yeah." She called them and let them know that she and Dane had eliminated Axel so they would get paid. Also the notification would go out to other hunters to remove him from their lists if anyone *had* recently picked him up to terminate.

Dane was just a little surprised that she had told the police that they both did the job. The police arrived in short order and took their statements and would dispose of what was left of the body. The would-be victim had also called it in, the officer said. Jacqueline grabbed the book the woman had dropped on the cement path and offered it to the officer so he could return it to the lady. But he shook his head and wouldn't take it. He motioned in the direction of the library. "She's back that way. The bounty will be paid to...?"

"Split between us," Jacqueline said, motioning to Dane.

"Okay, we've got your information. You're free to go."

Then Jacqueline and Dane walked back to the library on the brick path. "Quick reaction," Dane said, "and your vanishing act is really great."

"I've been practicing, figuring it could give me an edge."

"It does. I need to practice at it more."

"You do. Being able to move like that can be a real benefit to us in the fight against the rogues."

They saw the woman shaking, crying, sitting in the ambulance and they joined her. Jacqueline gave her a hug and Dane thought the world of her for being so caring.

"They...they say he's dead," the woman said, wiping away more tears.

"Yes, and good riddance." Jaqueline handed the woman her book. "Here. You dropped this."

"Thanks so much," she said. "And thanks to both of you for coming to my rescue. I didn't want to be turned."

"Which is why the vampire was on our terminal list," Dane said.

"Thanks again," she said as a blond-haired woman wearing nurses' scrubs rushed up to see her and hug her. She looked like a sister.

"Are you okay?" the blond asked her.

"Yeah, the hunters took down a vampire that tried to turn me," the woman said.

Hunters, Dane was thinking. They were no longer just hunters. How would the woman feel if she had known that they were both vampires also now? That was one of the things he hated. That he wasn't all hunter any longer. He wondered if Jacqueline felt the same way. In a way, meeting up with her and doing this together with a hunter turned gave him a gratifying feeling—that she didn't look at him with disdain for using a vampire's abilities, just like he was glad that she had them and could use them so successfully.

Then Jacqueline's ex-fiancé showed up and Dane knew he had come for Axel. Dane figured Van wouldn't have any other reason to be here at this time. Dane didn't believe in coincidences.

"Ohmigod, don't look now," Jacqueline said, and pulled Dane into a hot embrace, the breeze making her silky red hair wrap around him as she lifted her face to him and kissed him like they'd been lovers for months.

Okay, so he could *really* get into this, though he knew the reason why she'd kissed him like that. And it had nothing to do with really wanting to kiss him, but more to aggravate her ex. Maybe. But truly, he was all for it.

She finally pulled her mouth away from Dane's, but he wasn't ready to part company with her yet. He kissed *her* this time, initiating the delicious mouth-to-mouth contact, wanting to prolong the interaction between them, but not because her ex was here.

Just then her ex got a text message, read it, and frowned at them. "You killed Axel?"

"Yeah, before he turned the woman who is sitting in the ambulance right now," Jacqueline said.

Van glanced at Dane and then back to Jacqueline. "That was quick."

Jacqueline shrugged. "Just like you going after my best girlfriend was a fast turnaround for you." She took hold of Dane's arm and headed for the parking lot.

Dane wasn't used to a woman taking charge of him, especially one who had acted disinterested in him when they were at the therapy session. Well, except at the meeting when Stacey grabbed his arm but that hadn't been welcome. But with Jaqueline, this certainly worked for him.

But Van headed in the same direction, probably to his own vehicle in the parking lot.

"Did you get anything from informant Green last week?" Dane asked him, still wondering if one of the hunters the informant spoke to had anything to do with his being ambushed in that alley with Lucilla and her vampire friends.

"Yeah, about a vampire named Carrel, but someone else got the vampire."

"Not anything about a Lucilla?"

"No. Green never mentioned anything to me about her. Why?" Van asked, frowning.

Dane shrugged. "I was just wondering. He told me he sometimes worked for you too."

"Yeah, he does. I...didn't know he worked for you also. I hope it doesn't cause any difficulties for you," Van said, sounding arrogant, like he didn't care if it did or not.

It made Dane wonder if maybe Van had something to do with Dane being targeted in an ambush. But why? He barely knew Van.

Then Dane and Jacqueline headed for his pickup, and she said to him, "What was that all about?"

"I still think someone might have set me up and that's why I was ambushed. I can't imagine the informant Green would have done it on his own."

"The vampiress then?"

"Or another hunter who Green works for."

"Like Van? Oh, that would be awful," Jacqueline said.

"Yeah, I know."

"What would be the reason though?"

"If I ended up taking down a rogue vampire who paid a really big bounty, maybe? Lucilla was a huge bounty."

"Oh, wow, why didn't I hear about her so I could have gotten the case?" Jacqueline asked.

Dane smiled at her. But then he turned serious. "Then you would have been ambushed."

"Yeah, and turned. That would have been awful." She was being facetious. "Is there any specific reason why you feel that a hunter was responsible?"

"Lucilla said a hunter was the one who set me up. Now of course, she might have just said that to make me distrust other hunters, but still, I have to consider it's a possibility."

"For sure. I would take it seriously until I determined it wasn't true. Are you ready for the next mission?" Jaqueline got into his truck.

"Yeah, sure. I'm always ready to take down a rogue before they kill any more innocents." He liked that she seemed dogged to get the job done. He wasn't sure she would be ready for another one tonight, but he was ready to share the bounty on this one with her after she had shared the bounty on Axel with him like she had said they would.

"Okay, so you've got his address, right?" she asked.

"Yeah, using GPS now to check on it. It's out in the country on the north side of Dallas. Thanks so much for sharing the bounty with me, by the way."

She smiled. "You earned it."

"I guess your ex had the same mission as us."

"Yeah, and I know him well enough to recognize he was pissed that he didn't get the score."

"I'm glad we got there before him, but mainly because we saved the woman. Actually, you did most of the saving. We worked in unison to take him down after that."

Jacqueline glanced out the window at the dark sky. "How do you feel about humans believing we're just hunters still? Does it bother you?"

"Yeah. I hope to get over that feeling someday. But for now, I feel aggravated because we were the ones taking down rogues. Now people who have experienced trauma at their hands, or teeth, could feel we're just like them even though we're the good guys."

"I feel that way too. I guess that's why we still need to go to meetings."

He looked at her. "Yeah. I thought I would try one out and if it wasn't for me, I would just attempt to figure it out for myself."

"Oh, me too. What do you think of Stacey?"

He smiled. "She's hot to trot and not my type at all. You're hot, and definitely my type."

"Could you use help in figuring out who might have set you up?"

The question surprised him. He wasn't sure he wanted to accept her help should the person be a hunter. He had a couple of people in mind. But he didn't want her to be in harm's way if it turned out to be a hunter. He wasn't sure with their changed status if they could eliminate a hunter who had tried to have another hunter murdered...or in his case turned. He might have to have his brothers take care of it.

"Forget it. I'm helping you if you're willing to take down my... 'master,'" she said.

"Okay, you can help me learn the truth, but I think my brothers will have to take the hunter down." He swore he heard her growl a little.

"Because we're part vampire," she finally said.

"Yeah, and by law, vampires can't kill a hunter, no matter if hunter is a rogue or not or they're on a terminal list."

"Okay, fine, I'll help you learn the truth."

"Thanks. I appreciate it."

They finally reached Mabon's house, surrounded by trees and acreage, pulled off onto a side road leading out into the country, and parked.

She got out of his truck before he did. She was quick, he had to give her that.

He quickly joined her and then she vanished. *Shit.* He wished she would give him a heads-up. He wanted to know where she was going. Suddenly, she reappeared, seized his hand, and vanished with him. They ended up in the woods off to the south of the house and he felt totally disoriented, not like when he teleported himself on his own.

But at least they were together, and he was glad for the partnership again, even though he would have gotten the bounty for himself. There was something to be said about having someone along with him to help if they had to fight a rogue.

They saw a light on in the main living area and they crept closer to get a look. All the blinds were closed, but they would see if they could find an unlocked window.

He saw a balcony to a dark room on the second floor and was about to mention it to Jacqueline, but she had the same idea and vanished and reappeared there. He immediately followed her and ended up on the balcony.

She tried one of the double glass doors on the balcony and the door opened. Mabon probably figured that no one would try to enter his house from there. Jacqueline was clever.

They slipped into the room that was large and opulent, featuring a king size bed with a gold headboard and the rest of the furniture was golden, 18th Century Italian Baroque. Dane only knew because he had learned about Mabon and his hobbies and collecting antique furniture and decorations was one of his things.

Dane moved to the bedroom doorway, the door open and they heard Mabon on the phone downstairs. "Yeah, yeah, I got it."

They moved down the hallway to get closer to where Mabon was, and Dane began recording the conversation just in case the caller was contracting a hit. The police could track it down to the caller, and hopefully this time, Mabon wasn't in the process of killing anyone.

"Your husband has an insurance policy of a million dollars and a five-million-dollar estate, a two-million-dollar cabin, a yacht. Yeah, I do my research when someone wants to hire me for a hit. I want the money from the insurance policy." Mabon hesitated. "If you want to pay someone else less, be my guest. With me, it's a guaranteed hit." He paced across a tile floor. "Okay. So when does Mr. Dunlap get home from work? Seven. Be sure and have a good alibi. Do not be there when I am." Some more pacing. "Between seven and eleven. Hell, I don't know. Have a ladies' night out with a bunch of ladies, but don't make it look like you're trying to create an alibi. I want the money as soon as you're able to access it. If I don't get it...well, let's just say you will no longer be needing it."

Dane and Jacqueline began making their way down the stairs, glad it wasn't creaking. They heard Mabon in the kitchen opening the fridge and then pouring something into a glass. Jacqueline disappeared and reappeared next to a dining room hutch. Only Dane could see her. They had to be careful not to get too close to the vampire until they were ready to attack. Otherwise, he could hear their hearts beating, though they could hear his also when they were close.

Dane joined her and then the phone on the counter rang and Mabon picked it up and said, "Yeah? All right, Jerome. That's tricky. Your business partner has a penchant for blond hookers. Yes, I know all. I'll make sure he has one for the night in question... tomorrow night? Right, between eleven and two the next morning. So be home with your wife and make sure she can verify you're with her for the entire time..." He paced again. "I don't care if she goes to bed early. You need to have an alibi that proves you're home when your business partner meets his untimely death...no, that wasn't me. All right. Send the money to my account and when I have it, I'll make this happen." He set his phone on the counter. "Business is good," he said out loud to himself.

But Mabon's lucrative business was finally coming to an end, Dane was thinking.

4

S o far, so good, Jacqueline was thinking. As soon as Mabon finished his second murder-for-hire phone call, Dane shoved his phone in his pocket. She loved how he was proactive and was taking a recording of Mabon's business dealings before they terminated him. She hadn't even thought of that, but he was doing the right thing in doing so. Once they took Mabon down, the people who had hired him could still kill their partners, just by hiring someone else. So they needed to be convicted of trying to do a hire-for-murder scheme also and in the end, save their partners before they hired someone else to do the job.

Mabon turned and started to head for the living room, but he suddenly stopped and glanced in the direction of the dining room where they were standing. That's when Jacqueline realized she heard Mabon's heart beating. He could probably hear their two hearts beating at once.

She and Dane made their move, both of them vanishing and appearing in the living room. She had to admit she loved that she could vanish and appear in places like that. It really helped to get somewhere much more secretively. As hunters they would have to have moved quickly and decisively but they would have exposed themselves too early to the rogue vampire threat.

Even though she suspected that Mabon knew they were hunters, their movements said that they were vampires. He looked surprised, maybe like he was trying to figure out who they were and why they were there. He hadn't invited them, so he knew they were not there for fun and games.

Not when they were armed with swords and targeting him. Mabon threw his bloody cocktail at Dane, and he dodged it. The rogue immediately dove for an umbrella stand filled with sheathed swords and tried to pull one free but it was tangled up with four others.

Yes! Fatal mistake, *hopefully*, on his part. She wasn't going to let down her guard in the event he could finally free his sword or come after them with his deadly teeth. She'd never even let her vampire teeth down, not wanting to experience that part of her vampirism so it wasn't something she felt she could use in a fight.

Dane was on the vampire and before she could even engage Mabon, Dane removed the vampire's head. His body and head quickly turned to shriveled leather body parts. Her adrenaline was still racing through her blood, and she couldn't believe how easy that had been, all because the vampire had a tangled mess of sheathed swords in an umbrella stand. He should have just had one for easy retrieval.

She hugged Dane and whooped and hollered. He smiled at her, then kissed her.

"See? We make a great team," he said.

"Yeah." But Dane hadn't really needed her on the job this time, she felt. Just looking at him, their gazes meeting, she felt butterflies taking flight. She couldn't believe it. She had just finished a hunt, for heaven's sake. "Listen, you terminated him, and you can go ahead and claim him."

"No way. We're in this together. You could have been after

another bounty or enjoying the rest of your night off. Besides, having two of us here rattled him enough that he couldn't grab his sword."

"Well, thanks. I appreciate it." She had hoped Dane wouldn't take her up on the offer because she thought he deserved all the money, but she really thought the world of him for giving up half the bounty to her.

He called the police and reported the kill. "I also have a recording where he was making a couple of deals to be a hitman for a murder-for-hire scheme. Yes. We'll be here."

They always hung around until the police arrived and verified who the dead vampire was. Providing evidence that the rogue vampires were up to their usual shenanigans regarding trying to turn or kill people when the hunters took them down was helpful, but it wasn't absolutely necessary. The police already had enough evidence against them. They just needed hunters to terminate them.

They both went into the kitchen and found fresh bottles of blood. Because they were newly turned, they had to drink them occasionally, especially if they were injured and had lost blood. Dane poured them both a glass before the police arrived. It was better if the police didn't witness them drinking blood. It just kind of freaked some humans out.

"Have you extended your fangs yet?" she asked Dane, then finished her glass and washed it out.

"A couple of times."

"Oh?"

"When you kissed me the first time."

Her jaw dropped.

He smiled. "Apparently, when a vampire is aroused, his canines can extend. I suppose that if you are an ancient vampire, you would have more control over it. I've never kissed a woman since I became a vampire, so when we kissed, I wasn't expecting that."

"You hid them well."

"We didn't kiss deeply, or you might have noticed. Yours didn't drop down?"

"No. I thought they would, only if you were really angry."

"Yeah, then too, supposedly, but I guess I haven't been angry enough. And of course, they'll drop down at command if you want to bite someone or want to show them off. I had to show them to my brothers. They still didn't believe that the vampire had turned me until then. Of course, once I could vanish, they really had to believe it." Dane finished his glass and cleaned it and set it on a drying pad next to hers.

"I think it's nice that they are still close to you. But you don't hunt together."

"Sometimes. Like if we know a group of rogues need to be eliminated, we need more of us to do it."

"Well, I think it's great."

Then they heard the sirens and three police cars pulled up. Dane identified himself and Jacqueline to an officer and gave their statements. Another couple of officers were searching through a file cabinet and one said, "Holy, crap! We've got the mother lode."

"What have you got?" a homicide detective asked.

"Files on several people that Mabon murdered, including all the contract information—payout, details on where a key would be left for him to have easy access to victims' homes or offices, or when his target would be home or alone. Names, addresses, everything," the officer said.

Then the detective started looking through them. "Okay, we put the people who hired him on five of these robberies in jail, but there are another six here that we thought were home invasions, robberies that had gone bad, but now we know they were all murders. We'll get all the culprits who hired him." The detective thanked Dane and Jacqueline then and released them.

"Are you ready to go home?" Dane asked her as they headed out to his truck.

"Yeah. I'm tired. It's late. It's time to call it a night."

"What do you like to do for fun?" he asked as they got on the road headed back to their housing development.

"Terminate rogue vampires."

He smiled. "Other than that?"

"I used to like to dance at a hunter club close by."

"We could go there."

"We're vampires now."

"You mentioned a human club. They don't know what we are and vampires who are looking for blood bonds go to them, so we would fit right in."

She glanced at him. "You're not thinking of looking for rogue vampires at a human club, are you?"

"No. Unless of course one shows up who we know is trouble. But first, we need to get rid of *your* vampire."

"Not the others on our lists first? What if other hunters get them before we do?"

"We can always get more contracts, but we need to get the vampire who turned you so he doesn't force you to do something you'll regret."

"Okay, I agree." She had wondered how she was going to manage that on her own. But with Dane's help, she felt that he might be able to handle it. She was glad he thought they made a good team in a vampire fight. She thought she had done well when she'd fought alongside Van too, so she had really been surprised when he told her he preferred fighting beside his brothers instead.

"Since my place isn't too far from where you live, if you have any trouble with the vampire, let me know," Dane asked.

"Thanks." She was really glad he lived in her gated community. "Have...you tried talking telepathically to anyone yet?" She had been practicing with the disappearing and reappearing act because she knew how helpful that could be in a fight and because she could do it in the privacy of her home. Telepathic communication had to be done with a vampire who was willing to talk to her in that way.

"Not yet. I haven't really had anyone to talk to who is one like us. My friends Adonis Cameron and his sister were hunters turned. His mate is Rachael and her cousin, Zachary, was turned against his will. Adonis turned Rachael so she would be able to protect herself better from a rogue vampire who claimed her for his own. But they've been out in Florida taking care of the vampires that decimated the rest of Adonis's family. They're living out there now but come here to visit their family in Dallas too."

"Oh, wow, that's awful about what had happened to Adonis and the rest of his family."

Dane parked at her house. "Yeah, it was. They terminated the last of the rogue vampires in their territory in Florida though. If they had been here in Dallas still, I would have tried it with them."

"Well, maybe we can do it with each other."

"Yeah, I would like that."

Then she hopped out of his pickup truck. She wasn't going for another kiss and lead him on. But maybe later? She wasn't ready to get into a relationship with anyone after the ordeal with her ex-fiancé. Plus, because of the changes she faced with being a vampire, she just wanted to be more settled with her new self before she had any notions of courting anyone else in her life.

"About our other cases—" he said.

She let out her breath in a heavy sigh. "Okay, sure. You can take some of the cases we have left, or we can work on them together."

"What do you want to do?"

"Well"—she shrugged—"we did pretty well as a team for the last two missions. I'm good with doing it together until it doesn't work out any longer." Not that it wouldn't, but she wanted him to know that she didn't want him to feel obligated to work with her if he decided she was more of a liability than a team member.

"All right. Do you want to take some of the names and learn their locations and who they associate with, and I'll do the same with the others? Then we can go to the first one we can locate before other hunters get there to take care of the rogue."

"Yeah, that will work. We'll keep in touch then. Whoever gets a location first, will let the other one know and we'll take it from there."

"Sounds great."

She unlocked her house and turned to see he was still watching her, being a gentleman, making sure she got in okay. She smiled and waved, and he smiled back and waved.

Then she walked into the house and locked the door. Instantly, Princess came to greet her, rubbing her furry body against Jacqueline's leg and she reached down and stroked her. "Okay, I'm done with jobs for the rest of the morning. Time to go to sleep." She took a shower and dressed in pajamas, then climbed into bed and Princess quickly joined her.

"Well,"—Jacqueline stroked Princess's head—"that went fairly well tonight—the meeting, taking down one vampire on my list, and taking another down who wasn't. Good beginning to returning to work. And we even have a hunter who is willing to go after the vampire who turned me."

Princess purred, her nose turned up as she eyed her with her big green eyes, her chubby cheeks the cutest thing ever.

Then Jacqueline thought she heard a male voice in her head. She jumped out of bed, Princess leaping off the mattress at the same time as Jacqueline went to check the house and make sure that no one really was inside. She found no one. Why did the voice sound familiar? Though she hadn't made out what he had said. She didn't think it was Dane, but what did she know? She hadn't tried to talk telepathically with anyone, so it could be he tried to talk to her, and his voice would be different than when she heard it in his physical form.

She wasn't sure how to do this, but she tried in her mind to say, *"Dane, did you try to speak to me telepathically?"*

He didn't respond. Did she not do it right? Or maybe he was sound asleep.

But then she heard someone in her head saying, *"Go to 75692 Evergreen Drive. I'll be waiting."*

"Who is this?" she asked in her head.

But she didn't get a response. She got on her phone and called Dane. "Hey, did you try to telepathically connect with me?"

"Uh, no. I thought we would do it sometime when we're together to try and figure out how to do it."

"Someone told me to meet him at 75692 Evergreen Drive now. And it sounded like a man, but it was hard to hear, like he was a long way off."

"Is it the vampire who turned you? Is he forcing you to go? I mean, do you feel compelled?"

"Yeah, like I'll be in trouble if I don't go. I don't know if it's him. He never spoke to me when we fought, so I don't know what his voice sounds like."

"I'm going with you. He won't be expecting me."

"What about your brothers?"

Dane was silent for a moment.

She spoke again. "He might know I went on a hunt with you tonight. He might believe I would call on you. He didn't tell me not to say anything to anyone about going anywhere tonight. What if he's laying in wait to terminate you? Or maybe he can even force me to do it? What if he has a bunch of vampires at that location and you can't fight all of them on your own, particularly if he's controlling me? If your brothers could join us, maybe you and your family could take the vampire down."

"I'll call them. I'm coming right over. I don't want to lose you while I'm getting hold of my brothers."

"All right. Sorry about this. I'm sure you're as ready to sleep as I am. The same with your brothers."

"They'll be behind this all the way."

"Well, if you're wrong, let me know."

"I'll be there in a few minutes." Dane sounded determined to protect her.

She usually felt confident in her own abilities but there were too many unknowns in this case. Particularly with the problem of a vampire potentially being able to control her actions. She had kind of hoped Heskel wouldn't remember he had turned her. But that had been too much to hope for. She couldn't imagine it would be anyone else who was directing her to come meet up with him telepathically at this time of morning.

5

J aqueline didn't have to tell Dane twice that she could be in trouble before he was at her house. He knocked on the door and he could hear her running to answer it.

As soon as she opened it, he took her into his arms and hugged her in a way that said he was there for her. "We'll get this done. I promise you. My brothers are going to meet us at the house the rogue vampire told you to go to."

"Oh, wonderful." She sounded relieved.

There was no way he was going to let her do this on her own. No telling what the rogue vampire wanted her to do. "They will get there faster if they go from where they are. I'm sure you'll like Matt, Ryan, and Trey. Matt is the eldest of the bunch of us, and always takes the lead when we're all together. Ryan and Trey are twins— Ryan is the mischief maker while Trey is the serious one, and then there's me."

"Oh, you're the baby of the bunch."

Despite the seriousness of the situation, he smiled. "Yeah, I get that all the time from my brothers."

"Well, I'm the youngest between my brother and me so I hear that all the time too." Jacqueline and Dane climbed into her car because the vampire might realize that's what she was driving, so Dane didn't want to take his pickup truck.

"Is that the reason you were out on the case on your own when you were turned? Because you felt you had something to prove to your brothers?" she asked.

"No. My brothers were all on different jobs, but they were nearby, so we knew if anyone needed help, we could call for it."

"Yeah, right. Like either of us ever had that opportunity."

"None of us ever thought of that scenario." Dane hated to admit that he and his brothers had been arrogant in that regard.

"At least they still back you up."

"That's what families should do. Same with our friends, but like you, I've lost several of my hunter friends over this." He turned down another street. He tried not to take the betrayal personally, but it was hard not to do it sometimes.

"Some friends, though I can understand when it comes to me because the vampire who turned me could possibly make me turn on them."

"True, which makes it more imperative that they took him down. I mean, if they're truly your friends, they're there for you through thick and thin, not just when it suits them."

"Yeah, I agree. What did your friends that dumped you say about it?" she asked.

"Nothing, really. I learned hunter parties are coming up that normally I would be invited to and that's not happening any longer." He shrugged. "I could be irritated about it, but I figure they're not worth my attention." Which wasn't totally true. It was hard growing up with these hunters as friends, play-fighting, socializing with them, watching each other's backs. Now they treated him like he was a rogue vampire—the only difference being that they couldn't terminate him legally.

"What if they're at a scene that you happen upon? Are you going to help them? Or just let them deal with it themselves?"

"Well, I would help them, unless they threatened me. And then it is their problem. But yeah, despite their abandoning me, I wouldn't hold it against them if they needed my help. What about you?" Before she answered, he assumed she would step in to help them.

She shrugged. "If there was a reward for the vampire's expiration, I would help."

He chuckled. He was sure she would, even if she didn't get any bounty for it. Then he got a call from his oldest brother. "Hey, Matt, are you there already?"

"Yeah, we're parked down the street, but we're watching the house. How do you want to handle this?"

Usually, Matt decided when they would do a job, where, who would be involved, and how, during cases they worked on together. A lot of research was done first, and they did fight the vampires together when they had a rogue crew of them that they had to deal with. This was the first time that Matt had ever asked Dane to tell him how this was going down. Why? Because a fellow friend was involved? Most likely. Maybe also because she and he were vampires now and that might give them a different perspective.

"Hi, I'm Jacqueline Anderson, the huntress turned vampire, damsel in distress," she said.

Matt laughed. "From what Dane tells me, the only ones in distress are the vampires you're targeting."

She smiled at Dane. Yeah, he'd called his brother up to tell him what they'd done tonight together. He didn't usually check in but after that last fiasco with the vampire who had turned him, his brother had told him if he didn't call, he and his other brothers were coming after him.

"I'm really not sure how to handle this situation. If this is Heskel, who telepathically communicated with Jacqueline, he's probably expecting just her. Unless he knows I was with her tonight, eliminating a couple of vampires on hunters' lists and he hopes I'll be with her, and he can eliminate me."

"Because you're possibly an obstacle to his control over her," Matt said. "But should she go into the house alone? Shouldn't we keep her in one of the vehicles until we can take him out?"

"He might not even be there. It might be another situation entirely. We might blow the whole mission," Dane said.

"I'm going in," Jacqueline said. "Wait, let me test something out first." She took a deep breath and said, *"Okay, I'm talking to you telepathically to see if I can speak with you from inside the house."*

"Oh, hell, I can hear you in my head," Dane said, surprised to hear her speak to him like that.

"Yes, but talk to me telepathically so I can get feedback from you and you can tell your brothers what is going on. I need to know that you can do it too."

"All right. Can you hear my words when I try to communicate like this?" Dane asked.

"Yes. It's amazing, isn't it? Okay, I'll go in, and you stay in the car. I'll let you know who all is there and what's going on. If I say I need rescuing, don't hesitate to come to my aid."

He really didn't like that she would be going in alone, but they had to try this her way. "Okay. Matt, she's going into the house." He explained about the telepathic communication they had just shared.

"Why didn't you answer me the first time I talked to you telepathically?" she suddenly asked Dane.

"The first time?" Now he was worried since he hadn't heard her speak to him like that before.

"Yeah, before you came to the house. I tried reaching you that way and then I called you on the phone."

"I was in the shower. Maybe that's why?"

"I hope that's all it was and that it wasn't something like we were too far away from each other in the housing development."

"I'll just be in the car and we're right outside the house."

She nodded, then leaned over and kissed him. He sealed the kiss with a promise to be there for her. Then she got out of the car and headed for the house. It was completely dark, and he really had a bad feeling about this. She knocked on the door, but nothing happened. Then she turned the doorknob and it was unlocked. She glanced back at him, appearing confident, though he had smelled her anxiety before she left the car, and then she went inside.

"I can see, though the whole house is dark. I don't hear anyone's heartbeats. I don't think anyone's here yet."

"Okay, keep me informed." Dane relayed the information to Matt.

"Oh, he's here, sitting in the dark. I hear his heartbeat now. Steady. Calm. Like a hunter waiting for his unsuspecting prey."

Like he had nothing to fear. *"Is there anyone else there?"*

"No, it appears he's alone."

It was killing Dane not to go into the house right this instant and rescue Jaqueline. He knew nothing good could come of her meeting the vampire. If he sat tight and did nothing and the vampire murdered her or sent her out to murder someone else and made her a rogue, Dane would never forgive himself.

He rushed to the front door, and it was still open. His brothers hurried to join him.

6

"I've been busy so I haven't been able to really get to know you, Jacqueline. I didn't even know *who* you were when you killed my brother," Heskel said.

She was standing about ten feet away from where he was sitting on a brown and beige plaid couch, acting comfortable, like he had nothing to worry about. "He had been killing blood bonds when his temper got the best of him."

Heskel smiled a little, his expression sinister, his blue eyes chillingly cold. "We're twins. We both have that trait. It probably had something to do with our father who taught us all we know."

That's what she was afraid of and what was worse was she couldn't do anything to him like she so wanted to. "*Where are you, Dane? Take him down, now!*"

Heskel said, "Just in case you alerted anyone that I've called you here, we're going to leave."

She readied her sword.

"You can't kill me." Heskel's brows rose, and she suspected no one he had ever turned had challenged him before.

She swung her sword at him, and his eyes widened right before he leapt out of the way.

"You can't threaten me," Heskel said, his voice dark with condemnation, but it wavered a bit. He sounded a little unsure of himself.

It was just instinctive for her to react as a hunter to a vampire threat, but she couldn't believe she could even do that much when he had been the one who had turned her. He disappeared and reappeared at her back, and she heard his heart beating wildly. Hers was too as she vanished and showed up on the other side of the couch to put some distance between them. She loved how she could vanish and reappear like they could. Even though he couldn't turn her again, he could still kill her while she would be unable to terminate him.

"Huntress," he snarled, angry that he couldn't control her as much as he could humans.

That was great news to her. But when she flew at him to strike him, she felt his control stopping her. Still, she fought against his mental strength when she heard someone coming in through the front door. Heskel whipped around to see who had just arrived in the dark house.

Dane, her hero.

Heskel cast him a dangerously, evil smile. "So, you are the new lover? You can join my little pack." Then he bared his teeth and Dane swung his sword at the vampire.

Heskel vanished and came in for an attack at Dane's back. But Dane shoved his sword under his arm and into Heskel. He didn't manage to strike his heart, or Heskel would have collapsed in death as a wizened form of himself, but the vampire did howl in pain.

Then Dane's brothers rushed into the living room. They all had their swords unsheathed and hurried to take the vampire down. But he vanished.

Usually, vampires stayed and fought, being so arrogant that they thought they could fight any odds and win, but Heskel was playing it safe, the fight against four hunters too much to deal with.

Still, they waited, making sure he wasn't going to come back and try and pick each one of them off.

When he didn't, the brothers went in twos to check out the rest of the house, Jacqueline going with Dane and Matt. The twins stuck together. She was so glad Dane had cut Heskel and the vampire hadn't injured him. But she so wished they could have taken him down. She suspected Heskel was long gone.

It appeared that Heskel didn't realize Dane was a vampire too, which could be to their advantage. After they finished looking through the rest of the house, they returned to the living room.

"He's going to continue to come after Jacqueline, but since he can control her—" Matt said.

"I'm dangerous to be around," Jacqueline said. "I couldn't kill him, but I threatened him."

"Do you mind having some guests at your place?" Matt asked.

"Uh—"

"I could just stay there," Dane offered.

"No," his twin brothers said, and she thought it was wonderful Dane had all that family support. Trey and Ryan were both dark-haired like Dane, both green-eyed. Matt was lighter haired and had blue eyes.

"We can stay at my place," Matt said. "Or Dane's."

"I have a cat, Princess," Jacqueline said.

"She'll be welcome anywhere that she'll stay," Dane said.

"All right, but she sleeps with me," she said, waiting to see what Dane's response to that would be.

Dane smiled and all his brothers looked at him to see his take on it as if that's where their relationship was headed.

"Hey, that works for me," Dane said.

She sighed. She thought she would be staying alone in a bedroom—with her cat, but she guessed that could be dangerous if Heskel got to her and could take her with him right under everyone's noses.

"If we stay at my place"—which frankly she would have preferred—"Heskel would most likely know that's where I live."

"Yes," Dane said, "but if you would feel more comfortable with staying there, we'll do it. This is a really trying time for you with your 'maker' after you."

"Well, who has the bigger place?" she asked, smiling. She might as well get something out of this.

Ryan laughed. "You're my kind of girl."

"Dane does and he even has a swimming pool that we love to use," Trey said, his twin agreeing.

"Okay, well, it's close to my place so we'll meet you at my home first, I'll pack some things and Princess and then go to Dane's home with my cat?" she asked Matt.

"Yeah, let's go," Matt said.

They got into their respective vehicles and Matt followed them in his car, the twins with him.

"You're really all right with my cat sleeping in bed with me?" she asked.

Dane smiled at her. He had the most disarming and charming smile of any hunter she'd ever known. Why couldn't she have met him before instead of Van? She really liked him deep down so much more than her ex-fiancé. Dane was there for her no matter what.

"I'm fine with it. When I was a kid, we had a German shepherd and he slept with me. He always tried to sleep in the middle of the bed and would kick me when he was having doggy dreams."

She laughed. "Truthfully, Princess gets hot, and she'll leave the bed, but if there's another body in the bed, she might leave sooner."

"I have a king-sized bed, so maybe she won't feel too confined. On another topic, I want to talk to your parents too," Dane said.

That shocked her. "Why?" She couldn't imagine he was thinking of talking to them about dating her. There was no way Jacqueline felt her parents should have any say in her life from now on, unless they changed their tune about what she had become.

"I just need to get something off my chest with them."

Her jaw dropped. Then she frowned. "It's their problem."

"That's not good enough."

"All right. You do what you want." She wanted to be a fly on the wall when he did it. She could imagine her parents getting defensive, but she was also curious how he would handle it.

"Good."

She hoped he had let it be her choice, but he was his own person and in a way, she liked that he would stick up for her. It would be interesting to see if it had any effect on the way they treated her. On the other hand, she didn't want them to feel they had to be close to her again just because they were being forced to.

They finally reached her house, and Matt pulled up in his car next to hers.

Then she went to the front door and wasn't surprised when Dane and his brothers all went inside with her. They greeted Princess who had heard her car's engine so she was eager to see her. Jacqueline was so tired after hunting two vampires tonight and then going after Heskel, she just wanted to retire to bed.

"If you could grab some of Princess's food, her water dish, the litter box, and the bag of litter, I would be grateful," she said to the brothers. "Princess will not ride in a carrier, so we'll just take her in my car. I'll pack a bag."

She hoped it wouldn't take too long to terminate Heskel so that she didn't have to impose on Dane and his brothers' generosity for too long. She knew they had their own jobs to do.

When she came out of the bedroom, she smiled to see Dane brushing a very satisfied Princess's long soft, silky fur, stretched out on his lap on the couch, her big fluffy tail waving a little. Princess perked up when she saw Jacqueline getting ready to leave, pulling a suitcase. But making sure she wasn't going to be left behind again wasn't enough of an incentive to leave Dane's lap and the heavenly brushing she was getting.

"Traitor," she said to her cat, amused and glad she seemed to like Dane.

"I'll bring Princess, her comb and brush. Is there anything else she needs? My brothers hauled out everything else."

"Nope. I'm ready to go." Then she pulled her bag out the door with Dane following behind her with her cat.

Ryan quickly took her bag from her and put it in her car and then she got in to drive to Dane's place while he held Princess on his lap in the passenger's seat. She drove behind Matt's car since he knew where to go, though Dane could have given her the directions.

"She really likes you," she said to Dane.

"Yeah, I have a way with animals."

"You don't have any pets right now, do you?" She wasn't sure how that would go over with Princess. She hadn't been around dogs or other cats before.

"No. My ex-fiancée was allergic to everything. I'm not totally convinced that she was or if she just didn't like animals."

"Okay, so she wasn't the right one for you." She motioned to the way Princess was sitting on his lap, looking out the window. "She adores you and you seem to like her just as much. I can tell you're an animal person."

"I am and I agree she wasn't the one for me."

Then Jacqueline pulled into the driveway of his two-story, red-brick, Greek Revival home and parked next to Matt's car. Nice. Really nice. She loved the four pillars that reached up two stories high, white trimmed windows with white blinds filling them. Just beautiful.

Dane's brothers started hauling stuff out of his car to carry the items into the house. She got out of her car and started to roll her bag to his house while Dane carried Princess inside, but Trey returned to grab her bag. Ryan had opened the garage door.

"Matt said you need to park your car in the garage so that no one sees it here," Trey said to her.

"You mean Heskel or someone who works for him," she said.

"Exactly."

"Okay." She got back into her car and drove it inside the garage next to Dane's. It was actually a three-car garage which meant they had plenty of room.

"We're going to each take turns returning to our homes and grabbing a bag so we'll have what we'll need to stay here also," Ryan said.

"Thanks to all of you for doing this for me," she said, genuinely thankful to Dane and his brothers. They had even set everything up for Princess.

"No hunter should have to live under a vampire's control," Ryan said.

"I agree." It's just too bad all hunters didn't see it that way. And the thing of it was, they would get a bounty if they took Heskel down, so even if they didn't want to do it altruistically, why not just do it as another mission that they got paid for? Maybe they were afraid he would turn them too.

Trey closed the garage door, and they went inside the house. Matt was leaving first to get his bag packed. Princess was walking around the place, swishing her tail, like she owned Dane's home.

A seamless flow between the dining room, kitchen, and living room existed, covered in wood flooring and Turkish blue and ivory area rugs. The kitchen counters were white marble, and the cabinets were all white, very cheerful. Prints of longhorn steer and fields of bluebonnets hung on the walls. She was impressed. She hadn't known what to expect, but she hadn't thought he would have that much style. Her brother didn't and Van hadn't, so she just figured all bachelor hunters were like that.

The dark oak dining set was large enough for eight people and she figured that was because Dane and his brothers would take up half the seating without even inviting anyone else over. The living room had three blue-velvet, sectional sofas and four, high, wing-back chairs—all elegant, yet comfortable.

Through the floor to ceiling windows, she could see the indoor swimming pool with its aqua water and a rock waterfall at one end with fern plants growing between the rocks. The tile pool patio was a pretty gray slate. Just beautiful.

Then she sighed. "I'm so tired. Can someone just show me to the bedroom?" Jacqueline asked.

"Yeah, come this way. Your bag is in there. You're truly all right with me staying in bed with you?" Dane asked.

"Yes. As long as you don't snore."

He chuckled. "I don't. Does Princess?"

"Sometimes Princess snores."

Dane laughed.

"Night, everyone," Dane said to his brothers.

"Night," everyone echoed back.

As soon as Princess realized Jacqueline had entered the house, she followed her and Dane to the bedroom. Jacqueline wanted to see the whole house and the swimming pool. But for now, she just wanted to go to bed.

The king size bed featured a big fluffy black comforter with a box-pleated, blue and black striped bed skirt.

She sat down on a blue, velvet loveseat in the bedroom and removed one of her boots but before she could get the other, Dane crouched down and untied it, then pulled it off. Wow, that was nice. Van would never have done that for her.

"Which side of the bed do you want?" Dane asked.

She looked at his bedside table that had an alarm clock and a stand to charge cell phones and other electronic devices so she was pretty sure that was his side of the bed. She pulled off her socks and rose from the loveseat and pointed to his side of the bed.

He gave her a knowing smile, plugged his phone in, then stripped down to his boxer briefs. "Is this okay with you or do you want me to dress more?"

"Dress however you usually do."

He cast her more of a sexy grin this time and she suspected he usually slept in the raw.

"I'll be right out." She grabbed her pajama shorts and top and headed into the bathroom. Despite that he was sharing his bed with her to protect her from Heskel, they were *not* dating. So she didn't want to give him the impression that was how she was viewing this.

She brushed her teeth and changed into her pajamas, then carried her clothes out and set them on the love seat. She would organize her clothes tomorrow. Dane was lying underneath the black comforter on the bed and Princess was curled up beside him as if Dane was her newest best friend. It was true love.

Jacqueline climbed into bed, assuming Princess would move over and snuggle up to her until she got too hot, but nope, she stayed right next to Dane. Maybe Jacqueline *was* dating Dane, and Princess knew it before she even did.

"You're all right with me seeing your parents, aren't you?" Dane turned to face her.

"Yeah, sure. What are you going to say to them?"

"That you're their only daughter and they should be thrilled that you are alive at all. That family means everything, unless you had all parted ways some years ago."

"We hadn't."

"I hadn't figured you would. The rift between you has to do with you being turned."

"Maybe...maybe they're just worried that Heskel will force me to kill them or something, when they're least expecting it."

"Which is why they should have solicited all the help they could get to take the maniac down."

"I agree." She swore Dane looked like he wanted to hug her, to tell her that he was now in her life and would be there to protect her even if she no longer had family to aid her.

But they had one problem. She was actually changing her mind about dating him, and wanted that hug, if he was so inclined. Princess was the problem. She was cuddled next to Dane, keeping him from reaching her. It was probably just as well.

She reached over and squeezed Dane's hand. "Let's go to sleep."

"Yeah, in case we have any more trouble. If he communicates with you again, wake me."

"I will." Then she released Dane's hand and closed her eyes and finally fell asleep. Until Princess ran over her body and jumped off the bed. Then Jacqueline moved over and cuddled against Dane, and he wrapped her in his arms...before Princess could separate them again.

7

Dane woke to the aroma of eggs and bacon cooking in the kitchen, coffee brewing, a big fluffy cat sleeping behind him, and in front of him was the beautiful redheaded huntress whom he held in his arms in bed. He smiled. She was still sleeping, but she had moved against him as soon as Princess had left the bed. He was enjoying their deepening friendship and hoped it would continue.

Then he got a call on his phone on her side of the bed. He didn't want anyone to disturb her!

It was too late. She sighed, turned, kissed his mouth, then moved over to get his phone. When she got it, she glanced at the caller ID, and said, "Oh, it's Stacey."

"From the meeting?"

"Yeah. It looks like she's ready to hook up."

Dane laughed. "It's not happening." He took the phone from Jacqueline and answered the call. "Hello?"

For a moment, Jaqueline stayed in bed, but then she left the mattress, grabbed some of her clothes, went into the bathroom, and closed the door.

"Hey, Dane. I was wondering if you would like to go on a hunt with me tonight," Stacey said.

"Uh, I can't. Sorry."

Jacqueline came out of the bathroom, dressed in blue jeans, boots, and a blue floral shirt, raised her brows at Dane and smiled, waved, and headed out of the bedroom. She looked like spring and ready to have some fun today.

"My brothers and I are staying with Jacqueline—"

"Jacqueline from the meeting?"

"Yeah. The rogue vampire who turned her is still alive."

"Oh, no. I thought hunters had killed the rogue vampires who had turned all of us. I want to help take him down."

"Good. We'll sign you up. We need to locate him first. He went after her last night, so my brothers and I are staying with her until we get this done," Dane said.

"Wow. Okay, should we get hold of Anne too? I bet she'll want to help," Stacey said.

"Sure, that sounds good. I had thought of our group, but when my brothers said they would help, I figured that might be enough."

"What happened last night?" Stacey asked.

He explained what had occurred. He suspected since they were all so new at this business, she wanted to know how it would all go down. "She couldn't kill him, but she did pull her sword on him, which distracted him."

"Oh."

"And when he told her to meet him at a house, she didn't feel compelled to go. So maybe her hunter abilities have given her a little bit of an edge compared to a human who is turned," Dane said, getting out of bed.

"That would be good. Okay, well, I'm on standby and if you decide you need me, or if you can help me with my mission tonight, just let me know. I'll let you call Anne and tell her what's going on.

It's best it comes from the horse's mouth, rather than me pass along the news and get it wrong."

"Sounds good. I'll do that. Talk to you later." When they ended the call, he headed for the bathroom and hoped that Jacqueline didn't believe he was making date plans with Stacey.

After dressing in a blue T-shirt, jeans, and boots, he went downstairs and found everyone setting the table for breakfast. That was one of the things he was glad for. He could still eat regular food.

"So?" Jacqueline asked Dane.

"Stacey wanted me to go on a job with her tonight. I told her I was sticking with you because of the vampire issue you're having."

"You can go with her if she needs you. We can't abandon others like us if no one wants to work with us—making an exception of your brothers, of course," Jacqueline said.

Trey said, "A couple of us can go with her."

"I told her we're trying to track down Heskel, and she wants to help with that." Dane had no intention of seeing Stacey except when it came to meeting her at the therapy session or on a mission to take down vampires to help each other out. He was sure she wanted more of a relationship.

Jacqueline poured a glass of orange juice for everyone. "If she has a vampire that she needs help with tonight, I'm all for going with her too."

"All right," Dane said. If Jacqueline wanted to help, he was all for it. But also, he needed to make sure she remained safe. He called Anne to see if she wanted to go with them.

"Oh, I've got a family issue to deal with, but I'll be happy to help when that's resolved."

"Okay, we sure appreciate it. And if you need any help, just let us know."

"I sure will," Anne said. Then they ended the call.

"I did some research into Heskel to learn where he might go," Trey said.

"Trey is our private investigator when we're trying to learn all we can about a rogue vampire that we are after. What did you learn?" Dane asked.

Trey finished his slice of crunchy bacon and wiped his fingers off on his paper napkin. "The house we went to last night is owned by one of his blood bonds, a chef at a restaurant in Plano. He obviously wasn't home at the time. Heskel might have told him to stay away. Heskel has five other blood bonds and I have a list of their residences. I'm also investigating the whereabouts of his three close vampire friends. None of them are on any termination lists, so hopefully they'll stay out of it if Heskel goes to one of their places and his friends are there when we turn up."

"Okay, that sounds like a good start." Matt drank some more of his coffee.

"Call Stacey back and tell her we'll go with her tonight," Jacqueline said to Dane.

He smiled at her. "You know, I think *you* need to get in touch with her."

Jacqueline chuckled. "I will." She pulled out her phone and said, "Hey, Stacey, it's me, Jacqueline, from the meeting. Dane told us you want some back up on taking someone down. We're ready to help. Can you tell us more about the rogue?" She put the phone on speaker.

"Uh, yeah, and thanks. It's a woman, Italia, an ancient vampire. She has an ancient vampire boyfriend who strays quite often and every time he does, Italia tracks down his new human lover and then kills her. The police have pinned ten crimes on her finally and I ended up with the case to take her down."

"What about her boyfriend? Is he on a terminal list too?" Jacqueline asked.

"No. Franklin hasn't done anything wrong but gotten his side interests killed because of his jealous want-to-be mate. They've been together for centuries, but he won't agree to being her exclusive mate."

"I'm surprised that she doesn't kill him, instead of the women," Jacqueline said.

"She still wants him. According to witnesses, she always has," Stacey said. "I'm sorry about the situation you have with Heskel. I hope Dane told you that I want to help you get rid of him."

"Yes, thanks so much for offering."

"You should have mentioned it at the meeting. The rest of us had someone help to take out the rogues who turned us. We are a team."

Jacqueline swallowed hard and smiled. "Thank you. Where and when do you want to meet to take down Italia?"

"Seven tonight. Franklin goes to a vampire bar—the Blue Moon —every Tuesday night and Italia does also, but they go in separate cars. Then he leaves the club, goes to a human club, picks up a woman, and drives to her place. Somehow Italia learns where he has gone, possibly tracking him to the human club and lying in wait, then follows him to the victim's home," Stacey said. "We can meet at the grocery store half a block from the Blue Moon. The police suspect she has killed more women, but they couldn't prove it. They have proven she murdered the others."

"Okay, we'll meet up with you at the grocery store," Jacqueline said.

"Then we have to go after *your* vampire once we take down Italia," Stacey said.

"We're trying to find any location he might be at and then sure, that would be great."

Then they ended the call and Dane sighed. "I'm glad you called her."

"Do you think she's after you?" Jacqueline asked.

"Yeah."

Trey laughed. "Here we were so upset that Dane's fiancée

ditched him and he already has a couple of huntresses interested in him."

Dane gave his brother a look to cool it. He didn't want to lose whatever headway he had hoped he was making with Jacqueline.

"Oh?" Jacqueline said.

Trey's face reddened.

Dane suspected his brother thought that Jacqueline and he were already an item. He wished, but he had to take this slowly. He suspected all the changes to her life were making her hesitant to really get involved with another hunter who had been turned like her. He didn't blame her for feeling that way. Also the business of both of them being recently separated from the ones they were engaged to would make a difference.

Matt laughed. "It seems you stuck your foot in your mouth again, Trey."

Then Jacqueline smiled, to everyone's relief.

"You know we were talking earlier about how you liked to go to hunters' clubs for drinks and dancing. We shouldn't be banned from hunters' clubs," Dane said.

"I agree, but I'm sure that we'll have trouble if we go to one," she said.

"Tell us when you want to go there and we'll be there for you as backup," Trey said.

"You took the words right out of my mouth," Matt said.

"Yeah, I agree." Ryan toasted them with a glass of orange juice. "Just say the word. Between the two of you and the three of us, we'll change their tunes if anyone gets nasty."

"Exactly. You're both still hunters. You were born that way also," Trey said. "Sure, you're vampires now too, but you're part of our community, still taking down rogue vampires, just with additional skills the rest of us don't have. You're the good guys, like the rest of us are."

"But then if we wanted to go there, we would always have to go with you guys," Jacqueline said. "That's an imposition for you."

"No, not at all," Matt said. "The more you go there, the more they'll get used to you being there and realize you're not any different than you were before."

Dane would like to take Jacqueline to a hunters' club. If they hadn't been turned and they hadn't been engaged to other hunters, that was something he would have done without question. "I'm game." But he didn't want Jacqueline to feel uncomfortable about doing it if she wasn't sure.

"Yeah, I'm willing." She smiled at the brothers. "We'll have fun. And maybe we'll make new hunter friends who are more openminded."

"Right. That's who we'll want to be around," Dane said.

"Okay. We could go early when it's not as crowded. But we probably should wait until we get rid of Heskel. I would hate to be at a hunters' club and then worry that Heskel could control me and try to force me to hurt anyone. That would undo our effort at proving we're still hunters and like the rest of them. And that we should be allowed to go to a hunters' club." Jacqueline drank some of her orange juice.

"It's a date," Dane said. They just had to get rid of Heskel.

"All right. That sounds good," Jacqueline said.

After they finished breakfast, she said, "Okay, I need a tour of the house."

"Uh, I didn't make my guest bed," Ryan said. "And I probably left my dirty clothes on the floor."

She laughed. "Dane can show me the rest of the house, and not the rooms you're staying in."

"Let's go." Dane was proud of his home that he had purchased with the idea of finding a huntress mate and eventually raising a family there. He had bought it before he had met Wendy, his now ex-fiancée, so it wasn't like they had purchased it together. Though she loved the home and planned to move in. She'd had the nerve to tell him he needed to sell the place and give her half the proceeds, as if they'd been married already and were getting a divorce. To which he'd said no way.

He showed Jacqueline the den and the sunroom which had windows that faced the swimming pool.

"Oh, I want to swim."

"You're welcome to anytime you want," he said.

"Thanks. I brought my swimsuit."

"Great." He showed Jacqueline the laundry room and then his office. "And of course there are the three guest rooms my brothers use when we're going on a mission together and want to watch each other's backs." Then he showed her the other two bathrooms.

"I guess your brothers believe we're dating, but we both had relationships that had ended abruptly because of what we have become."

"Yeah, but we are much more suited to each other because of it." He truly believed it.

She shook her head. "Until Heskel is eliminated, I don't feel anyone who is close to me is safe."

"Yeah, but we always run that risk, even when we were just hunters."

"Well, that's true, but we still had control over our own actions."

He couldn't argue with that. He sure didn't want her to feel unsafe and he didn't want Heskel to control her. More than anything, he wanted to get rid of the menace to her. But until they found Heskel, they couldn't do much about him.

"I'll tell you if he communicates with me again," Jacqueline said as they walked out to the patio and stood looking at the aqua pool.

"Good." He knew she would, as long as she was able to and Heskel didn't stop her from doing so.

"Is it...too early to go swimming?"

"Anytime is great for swimming. As hot as it is already in

Dallas? No. And since it's indoors, even if the sun is fully out, we're fine."

"Great. I'm off to change. Coming?"

"Yeah, I sure am." He was thinking he needed to do some fun things with her and not just prove to her that he could make a great hunter companion on hunts. He was right behind her when she vanished. He chuckled, his brothers smiling at him.

"She's tenacious," Matt said.

"That she is. We're going swimming."

"Enjoy!" Ryan said.

He would.

To give her some time to change into her bathing suit, he headed up the stairs, instead of vanishing and reappearing in the bedroom. When he reached the bedroom, she was already changed, wearing a bright teal, high-waisted bikini and she smiled at him. The bikini top caressed her breasts, her bottoms fitting her shapely form beautifully.

Before he could tell her how much he loved the bathing suit on her, she vanished. He laughed. He would never get used to that. He hurried to strip out of his clothes and yanked on his swim trunks. He wanted to join her quickly, so he teleported himself to the indoor pool and found her already in the pool, swimming.

He jumped in so that he could be in her path, making a calculated strike. She saw him, just before she swam into him. He captured her in his arms and kissed her.

"Hmm, as a hunter, were you this persistent in dating a huntress?" she asked.

"Is it working?" he asked, kissing drops of water off her cheeks.

She laughed. "I think you are doing just fine, despite me trying to keep this on a more professional level."

"Hell, yes! I was so afraid I wasn't doing this right. As to dating others? I never was successful at dating and truly, I don't know how I ended up with being engaged to Wendy."

"She didn't deserve you."

"Yeah, in retrospect, I realize that's true. The same with Van being engaged to you." Then Dane kissed her again, and she deepened the kiss. Oh, yeah, she was incredible and way too good for the likes of any hunter like Van. "I can't imagine anyone giving you up. And we truly make a great team on a hunt."

"Oh, yeah, I was thinking the same thing about you." Then they kissed again.

After they separated, they began to swim and tackle each other. Then his brothers came out to the pool wearing swim trunks, and Jacqueline and Dane laughed. He loved his brothers, and he knew they wanted to kind of slow things down between Jacqueline and himself because they wanted to make sure he wasn't just having a case of rebound, just like she wasn't after they were no longer with their ex's.

He knew they would help them to be in the relationship, to back them, but just to take it more slowly. He hoped Jacqueline was okay with it, and she appeared to just be amused and happy to see them. Maybe she was thinking the same thing. He figured if it was meant to be between the two of them, it would be.

He chased after her, ignoring his brothers as Trey cannonballed into the pool, and Matt dove in. Ryan soon joined in, and the three brothers began wrestling each other in the pool, splashing water everywhere. But for now, Dane preferred playing with Jacqueline in the pool when he usually loved to horse around with his brothers when they went swimming together. Yeah, he wasn't giving up on her that easily.

8

Jacqueline loved Dane's brothers. She thought they were the greatest. She loved that they were willing to back them on going to a hunters' club. She didn't want them to tarnish their reputations as hunters, but she thought the world of them for offering to be there for both of them. And she was completely amused that they would come and insert themselves during their pool time to cool things down a bit between her and Dane. She knew they had his best interests—and probably hers—at heart.

She got a kick out of the brothers all wrestling in the pool. They were fun. But Dane wasn't playing with them. He stayed with her and kept her company, chasing her, or she chased him, diving under the water, treading water together.

She and he finally got out of the pool and sat down on a couple of lawn chairs to dry out. "It was good that you have an *indoor* swimming pool once you were turned."

"I know. It really was fortuitous. I just figured we could use it all year round, even in winter if it was enclosed. But it was really good that we can use it any time now, even if it's fully sunny out."

"*Where are you?*" a voice said in Jacqueline's head suddenly. "*You're not at home.*"

Jacqueline grabbed Dane's arm. "It's him."

"Heskel?" Dane took her into his arms as if to protect him from the monster.

His brothers stopped playing and watched them, having heard him mention Heskel's name.

She nodded. "He asked me where I'm at."

"He knows you're not at home?" Dane asked.

"It appears that way. Do you think he sent his blood bonds to come for me?"

"It sounds like he has sent someone to check on you or grab you."

"But he doesn't know where I am now. No one must have been watching my house when we returned there, packed up, and left. Which I'm glad for."

"Me too."

"Can he force you to tell him where you are?" Matt asked, treading water in the deep end of the pool.

"I haven't answered him. I didn't before when he told me to meet him at his blood bond's house either. I just told you and we went there."

"Okay," Matt said. "So he can't read your mind."

"No. He can talk to me telepathically, but he can't seem to force me to tell him what I'm up to. And he can't make me telepathically communicate with him. But I'm sure he'll be trying to learn where I am."

"Did you feel forced to go to Heskel's blood bond's house?" Trey asked.

"I did. Not like I had to leave right that second, but I felt I had to do it. I couldn't kill him, but I actually threatened him with my sword. I couldn't believe I could do that. I keep hoping that as a huntress, I'm able to fight his control. Maybe not all the way, but enough to keep him from making me do anything against my will."

"We need to take down this bastard," Trey said, everyone agreeing.

God, how she hated that the vampire who had turned her had any control over her life. It had been turned upside down enough already!

"Maybe we should go to a vampire club and see if we can track him down that way," Dane said.

"Do you think vampires who are strictly vampires would turn on one of their own?" she asked, afraid they would just as soon tell Heskel the hunters were at the club looking for him.

"Not necessarily," Dane said. "The vampires who aren't rogues don't want to have their own names blackened. Though if friends of Heskel are there, or other rogues, they might feel compelled to tell him that we were looking for him."

"Well, also, I suspect that they won't want us in the club either because we're still hunters," she said. "I'm going to change clothes."

"See you upstairs in a minute," he said.

She vanished and reappeared in his bedroom, changed into jeans and a T-shirt and headed downstairs. "How does sea bass sound for lunch?" she asked.

"Delicious. I'll be right down," Dane said and vanished.

Then the brothers left the swimming pool, went upstairs to change, and they all joined her downstairs. They ended up having sea bass, fried potatoes, tomatoes, and green beans.

"Let's go to the park and take a hike," Jacqueline said.

Matt asked, "All of us?"

"Sure," she said.

It was cloudy out, but for now, there was only a low chance of rain. After eating lunch, the brothers cleaned up, then they all went for a drive to a park to hike a ten-mile trail. Dane walked with Jacqueline while Matt walked way ahead of them, and Trey and

Ryan walked way behind them—there for them in the event anyone caused trouble for them.

Once they returned to Dane's house, Jacqueline said, "We ought to go to a humans' club. We should be able to dance and enjoy ourselves at one without any incident." She felt that she couldn't be locked up while waiting for a chance to take down Heskel.

"Yeah, I'm ready for it," Dane said.

"I'm going to pick up a huntress I wanted to ask out. Hopefully, she'll be free," Matt said.

"Who?" Jacqueline asked before the others could ask.

"Marissa."

"Marissa Overlander?" Jacqueline asked.

"Yeah, do you know her?" Matt asked.

"Just by name. I've heard she's kind of a maverick huntress," Jacqueline said.

Matt smiled.

She got the impression that he liked that kind of a woman.

Then Matt called Marissa and said, "Hey, this is Matt Edmonton. Yeah. My brothers and a huntress are going to a human club. Do you want to go with us? I can pick you up and take you?" He shook his head. "Okay, no problem. Maybe we can make it another time then. Sure, bye." He ended the call.

"No, deal, eh?" Dane said.

"She said the notice was too short but that she was happy to go out some other time—if she has enough notice."

Jacqueline laughed. "She probably had other plans."

"She'll take you up on the next offer, if you don't call her at the last minute," Trey said.

"Yeah," Matt said.

Dane said, "I'm lucky that Jacqueline loves to do things on the spur of the moment."

"Yeah, but truly, Marissa could have had some plans she couldn't or wouldn't change for a date with a hunter she has never dated before," Jacqueline said. "I mean, if I had plans to do something and couldn't get away for a spontaneous date. I would have said the same thing."

"Nah," Dane said. "You would have dropped any of your plans to go out with me."

His brothers laughed.

"You are so sure of yourself," she said, kissing his cheek. She realized he might be right though.

Trey said, "I'll ask Denise if she and two of her huntress friends can go with us." He got on his phone and called her. "Hey, my brothers and I and a huntress are going to a human club. Do you and a couple of your huntress friends want to join us?" He smiled at Matt. "Okay, we'll come and pick you up...yeah, now. See you in a few." He said to them, "Okay, we all have dates."

Matt slapped him on the back. "Good going."

"Is this going to mess you up with plans to date Marissa later?" Jacqueline asked.

"I've never dated her before so there may never be anything there between us," Matt said.

But Jacqueline wasn't sure that Marissa would feel that way if she learned that when she said she couldn't go out with him, he just picked up another date for the night.

Then Dane's brothers went to pick up the other women while Dane and Jacqueline dressed.

"I was going to say *you're* a maverick huntress," Dane said.

She chuckled. "I am. Okay, I'm going to wear this off-the-shoulder black dress and heels."

"Oh, I love that. I've got this black shirt, black jeans, and dress shoes."

"Perfect." Once he pulled off his shirt, she ran her hands over his bare chest. "I guess we can't skip out on your brothers and their dates."

"Sure we can."

She laughed. "We'll do it after we check out the human club." She really loved dancing and she wanted to know if maybe human clubs would be the best way for them to go when they wanted a night out to dance. Humans wouldn't know what they were, most likely.

Then they finished dressing, petted Princess goodbye, and headed out to Dane's truck. Matt gave Dane a call on Bluetooth. "We're dressed, have picked up the ladies, and are on our way. What about you?"

"We are too."

"Good. We were afraid you might have gotten sidetracked," Matt said.

Everyone in the vehicle laughed.

Dane and Jacqueline smiled.

It wasn't long before they all arrived at the Stardust Club. The exterior was a stone building with a big green metal roof, lights in the shape of stars all outside the club lighting it up, a fountain with a fish pouring water into it sitting near the entryway. Inside, they found a couple of large tables to grab and pushed them together. Disco lights were flashing inside, and the building was atmospherically dark. Everything was a western theme in there, including the serving staff who were wearing blue jeans, red and white gingham shirts, cowboy boots, and cowboy hats.

Lasso ropes, cowboy hats, boots, paintings of cattle drives hung on the walls. The furniture was all heavy oak. It was a fun place to go.

They introduced Jacqueline and Dane to Denise, Kelsey, and Sandy. They soon had drinks and started dancing. They were having a great time.

"Hmm, you are such a great dancer," Jacqueline said to Dane.

"You bring out the moves in me," Dane said, holding her close, dancing to the beat, turning her on.

When she had danced with Van, it was like they were two separate people, doing their own thing. But with Dane, they were dancing nice and close, like they had been forever, like this was where they belonged. He made her feel sexy and desirable. And she could feel where she was arousing him. But then her teeth began to elongate, and she felt embarrassed. Why would they do that now? She didn't want him to see that her teeth had come down or he might think she was mad at him.

But then they finished their dance and they returned to their table so they could drink their cocktails and she hoped she could get her teeth under control. The others all joined them and ordered fresh drinks when a blond-haired guy came over to the table and asked Jacqueline to dance with him.

"Uh, no, thanks. I'm with my partner." Jacqueline patted Dane's arm.

"You are lucky," the man said to Dane. Then he reached his hand out to Jacqueline as if she hadn't just said no to him, his blue-eyed gaze focused on her eyes.

She picked up her drink and took another sip. She wasn't going with the guy. None of them had their swords with them since no weapons were allowed in any of the clubs. Her canines were still extended, but she didn't want to expose them to him.

Dane said, "She said no."

Then the man turned his attention to Dane. He was just staring at him, as if he couldn't believe that Dane would say that to him.

Then the man grabbed Jacqueline's wrist and Dane was out of his seat before anyone could see his response. He slugged the man in the jaw, knocking him back and the guy lost his grip on Jacqueline.

Then suddenly, the man backed off, rubbing his jaw where Dane had punched him, frowning. "What are you?" Then he paused. "Hell, you're hunters."

Dane smiled, but his canines were fully exposed.

"My mistake," the guy quickly said, and hurried out of the club.

"What was that all about?" Trey asked.

"I'm sure he was a vampire, probably looking for a blood bond, who was enamored with Jacqueline, and figured she was the perfect conquest. I'm sure he was trying to convince Dane and Jacqueline through vampire persuasion that she would dance with him," Matt said.

"But then he thought they were hunters," Ryan said.

"Yep, because he wouldn't have been able to control them then, but then Dane had to show off his fangs," Matt said, chuckling.

"I had to make the point that I wasn't just a hunter," Dane said.

She could have shown off her fangs also, but after her hot dancing with Dane, and then cooling off with drinking their cocktails, they were already back to their normal size. She was glad that they weren't always long fangs at least. She was relieved Dane had shown off his fangs to the other vampire.

She smiled up at him and he kissed her. So much for safely going to a human club. But she realized that this was probably a place vampires *would* come to for a blood bond.

"I'm glad you showed off your canines," she said to Dane.

"That's the first time anyone has made me angry enough to show them off in a confrontation. Besides, I figured he was a vampire at that point, and I assumed there might be a code of honor between non-rogues that a woman who was with me was off-limits unless she wanted to dance or be with him," Dane said.

The huntresses with them just stared at the two of them. The one said, "You're vampires?"

"Hunters turned, yes," Jacqueline said, trying not to sound annoyed. Why couldn't they have just gone dancing and enjoyed themselves like other people were doing?

Their second round of drinks were delivered to the table and Jacqueline drank some of hers, then said, "Let's dance."

"I'm all for it." Dane drank some of his drink, and then took her hand and they headed back to the dance floor.

She was sure Dane's brothers would be explaining to the women what had happened to them. Maybe even not to bring it up.

"Well, that went over well," Jacqueline said to Dane as they danced nice and close again and she really needed this affirmation that she was all right as a hunter turned.

"You mean with the vampire?"

"No, with the women who came with your brothers to the club."

Dane smiled down at her. "I think they were in awe."

"I think they were in shock."

"Well, now they know, and all that matters is that we're having a good time," Dane said.

"That's true! I sure am. But yeah, the confrontation with the vampire sure went well."

When everyone was done with their drinks and dancing, Matt said, "We're taking the ladies home."

"We're headed to my house," Dane said.

Jacqueline wanted to know what the women thought of them, though she shouldn't have cared. That was something she was having to deal with—letting go of whatever others' thought of her now that she was turned.

Then finally they arrived home and started making a dinner of chicken enchiladas and rice.

Not long after that, the brothers joined them for dinner.

"So what did the women say about Dane and me being turned?" Jacqueline asked Dane's brothers at once.

Matt smiled. "They thought it was really cool. They didn't want to make either of you mad."

Relieved, Jacqueline said, "Good."

Dane rubbed her back. "Yeah, if they hadn't been cool with it—"

"They would be history," Trey said. "I mean as far as us dating them."

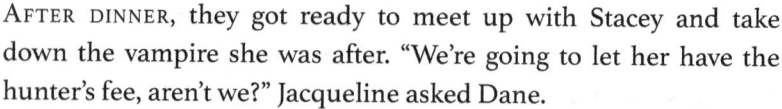

AFTER DINNER, they got ready to meet up with Stacey and take down the vampire she was after. "We're going to let her have the hunter's fee, aren't we?" Jacqueline asked Dane.

"Yes. Stacey asked us to help her so I think that's only fair," he said.

"You took half of my bounty fee for getting rid of Axel."

"You took half of my bounty fee for getting rid of Mabon." He smiled at her.

She smiled back at him. His brothers chuckled.

"What do you all do when you go after a rogue together? Split the bounty money between the four of you?" Jacqueline asked.

"When we go together, we're usually after a gang of rogue vampires, so yeah, we split the proceeds because there's enough money to go around. Though we get paid a lot for every case because of the danger of taking them down," Dane said.

Trey said, "I would have given you the full bounty on Axel, Jacqueline."

Dane laughed. "Hell, he was on my take-down list also."

"Dane earned it. We both did. And he did pay half of his bounty on Mabon when *he* did all the work." Jacqueline squeezed his hand.

Then they arrived at the grocery store. Stacey got out of her car and gave all the guys a hug first, then finally hugged Jacqueline. Jacqueline knew where she stood on the totem pole—on the bottom—because Jacqueline was into handsome guys. Dane and his brothers were all real lookers.

"Thanks so much to all of you for coming to help me with this. I thought only Dane would be, but I understand how he was stepping in to help a fellow therapy group member."

Jacqueline was amused. Stacey *really* liked men.

"Okay, so I put a tracker on Italia's car and also her mate's.

They're at the Blue Moon vampire club. They take separate cars when they go there so they can leave when they feel like it. I thought we could wait there and watch for them to leave. If Franklin leaves first, we need to have one vehicle follow him, and then the other needs to follow Italia. She'll probably wait for him to leave and then go right after that," Stacey said.

"Who of us is going after whom?" Matt asked.

"Since Italia's the one we have to eliminate, I want to follow her and then Dane can see where Franklin goes. If he picks up a woman, he'll be with her, then he leaves her house, the police believe he returns home and then Italia kills the woman her mate had been with," Stacey said.

"Okay, that sounds good." Now Dane understood why Stacey had needed someone to help her with the case. They never knew how they would have to take down a rogue until they did their research. He was glad they had agreed to help her. Stacey couldn't have done this alone.

"We'll divide up and some of us will go with Stacey and the others will go in Dane's truck," Matt said.

"I'll go with Stacey," Trey said.

Ryan said he would go with them too.

Then Trey and Ryan got into Stacey's car with her. Jacqueline was glad that they were there to protect her if anything went sideways. She was also glad Dane wasn't going with her in her vehicle.

As they followed Stacey's car, Matt said, "She's intriguing."

Dane glanced at Jacqueline. "She's a nice person, but I'm not interested in her."

Matt laughed. "She would be a handful."

"Yeah, too much of a handful."

"Maybe *I* would be," Jacqueline said.

Dane smiled at her. "*My* kind of a handful."

"That's what you think." Jacqueline wanted to make sure he understood that them being a couple wasn't a sure thing yet!

When they arrived at the vampire club painted a cornflower blue and featuring a large white moon, Stacey called Dane and he put it on speaker. "Italia's car is that red Cadillac. The blue Jeep on the other side of the parking lot is Franklin's. According to when I saw them going inside the club, they've been there for about a half hour."

"We're used to waiting to take down rogues, so no problem," Matt said.

An hour later, Stacey called Dane again and he put it on speaker. "The man in the black jeans, checked shirt, black cowboy boots, and hat, that's Franklin. Some say he was a cowboy a couple of centuries ago."

"Okay, we're following him." Dane waited to start his vehicle until Franklin drove off. Then he followed him. "I guess he never picks up a blood bond at a vampire club while his mate is there."

"No, he appears to be sneaky about it. Maybe it's always a one-night stand and he never realized that his mate eliminates the woman afterward," Jacqueline said. "But what if he's all in on this? It spices up their life? He gets to do what he wants, and she gets to do what she wants. It's a mutual game between them and he knows all about what she's doing."

"Uh, yeah, I agree with Jacqueline on that," Matt said. "I wonder if he's on any lists."

"Unless it can be proven that he and his mate are in collusion, then maybe not," Jacqueline said. "He may know exactly what she's up to but proving it could be difficult to do without questioning both of them separately. I suspect questioning either of them isn't going to be an option. Especially with Italia because she's already on a list. She'll only have one thought in mind—kill the hunters who come after her and keep from being eliminated. And if she's loyal to Franklin and doesn't want us to go after him next, she won't tell us that he is part of this whole murder scheme."

Then they saw him stop at a home in a nice residential area.

"No," Jacqueline said.

"Yeah, blood bonds come from all walks of life," Dane said.

A woman came out of the front door wearing a silky, red nighty and smiled at Franklin. She was about thirty, her brown hair streaked with blond strands, and she didn't know what she was getting herself into.

Franklin parked his car while Dane parked curbside a few houses down. "What if Franklin takes part in the killings? Maybe just his mate is blamed for them, like she's jealous he would see another woman behind his back?" Dane said.

"That would be even more insidious," Jacqueline said. "But it could give the human woman more of a sense of security if she thinks she's only going to be with a male for a good time."

"Do you think she might not even know that Franklin is a vampire? I mean, he's a good-looking guy and she might just think he's human," Jacqueline said. "It would be easy for him to convince her of it."

"Let's make sure that he isn't the one who is responsible for killing the victims," Dane said.

They left the pickup and headed for the house, skirting around the right of the one-story stucco house with a large water fountain out front, a green boxwood hedge all around, until they moved to the back door. Matt had a lockpick and unlocked the door. He carefully opened it.

They heard a man and woman talking in the living room and they headed in that direction to make sure the woman was okay. The thing was, they couldn't do anything to him if he was just having sex with her, just biting her, and giving her pleasure. But if he did it against her will? That was another story.

WHEN THEY SAW Franklin kissing the woman, Jacqueline felt like a voyeur. She glanced at Dane. He was frowning at the couple. Suddenly, the front door was thrown open and Italia flew into the room with murder in her eyes. Jacqueline thought Franklin would stop his mate from hurting the woman, but instead he stepped back and the human woman screamed. Then the human collapsed on the couch in a faint. At the same time, Jacqueline appeared in front of the woman to stop the vampiress from hurting the human. Both Italia and Franklin looked shocked to see the group of hunters in the living room and then Dane transporting himself like a vampire.

Stacey had finally moved in the same way to reach Italia, and she quickly shoved her sword into her heart. Italia turned into a wrinkled, dehydrated prune. Franklin jumped away from the human woman and his mate's body, throwing up his hands as if he wasn't doing anything bad, and that he had nothing to do with hurting anyone.

Now Jacqueline wondered if he was just as involved but when she had stopped Italia from ripping the human's throat out, he decided to play the innocent.

Matt was texting on his phone and then he said, "You're lucky this time. You're not on any termination lists, but if you hook up with another vampire who kills humans that you're luring into a situation like this, you're going to be eliminated."

Franklin glanced at his girlfriend's body, then vanished, not waiting for the hunters to change their minds. They heard his car peel out of the driveway. The police would have Italia's car towed and impounded. A couple of officers were coming to take their statements.

Jacqueline revived the human woman, who looked horrified to see the dead body on her floor and the hunters peering down at her. "Did you know Franklin was a vampire?"

She shook her head vigorously.

"Have you met him before?" Jacqueline asked.

"On a dating site. Don't tell my husband, please."

Jacqueline raised her brows.

"He's always away on trips. I know he's seeing other women. It's...it's the first time I even tried anything like this."

"It would have been your last if we hadn't intervened on your behalf," Jacqueline said.

The police and two homicide detectives arrived then and everyone, including the woman, gave them their statements.

"We'll keep an eye out on Franklin and if he's involved in any more cases of murders of women, we'll add him to a list," the homicide detective said. "And, miss? You're lucky these hunters have been following the rogues' movements. You can never be too careful."

Lipstick was smudged around her mouth, and her mascara was running down her cheeks in black rivulets.

That's when Jacqueline saw a dollhouse sitting in the corner of the living room against the wall. "Do you have children?"

"A boy and a girl, age seven and nine."

"You're lucky we found you and rescued you before the vampiress killed you. No telling what she would have done to the kids," Jacqueline said, wanting the woman to realize the danger she had put them in even if she didn't care about her own safety.

Then the police finished up with them, and one of the detectives said to the woman, "Do you have anyone you can call to stay with you? We've notified your husband, but he can't get here any sooner than tomorrow night on a flight home."

"My...my mother."

Jacqueline wondered how her mother would take this whole business. But that's when she got a communication again from Heskel. *"Where are you? I learned you took down a couple of vampires last night and then you just vanished. I know which vampires are on your target list still, but you haven't gone anywhere near them."*

"It's him, Heskel," Jacqueline said to Dane. "He wants to know where I am again. He said he's watching my target list of vampires, which he can't do on his own, so he must have vampire friends or blood bonds watching them, waiting for me to show up."

"Ask him where he is," Stacey said.

Would it be that easy? Jacqueline doubted it. "I don't want to communicate with him. What if he can learn where I am if I did?"

"Hmm, like GPS? Maybe. I don't know," Stacey said.

That was the thing. None of the turned hunters knew enough about it.

9

"I have Heskel's home address," Dane said to Jacqueline, Stacey, and his brothers. "We talked about his blood bonds and vampire friends—where *their* homes are. But what about *his* home? Maybe that's where he is, believing we'll be searching for him every place else, not believing he would be home."

"Let's go there," Jacqueline said.

Everybody was agreeable. Dane sure hoped they could take the rogue down tonight.

Then they got into the two vehicles and headed to the house that Heskel owned. His home was surrounded by about five acres, half an acre in front, about four acres in the back and some land on the sides, but not that much between homes. His home was maybe about seventy-five-hundred square feet, all brick, lots of windows, but all were covered with beautiful hurricane shutters. Typical of a home that was owned by a vampire who had to keep the sun out when it was shining bright during the day.

Even Dane kept his blinds closed now that he was a vampire, and he had noticed that so did Jacqueline.

"Wow, what a house," Jacqueline said.

"Yeah, these ancient vampires often have a lot of money. They've been able to save money for centuries, not like the rest of us," Dane said.

"Yeah," Matt agreed. "He'll have security cameras since he can't watch out the windows. Because there are three cars sitting in the driveway, and not in the three-car garage, I suspect those are blood bonds. Though they could be Heskel's vampire friends."

"I agree. And if they're here, there's a good chance that their master is also. At least I'm hoping so," Dane said. "Let's go."

Trey, Ryan, and Stacey joined them at the car. Then they all discussed what they were going to do.

"We go in twos," Matt said. "One person to watch each other's back. Who wants to go with whom?"

Dane immediately said, "Jacqueline is with me."

Trey said, "I want Stacey with me because she has some cool vampire moves. You're on your own, Ryan."

Ryan smiled. "I'm with Matt."

"Did I just get picked last for teams?" Matt asked.

Everyone smiled.

"We don't take out blood bonds," Matt said. "If there are other vampires in the house and they stand back, we leave them alone. If they come after us, they're dead. We'll go in the back way together. Even though I like the idea of going in from different directions, and not getting backed into a corner, I want us to stick close to each other so we all have each other's backs. But your partner is the one that you'll be concentrating on. Does anyone have any different ideas?"

"We need one of those infrared cameras to know where everyone is in the house," Stacey said.

"Yeah, we tried it once, but when we go into a fight, we often don't have time to use one before we're in attack mode," Dane said.

"Completely understandable. Let's go," Jacqueline said, and Dane knew she wanted to get this over with if they could tonight.

They saw some security cameras, but the hunters skirted them, while the hunters turned vampires all vanished and reappeared in the backyard where they could check out the security cameras in the backyard. Heskel didn't have any. *Score!*

But Dane couldn't deny how much he worried about Jacqueline. He knew she was a good huntress, but she was also the one that Heskel could control—to an extent. They still didn't know how much if he really put his mind to it, or how much she could fight against it.

Matt was in the lead with Ryan.

They heard loud laughter and talking inside.

How many were inside? And were they a mix of vampires and blood bonds? But mostly, would they fight the hunters and put their own necks at risk?

Matt used the lockpick and carefully opened the door, and they were all glad it didn't squeak. Dane couldn't stand squeaking doors and was always putting grease on his when they did that. But in a way, a squeaking door could act as an early warning system.

The laughter and talking was coming from deeper inside the house. The back door led into a den, and it was beautiful, the lights on in there showcasing oil paintings of ranches and cowboys, of cattle drives, and fields of Indian paintbrush. The couches were all brown leather and marble-topped tables with wrought iron legs.

Then they moved toward the room where all the conversations were coming from. They kept Dane and Jacqueline in the middle to begin with and Dane knew they were trying to keep anyone from hurting her.

"That's him," Jacqueline whispered to Dane, but Matt turned to look at her too. "In the room up ahead. I recognize his voice. It sounds just like his telepathic voice," she said.

"That's who we'll concentrate on then," Matt said.

They went slowly though, not wanting to alert everyone they

were coming. Though it was killing Dane not to be able to rush in and kill the vampire to free Jacqueline from his control.

They reached the end of the hall where Matt could see what was going on, the rest of them holding back. Matt moved back to speak to them privately. It was so noisy in the living area that no one could hear them speaking.

"Five vampires—two on my list besides Heskel," Matt said. "The one kind of in the middle of the whole group is Heskel. And it looks like about seven blood bonds are here. Ryan and I will go straight into the mess of them and target Heskel. Romanoff is off to the right near the fireplace holding a bloody cocktail and wearing a black tux. He's a vampire on my list. Vandenburg is off to the left of the group feeding on a blood bond, both sitting on a forest green couch."

"We'll take out Romanoff," Dane said, Jacqueline agreeing.

"We'll aim for Vandenburg," Trey said, and Stacey was ready for it.

"Let's go," Matt said, and he rushed into the room before anyone even noticed he shouldn't have been there.

Stacey and Jacqueline vanished and appeared right next to their targets. Dane had to get with the program when it came to moving like that and quickly joined Jacqueline as she aimed her sword at the tux-clad vampire.

Trey was racing to catch up to Stacey as three of the blood bonds screamed out and ran away. They appeared eager to get out of the hunters' path and live another day. As soon Romanoff saw Jacqueline with her sword aimed at his heart, he disappeared and came around behind her. But that's when Dane came behind him and thrust his sword into the vampire's heart. Dane was beginning to think this was a winning way for him to team up with Jacqueline. Romanoff turned into a baggy skinned skeleton while Matt was fighting Heskel and Ryan was fighting an overzealous and loyal blood bond.

Dane immediately flew to help Matt to take Heskel down, knowing he had to be their prime target.

Ryan killed the blood bond he was fighting, and the rest of the blood bonds rushed off through the front door and left. Trey and Stacey had managed to eliminate Vandenburg, the other three vampires who had been there quickly vanishing. Then Dane cut Heskel's arm, and he immediately disappeared. "Damn it." Dane looked around for Jacqueline, but she had vanished too.

Hell. "Jacqueline!" Dane tried to contact her telepathically then. *"Jacqueline!"*

The house had been vacated except for the dead body of the blood bond and the remains of Vandenburg and Romanoff. Matt was immediately on the phone with the police to verify the two rogue vampire kills.

"I'm at the house," Jacqueline said to Dane. *"Heskel was trying to make me turn on you. I had to get as far away from you as possible."*

"I'm coming. We didn't kill him." Dane said to Matt, "Jacqueline's at my house. I'm going to join her in the vampire way."

"I'll drive your vehicle home when we're done with the police here," Matt said.

"I'll go with you, Dane. Trey can drive my car there. What's your address?" Stacey asked.

He told her the name of the residential area and gave her the address. She looked at her phone and found the directions for it. "Okay, I'm going with you."

Then they both vanished and when they reached his place, he saw the whole house was dark. He didn't like the looks of this.

He went inside and called out, "Jacqueline?" Then he tried telepathically communicating with her. *"Jacqueline? Where are you?"*

"At home."

"Your home?"

"Yes, that's what I said."

"Sorry, I...forget it. Stacey and I are on our way." He told Stacey,

"Jacqueline's at her house, not mine." Then he gave Stacey Jacqueline's address, and they headed over there. He knocked on her door, at the same time saying, *"It's just me, and Stacey is with me."*

Jacqueline hurried to open the door for them and pulled them inside. "I'm sorry I left all of you behind, but Heskel tried to force me to turn on you, Dane. I think that when Matt was cutting at him, Heskel couldn't concentrate on forcing me to do any harm to you, but I didn't want to worry that I might injure or kill you if he managed to hurt your brother and attempt to gain control of me again."

"Did he get control of you?" Dane asked.

"He tried. I was fighting it the whole time. Until he was too distracted and then that's when he left. So he's still alive?"

"Yeah," Dane said with regret. "We tried to take him down, but then he vanished. We did manage to take down the other two rogue vampires on Matt's list though. Why did you come here and not go to my home? I was afraid he had gotten ahold of you."

"It was just natural for me to go here. Plus, I was afraid he might follow me to your house. I don't want him to know where you live."

Dane hugged her. "You know, you nearly give me a heart attack every time you vanish like you do and suddenly appear where the vampire is that you're trying to take down."

Jacqueline smiled. "You need to learn to do that so that it comes naturally in a fight. It gives us a real advantage over rogues when they don't expect us to have that ability."

"Yeah," Stacey said. "I think Trey was surprised too when I left him behind to fight Vandenburg."

"I'm sure of it," Dane said. "He wanted to be right there with you helping to take him down, not putting yourself in danger. Do you want to go to my house, Jacqueline?"

"Yeah. Now that you're going to be there too."

Then the three of them headed over there using their vampiric ability. It saved on driving a vehicle places!

When they went inside the house, Princess purred and rubbed up against Dane first, then Jacqueline. "You know you can be replaced," Jacqueline said to her cat.

Dane chuckled.

"I take it that she's your cat, Jacqueline," Stacey said while Dane got them all glasses of water to drink.

"Yeah, but she has fallen totally in love with Dane." Jacqueline sat down on the couch and Princess jumped onto her lap because Dane was putting the glasses of water on the coffee table.

Then Dane got a call. He put it on speakerphone.

"Hey, we're almost done with talking with the police here. We're letting Stacey have Vandenburg's bounty. You and Jacqueline can split Romanoff's bounty," Matt said.

"No. We agreed we would split the bounties between us. We never know who we're going to be taking down and we're all at risk," Dane said.

Stacey and Jacqueline agreed.

"All right. We'll split the money when we get there. You can tell us what happened when we arrive," Matt said.

"See you soon," Dane said.

"Do you usually team up with a hunter to fight vampires?" Jacqueline asked Stacey.

"Uhm, I'm more of a lover than a fighter," Stacey said.

"Of vampires?" Dane couldn't help frowning. Not that some hunters hadn't fallen in love with a vampire and even been turned to be with them forever, but they hadn't been rogues and he could see how it could happen in some cases, like with Rachael falling in love with Adonis. Then again Adonis had been a hunter also.

"Uh, no, I mean with hunters. I don't usually go on hunts all that often."

Which explained how Stacey had been turned by a rogue vampire while making love with him, and not when she was engaging with one in combat.

"But you looked like you really had a handle on fighting," Jacqueline said. "We wouldn't have put you in the position of having to fight anyone if we had known you don't like to hunt rogues down."

"Oh, I'm fully qualified as a fighter. I love practicing fighting with a fellow hunter. My brother usually. And the thing of it is that once I was turned and had these special abilities, I felt changed about that too. Like I wanted to help the hunters' cause, and I wanted to help the police take down the villains, and I wanted to help protect humans. It made me realize how ruthless rogue vampires are and how manipulative they can be," Stacey said. "I think before that, I was kind of living in my own little bubble. Playing at being a hunter, until the vampire turned me."

Then they heard two vehicles drive up and recognized they were Stacey's car and Dane's truck. Matt parked Dane's truck in the garage and Trey parked Stacey's car in the driveway, then Dane's brothers all joined them in the house, everyone giving each other a hug for a job well done. Dane gave them glasses of water and then strawberry margaritas after that for all of them to celebrate.

"At least we took two down on my list," Matt said, "though more than anything, I wished we could have taken down Jacqueline's vampire."

Everyone agreed.

Then Dane got a call from Zachary Bremerton, and he wondered if he'd heard Dane had been turned. Zach had and had been so distraught when he had been turned that he had wanted to die. But that had all changed for him when he met the huntress of his dreams. "Hey, I'm putting this on speakerphone. My brothers are all here and so are two of my friends who are huntresses who have likewise been turned, if that's what you're calling about."

"Yeah. Adonis, Rachael, Pasha, Michael, Danai and I are back in Dallas, and we learned what had happened to you. How are you and the huntresses doing?" Zachary asked.

"Well, we kind of have a problem. Jacqueline's maker is still alive." That's all Dane needed to say. Adonis had mated Zachary's cousin, Rachael, and had been a hunter before he was turned. He couldn't kill his maker either, who had been trying to force him to hand Rachael over to him, but with Zachary and other members of the family's help, they had finally eliminated Adonis's and his sister's maker and rescued his parents and younger sister. But his older sister, Danai, was dating Zachary's older brother, Michael. So Adonis and his older sister had known just how hard it was to be hunters who were turned and then forced to do their maker's bidding.

"We'll help you with this," Zach said.

"Thanks," Jacqueline said. "I'm Jacqueline and met Dane and Stacey at a group therapy meeting to deal with being hunters turned."

"We heard about that too. We'll be at the next meeting to share our experiences, though I think for the most part, we're dealing with it the best way we can. But if we can speak about what happened to us, maybe it will help others to realize what we have become doesn't have to be a curse," Zachary said.

"We were talking about going to a hunters' club and getting drinks and dancing," Jacqueline said.

"We will be there to back them up," Matt said.

Zachary laughed. "Well, we haven't tried that since all this happened. We've been in Florida taking down rogue vampires for the family, so, yeah, sign us up. I'm sure Adonis and the rest of us would all be for it. What's the worst that could happen? A bunch of narrow-minded hunters kick us out? Maybe someday we'll have a club of our own. But until then, we're still hunters, right?"

"That's exactly what we were saying," Dane said.

"Well, my family will be there backing us too and they have a lot of sway in Dallas," Zachary said.

"Okay, we'll make it a date. Though Jacqueline wants to wait until we take down her maker," Dane said.

"We'll help you with that too. What's his name?" Zachary asked. Dane said, "Heskel."

"Hell, he was Piaras's friend. When Rachael killed Piaras, she had ended the rogue vampire's reign of terror. Piaras was the one who had turned Adonis and his older sister, Danai, and had wanted to turn Rachael to be his own mate. Heskel wasn't at Piaras's house when the hunters went there to eliminate him. It appears, Heskel didn't have designs on Jacqueline, like Piaras had on Rachael, since the time that she was a youngster."

"Yeah, she had killed Heskel's twin brother, and he caught her at it. Instead of killing her, he turned her. We've tried twice to take him down, but he just vanishes before we can do it," Dane said.

"We'll add him to our list."

"Okay, thanks. We can use all the help we can get on this," Dane said.

"You're welcome. We'll talk soon." Then Zachary and Dane ended the call.

"That's great news about the other hunters helping us," Jacqueline said. "I've never met Zachary or his family, but his family are well-known in Dallas."

"Yeah, when some of them were turned, it really rocked the city. Some hunters still were their friends, and others dropped them," Dane said.

"Like what had happened to us," Jacqueline said.

"Oh, yeah, the same with me," Stacey said, then finished her margarita. "Thanks for helping me take down my rogue."

"Thanks to you for helping to take down one of our rogues," Matt said.

"If you need any help with anyone else, Stacey, just give me a call," Jacqueline said.

"Thanks. I will." But Stacey glanced at Dane as if she fully intended to call on him, not Jacqueline. "Oh, and if you get an idea where Heskel might be, call me and I'll go with you. We have to free Jacqueline of the curse."

"Do you need one of us to follow you home so you get their safely?" Trey asked.

"No, I'm good, thanks so much!" Then Stacey gave everyone a hug, Jacqueline last, of course, and then she left.

10

I t was late when the brothers and Jacqueline finally retired to their bedrooms to sleep.

Princess had made friends with all the brothers and instead of going to bed with Dane and Jacqueline this evening, she had gone to stay with Trey in his bed. Jacqueline suspected the brothers had colluded with each other to make sure Dane and Jacqueline didn't have any interruptions, and she thought they were so cute to do that for them.

She sat down to pull off her boots and Dane came over to remove them for her.

"You know, we don't have an impediment to sleeping close tonight together," he said, nuzzling her face, then kissing her knee.

"Yeah, which I suspect was planned and I'm all for it." Her gaze locked with his and he smiled that arrogant kind of sexy smile that she loved.

Then he yanked off his T-shirt and worked on his boots while she pulled off her shirt.

"I had no intention of dating anyone anytime soon," she said.

"I had gotten that impression from the first time I had laid eyes on you."

She smiled. "And you ignored that. Which was the big draw to me. Except for Stacey's interest in you. I thought the interest in her was mutual for you."

"Not in her." Dane unbuckled her belt while she unbuckled his.

"Yeah, that was soon apparent, which was your saving grace."

He chuckled. Then he cupped her breasts still confined in her smooth, silky bra. "I'm damn lucky I went to that meeting. After fighting the vampire, I almost didn't."

"Then"—she ran her hands over his bare chest—"you had to show off your beautiful chest."

"Which you were not impressed with."

She licked his nipples, and he sucked in his breath. "Ha! You knew I was," she said, "and you wanted me to say so."

"I loved teasing you."

"I loved that you did." She really was amused that he would. Then she removed his pants.

He yanked off his socks and then slid hers off her feet. Then he pulled off her pants. She hurried to ease his boxer briefs down his hips, though his arousal was so full, she was having more of a time getting the briefs over it. Which she loved.

He smiled down at her. She looked at him and shook her head. "Next time, the boxer briefs come off first."

He laughed. And then he was unfastening her bra, tossing it, and slowly removing her panties, tantalizing her. He skimmed his hands over her naked breasts. The pressure of his hands on her flesh made her heartbeat quicken and she sighed with pleasure. Her sensitive nipples were aroused, and she treasured his hands rubbing against them. Never would she have thought she would be doing this with a new man in her life after she and Van had become history—like a week ago!

But Dane was tantalizingly sexy, and she loved the way he touched her, like he was enjoying the intimacy before they went all the way, and she was glad for that. She heard his heart beating harder and she felt her canines extend, just like when they had danced at the human club. It was amazing, especially now that they were here, alone, and no one else could see them. She immediately kissed him, pressing him to open his mouth to her. She wanted to see if his own canines had extended. As if he knew what she was checking out, he smiled and showed her his devilishly sexy smile and his beautiful, elongated canines.

He cupped her face, and they began stroking each other's canines with their tongues. There was just something intimate with caressing each other's canines, sharing the knowledge that they had been changed, but that they were navigating through all this with curiosity and intrigue.

She nibbled his bottom lip, and he slid his hands to her buttocks and caressed. He lifted her and put her on the bed and then he was beside her, kissing her breasts, licking her nipple, kissing it, and starting on the other. Her body responded to his gentle and passionate kisses, his mouth moving over her breastbone, his extended canines teasing her throat with a gentle touch, not cutting.

She started to use her teeth on his neck, the experience so new to both of them, but they were enjoying the exploration. Neither wanted to cut each other or drink each other's blood. Maybe later when they were more used to all this vampiric stuff. But for now, they were just embracing their new abilities.

She swore she felt more alive than she'd ever felt before. She ran her hands over his biceps, loving the feel of his strength, his muscles well-honed from all the sword fighting he did. She was so wet for him, so eager to have him penetrate her between her legs, aching for him.

He slid his hand over her belly, lower, yes! She was so eager to have him embedded deep inside her. But he was beginning to stroke her between her legs. She was shooting to the heavens. Then she remembered his brothers were staying at the house, and she swallowed the cry of delight that nearly escaped her lips.

Then he was pressing his full erection into her and thrusting. She arched and he filled her. She moaned. Their hearts hammered at the same pace, and she felt the unfathomable connection to him. Both were now something more than just hunters and she wondered if that was what made them feel so right for each other.

He groaned with climax, staying inside her for a bit longer, and just pressed his body against hers. Loving the closeness, she ran her hands over his muscular back. "Amazing."

"Good?"

She smiled. "Yeah. Good."

"Great?"

She chuckled. "Quit fishing."

He rolled off her, pulled her into his arms, snuggled with her, and kissed the top of her head. "Great."

After all they'd been through, for the first time since being turned and Van ditching her, she felt truly at peace and with a hunter who might even turn out to be the one for her. Only time would tell.

EARLY THE NEXT MORNING, Trey surprised Jacqueline when he came into the master bedroom to wake Dane and her before they were ready to wake. "Hey, I got information of where Heskel might be. Remember Zachary telling us that Rachael had killed Piaras at his estate? Several other rogues were also eliminated. The house was sold, and the proceeds went to the hunters who risked their lives to bring the rogues to justice. The house was sold to a human, but when I was doing some research, I discovered that she wasn't truly the owner. She was given the money to purchase the property.

Heskel was behind it all. We're all gathering to go to the estate now to see if he's there."

"Uh, okay, thanks. We'll join you downstairs," Dane said, already getting out of bed, sans clothes.

Jacqueline was so hoping they would get the bastard this time. As soon as Trey was gone, she left the bed and hurried to grab her clothes out of a drawer and Dane's closet. He'd been a sweetheart to give her so much room to sort out her clothes.

Dane was dressing and then once she was also, he hugged her. "We'll get him."

"I know we will. Either this day or another. We will." Or one of the others would, though she wished she could take him down herself.

"About last night—" he said.

"I want a repeat tonight."

Looking relieved, he said, "You got it."

Then they gathered downstairs, and she was amused to see someone had gotten a big box of fresh donuts.

"Breakfast for champions, right?" she asked, snatching a chocolate icing covered one before the chocolate donuts were all gone.

Ryan laughed. "Yeah, when Trey said we wouldn't have time to make a breakfast, I hurried off to get the donuts, hoping I got enough of a variety to make everyone happy."

"All you needed to get was chocolate-covered ones," Jacqueline said.

The brothers all smiled at her. Ryan said to Dane, "Looks like I need to make sure you both get enough then."

"Who all is coming with us?" Dane grabbed one of the chocolate-iced donuts and smiled at Jacqueline.

"I called Zachary. He said his brother Michael, Adonis, and others would join us at the estate. Rachael wanted to, but Adonis's and her baby girl is six weeks old so Rachael is nursing her and not hunting yet," Ryan said.

"Oh, wow, okay," Jacqueline said.

"I called Stacey. She's meeting us there as well," Dane said.

"Okay, so"—Jacqueline grabbed another chocolate-iced donut —"I'm ready."

"Is that all the fortification you need?" Dane asked, getting her a cup of coffee.

She laughed. "Yes, that's all I need." Then she drank her coffee and Trey glanced at his watch.

"Let's get armed. It's time," Matt said.

They all grabbed their swords, throwing stars, and daggers, and then they loaded up in Dane's truck and headed out.

"Don't go inside the building on your own," Dane said to Jacqueline.

"I won't." She knew he was referring to her vanishing and reappearing next to the rogue vampires. But she wasn't moving into the house on her own. She would wait until everyone was inside the house with her and then she would use her vampiric abilities to move to her advantage.

She had been amused that Dane had been practicing moving from the bedroom to the bathroom and from the bedroom to the first floor, using the vampire way, as if he was trying to catch up to her using the ability.

"Are you really ready for this?" Dane asked her.

She smiled at him as he drove toward the estate. *"You are practicing telepathically communicating with me too?"*

He chuckled. "You're so good at all this stuff. I guess I haven't really been embracing the vampire abilities."

"Because you were upset that you were turned," she said, not asking a question. She had totally been unsettled by the whole business, but then she had decided that there was no way of going back to the way it was and she needed to just accept her new abilities. Maybe she could use them to her advantage in a fight against a rogue vampire.

"Yeah, but you've shown me how important they can be."

"Well, just don't get ahead of me when we're in the house and see a rogue we need to take down."

He just laughed and she knew then that was just what he planned to do. Not because he wanted the kill, but because he wanted to protect her. That was such a refreshing notion that she loved him for it. Van figured she could protect herself because she was a huntress. Even huntresses, and hunters, needed someone else to provide protection for them at times.

When they finally arrived at Heskel's estate out in the country, she envisioned what it had been like when Adonis and his mate and family were there in the fight against evil. It was an overcast day, still early in the morning, and they saw six cars in the circular driveway.

An ornate wrought iron gate was open, as if it was sinisterly welcoming them in. The two-story, rambling Spanish-style mansion was surrounded by young pine trees that looked like they had been planted since Piaras's termination. Beautiful boulders were scattered around the property. Since Piaras had been so malevolent, she had expected to see a dark, vile place, but it was light and airy looking, a large fountain spilling water into a basin in the center of the circular drive.

The sides of the home were coated in ivory stucco, but exposed areas revealed pink brick quarried nearby to give the impression of an antique building. An old spoked, wagon wheel rested against a live oak. The oak was so large, she figured it had been there for over a hundred years.

"Pretty, not evil looking like I thought it would be," Jacqueline said.

"Yeah, when it comes to some of these rogues, they can really make it appear as though they are just like the rest of us. When it's the furthest thing from the truth," Dane said.

"Whereas others cloak themselves in darkness, whether it's

wearing Gothic garments or living in a house that looks like it should be in a haunted horror flick," Matt said.

"Right," Trey said. "One of the worst vampires I ever took down —a female—had a pink house, literally, from her furniture, walls, drapes, and even to the outside of the house with its gingerbread style roof and pink siding. Her neighbors felt it was an eyesore. Her garden was filled with pink roses. She wore long pink lacy dresses, pink lace gloves, pink flowery bonnets, pink high heels, or patent leather flats. Yet despite all outward appearances, she was evil to the core. After she had eliminated fifteen men who had looked at her the wrong way—her words, not mine—I terminated her. The neighbors wanted the house torn down and to leave the lot vacant. But the homeowner's association wouldn't go along with it. So some house flippers bought the house, repainted the whole place white, inside and out, and redid the entire inside with large windows, white blinds, very modern chic style. They'd had an open house, and we went in to see it. She hadn't killed anyone there. Sometimes they raze a house where so many murders have been committed, no one wants to buy the house, and it would be condemned. But it was beautiful, and it sold right away."

"I couldn't even imagine a female vampire like that. The only ones I've taken down have been more femme fatales, wearing black or red, sexy, evil. But a vampiress in pink reminds me of a witch and her gingerbread house covered in sweet treats," Jacqueline said.

"Yeah, that's exactly what she was like," Trey said.

They didn't drive onto the estate but parked out of view of the security cameras. All the hunters got out of their vehicles. The Bremertons introduced themselves—Zachary, his brother Michael, Danai, her brother, Adonis, and their sister, Pasha—all of them ready to take on any friend of Piaras who was like him in turning a hunter.

"We need to go around the fence," Adonis said, since his family had been confined here. He, Pasha, and Danai knew the layout of the estate the best, though Zachary and Michael had been there during the fight against Piaras and his friends and minions also. They skirted around the fence surrounding the property, looking for an easy way to get in, or at least for the hunters. For the hunters turned, they could just vanish and reappear on the other side.

"You can climb over here. No one can observe you from the house. Everything is shuttered and they don't have any security on the backyard," Adonis said. "All the cameras are focused on the front of the yard." Then he vanished and reappeared on the other side of the fence.

Zachary, Danai, Pasha, and Dane quickly joined him. Stacey and Jacqueline appeared next to them while Dane's brothers climbed over the fence. Then they all ran toward the back door of the house.

Urns sat on the entryway to the patio that was bare of furniture. Then Adonis vanished and the door opened. Jacqueline hadn't expected him to do that.

They hurried into the house. It was quiet, even though there were so many vehicles parked out front. Were the occupants of the house sleeping?

Adonis said to Jacqueline, *"They're sleeping."*

She wondered then if he had told the other vampires that too, or just the ones who might not have known what was going on.

Then a man walked into the living room, and Adonis swiftly moved to him and put his fingers to his mouth, telling the man to be quiet, to not make a sound. Then Zachary joined Adonis and took the man outside.

What was he? A vampire? A blood bond?

Danai and Michael headed down a hallway. Zachary returned to the group of hunters and said to Jacqueline, *"They're checking out the wing where Danai's parents and sister had been kept hostage."* He motioned to another wing. *"That's where vampire guests stay. Upstairs is the master's suite."*

Dane nodded and Jacqueline realized he had told Dane, and probably Stacey, the same thing.

Jaqueline thought they should go upstairs first because they had to take Heskel out first and foremost.

"Normally, we would take out everyone on the lower floor first," Zachary said, *"but we know Heskel is the priority just like Piaras was. We can't allow a vampire to control a hunter."*

"I want to go upstairs and get him if he's up there," Jacqueline said, though she knew she couldn't actually eliminate him.

"I'm with you, Jacqueline," Dane said.

"Me too," Stacey said.

Zachary said to Matt, "Can you, Trey, and Ryan take care of anyone in the rooms down this hallway?"

Matt inclined his head.

Then Adonis joined them. "The man was a blood bond. He took one of the cars and left, not wanting any part of getting himself killed over this. He said Heskel is with his girlfriend upstairs. I'll go with whoever is headed to the upper floor and then the others will handle whoever is down here."

Jacqueline wondered what was going on with Michael and Danai, but then Adonis disappeared, and Jacqueline did the same thing to join him at the landing upstairs.

Dane, Zachary, and Stacey joined them. The others stayed down below to take care of anyone in the hallway who might be a threat.

Once they were all upstairs, Adonis motioned to the door of a room left open.

"The master's bedroom?" she telepathically asked Adonis.

He inclined his head. Then Adonis vanished and appeared inside the room. She wanted to go in there so badly, but she was afraid then that she would sabotage the mission. She said to Dane, *"Go! I'll help the others downstairs."*

He hugged and kissed her. *"Stay safe."*

"And you."

Then she vanished and ended up downstairs with the others. They were waiting at closed doors, and she suspected it was because they didn't want to wake anyone and alert Heskel. She was used to going in and fighting, not this breaking into a vampire's lair and waiting. Her heart, and everybody else's, were beating like crazy.

She heard someone coming and turned to see Michael and Danai joining them. Jacqueline was actually glad to have some other hunter-turned vampires with her to help fight the battle if they got into it. Suddenly, all the doors began being thrown open and she heard fighting upstairs at the same time. Heskel must have alerted the occupants down below that he was in a fight, and to come to his aid. But they hadn't expected to find hunters right outside their bedrooms.

Five of the vampires were wearing pajama shorts, two were naked, but they all were armed with swords. They immediately hissed at them, showing their deadly fangs. That was an indication they were all rogues. If they hadn't been, knowing the ones they faced were hunters, they would have put their weapons down. Instead, they had shown their fangs, indicating they were dangerous and ready to battle it out with them.

Three of the vampires were on Jacqueline's and Dane's terminal list: Maggard, Quillon, and Paine. She went after Paine. He was a tall blond wearing black PJ shorts and he immediately thrust his sword at her. She vanished and struck at Quillon, a redhead, who was just as shocked as the other rogues who hadn't expected any of the hunters to be vampires too.

Just as quickly, Paine came at her back, and she vanished. Paine struck Quillon in the heart with his sword, not anticipating she was going to hear Paine behind her and that she could move like that. Now that was the perfect tactical move!

Trey and Ryan had already taken down a vampire each as she

fought Paine, who was so angry that she had outmaneuvered him that he was slashing at her without using the control he needed to be successful. She was alternately striking his sword and vanishing and appearing in a new location, which meant he was constantly trying to anticipate her moves and he wasn't doing a good job of it.

Matt took down Maggard, who was one of the guys on her and Dane's list. It didn't matter. They had to just come out victorious, no matter who took down which rogues.

To her shock, Heskel suddenly was in front of her, and she thought Paine was going to stab him like he had Quillon accidentally. But then Heskel said, "You're coming with me," and he grabbed her wrist and vanished.

"He has got me," Jacqueline said to Dane, knowing he would tell the others.

"Where are you now?" Dane sounded levelheaded and not panicky, which she was glad for because *she* was panicking.

"I think somewhere else in the house. A...a cell."

"Adonis said that's where his parents and his younger sister had been locked up. We're on our way." Dane showed up in the room where a cell was located.

Heskel smiled wickedly. "Kill him," he commanded Jacqueline as soon as Dane came to fight him.

But a whole swarm of hunters showed up and Dane thrust his sword into Heskel's heart before the rogue could vanish, instantly breaking his connection over Jacqueline. Heskel's body wizened like a grape wizened into a raisin. Jacqueline likewise collapsed and Dane rushed with his vampiric speed to gather her in his arms before she hit the floor and kissed her. "Are you okay?"

"God, yes. He was trying to force me to kill you and I was fighting the command. I would never have forgiven myself if I had hurt you. When you terminated him, his control over me was broken, but at the same time, I blacked out briefly."

"We need to call this in," Matt said, usually the one to call the police and have them come for statements. "Do we know who all of the vampires were?"

"Yeah, three of them were on my termination list," Jacqueline said, Dane helping her to her feet.

"Hmm, that means three of them were on my terminal list," Dane said, a twinkle in his eye.

"There were eight in total," Matt said.

"Well, four were ours," Jacqueline amended. "Heskel was on our list too."

"Right," Dane said.

Joining them, Pasha said, "I got one." She was wiping blood off five throwing stars.

Trey said, "The one I took down was on mine and so was the one Ryan eliminated."

"I took down one," Matt said. "He had been on Ryan's list."

"I got another one. He wasn't on my list yet, but he wasn't going to give up," Stacey said.

"There were two more in the room off the cell," Adonis said. "Danai and I took care of them. They were part of Piaras's former staff. We thought we had eliminated all of them, but those two must have escaped and slipped back here when Heskel took over."

"Good," Zach said. "We eliminated the vampiress who had been in the bedroom with Heskel, and we were fighting Heskel, until he realized Jacqueline was nearby and vanished. We thought he had just fled like you said he had done twice before, until Jacqueline warned Dane that Heskel had grabbed her."

While they waited for the police, Matt said, "Man, I feel like this place is just a vampire haven."

"Yeah, since the rogues keep setting up housekeeping here," Adonis said.

Trey said, "All I've got to say is the hunters who have been turned are unbelievably good at fighting the vampires. You should have seen Jacqueline. Two vampires had her pinned down. I wanted to go to her aid in the worst way. One came at her back, but I was still fighting one and he wasn't letting me move. Then Jacqueline just vanished, and the rogue killed the other one she had been battling. The look on his face was precious until she came back to fight him some more."

"Yeah," Stacey agreed. "I told you guys at the therapy meeting how much I love the new abilities we have. I probably would have been a gonner if I hadn't been able to move like they do."

"I need to practice so that it comes naturally to me," Dane said.

"We can practice fighting each other like that," Jacqueline said.

"I'm game." Stacey smiled at Dane.

Jacqueline wasn't including Stacey, but then again, if they could all help each other, it could be worth it. "Hey, maybe some of the hunters who have been turned quite a while ago can help us navigate this new world we belong to."

"I'm all for it," Adonis said. "Though we're here just for a visit."

"So about going to the hunters' club," Stacey said.

"Oh, I want to do it early, like five? I think this calls for a celebration. I'm free from Heskel's control now," Jacqueline said.

"At five then. We'll meet at the Starlight parking lot," Adonis said.

Then the police arrived and took all their statements, but just as they were doing it, Van and Jacqueline's best friend, Lettie, and Van's two brothers showed up to fight the vampires in the house.

"You're too late," Jacqueline said, glad they beat them to the bounties. But mostly, she was thrilled Heskel was no longer a problem. Even though her life was still topsy turvy, at least that very major issue had been taken care of.

11

W hen Jacqueline's ex arrived at Heskel's house, Dane wanted to slug Van for abandoning Jacqueline after she had been turned when she'd needed him the most. But now Dane realized that since Heskel had been eliminated, Jacqueline no longer had a reason to stay with him at his house. He was disappointed about that. Though getting rid of Heskel had been tantamount.

Once they were done there, Van learned who all they had taken down, and looked mighty pissed for missing out on so many bounties. Jacqueline's former best girlfriend appeared sheepish, trying to avoid eye contact with Jacqueline all the while. Dane and the others with him left the house.

Stacey shook her head. "Boy, if that had been my fiancé, I would have had some choice words to say to him."

"He's not worth it," Jacqueline said.

"Was Lettie your best friend?" Stacey asked.

"Yeah, she isn't worth another thought either."

"She needs to be turned," Stacey said.

Jacqueline smiled. "Wouldn't Van be upset? And Lettie too."

Stacey shook her head. "She wouldn't be welcome in our meetings either. Not after betraying you and taking up with Van."

Dane didn't want Stacey bringing all this up if it was upsetting Jacqueline, but she didn't seem bothered by it, for which he was thankful. He guessed it was such a relief to get rid of Heskel, nothing else mattered at the moment.

"See you at the club," Adonis said, and he and his kin left in their van.

"See ya," Stacey said.

Then Dane and his brothers and Jacqueline got into his truck.

"We'll grab our bags from your house and head to our homes then," Matt said.

"Yeah, and we'll see you all at the club at five," Trey said.

"Everyone did a great job. We need to go on more hunts like this as a group," Ryan said, everyone agreeing.

Dane didn't bring up Jacqueline returning to her house, but when he drove into his driveway, Matt said, "We can help you take all of Princess's things to your place, Jacqueline."

"You can just grab your own bags and I'll help her," Dane said to his brothers. "It won't take any time at all."

"Thanks to everyone for all your help with this," she said.

"We wouldn't have left you alone to deal with this on your own," Dane said.

When they arrived at the house, his brothers helped him pack the cat's things into her car while she was gathering her clothes upstairs. Dane really figured his brothers would just grab their own bags and leave, but they wanted to help more.

Dane figured he would just ride with her, help her get everything settled, and then use the vampire way to get back home. He had to keep practicing at it.

While Jacqueline was upstairs, Princess had gone up there with her.

"She needs time to be one with what she's become, just like you need to before you get into a relationship that means forever," Matt said to Dane.

His brothers didn't understand that Dane and Jaqueline had a connection that no one else would have unless they'd been turned against their will. And both had lost their future mates over it.

Then again, Dane didn't need to prove anything to his brothers. They would eventually see that he and Jacqueline were really suited to each other, hopefully for the long term.

"And then there's Stacey," Trey said, chuckling.

Smiling, Dane shook his head. The woman might be interested in him, but the feeling *wasn't* mutual.

Then Jacqueline appeared next to her car with her bag in hand. He swore he would never get used to her vanishing and reappearing like that.

"We're dressing formally for the club, right?" she asked.

"You better believe it." Dane would love to see Jacqueline in a slinky gown, and he really wanted to dance with her.

"We're dancing all the dances, right?" she asked Dane.

He smiled, but before he could say anything, Matt said, "I would be happy to dance with you when Dane gets tired."

Dane quickly said, "I won't get tired." He wanted to be the only one dancing with her. On the other hand, it wouldn't hurt for other hunters to see that his brothers, who were purely hunters, would be interested in being with her. Not that he really wanted anyone else to be with her. He realized how possessive he was already feeling about her, but still, for her own feelings of acceptance and fitting in, he wanted her to be able to dance with hunters and prove she wasn't a blood-thirsty vampiress now. He would do anything to help her feel accepted by hunters again, if that was something she really needed.

Trey smiled finally and said, "I'll dance with you."

"So will I," Ryan said.

She laughed. "Good. I'll hold each of you to it."

"Hot damn," Ryan said.

They agreed to meet them at the club at the appointed time and they gave her and Dane hugs, then left.

Dane said to her, "I'll go with you and help you unload your car at your place and then return home, via the vampire way to get in some more practice."

She agreed to the deal. "You know I only want to dance with your brothers at the hunters' club to prove how nice they are to us when other hunters might not treat us well."

"Yeah, and I want you to dance with them for that reason too."

"But no other hunters, right?"

Dane laughed.

"I'll grab Princess and then we'll head over to my place." She vanished and returned with Princess in her arms, then she handed her to Dane.

They climbed into her car and drove over to her place. "I won't lie about it. After no one came to your aid, I feel the hunters don't deserve you," Dane said.

She smiled. "If it hadn't been for your brothers being so helpful and to prove a point to the other hunters, I wouldn't be dancing with anyone but you tonight." Then she glanced at Princess curled up on his lap. "She's going to miss having you to cuddle with her tonight."

Dane smiled. "You might be right, but I believe it was only because both of us were there together."

She scoffed. He laughed.

Then she drove into her garage, and he took Princess into the house while she rolled her bag inside. He carried the cat supplies inside while she put everything where it belonged. Princess was checking the place out as if she hadn't been there in eons and something might have changed.

After they were finished, Jacqueline pulled Dane into her arms. "Thank you for saving me earlier today."

"Thank you for not skewering me."

She sighed. "I really was fighting Heskel's commands. I think it made him even angrier that he didn't seem to have the control over me that he thought he would have."

"Adonis was the same way. He couldn't kill Piaras, but the rogue vampire had told Adonis that he couldn't fall in love with Rachael, that she was Piaras's. Of course, Adonis was in love with Rachael from the moment he laid eyes on her and Piaras had no control over it."

"Wow. I didn't know that."

"Yeah, so I don't think they can completely control hunters like they can humans. But it elevates them in the rogue vampire community to say they have a hunter at their beck in call. In Piaras's case, two, Adonis and his sister, plus he was holding their parents and younger sister, Pasha, hostage. Non-rogue vampires, had they have known, would have wanted to have taken Piaras down themselves. They don't want their reputations sullied by a rogue like that. But the rogues? They really looked up to him," Dane said.

"I would have helped them if I had known."

"Adonis couldn't tell anyone. Not even Rachael's family. They were all hunters, and they wouldn't have been happy if they had learned a hunter turned vampire wanted her for his mate. Worse, that he was supposed to turn Rachael over to Piaras who promised to release the rest of his family."

"But I suspect Piaras wouldn't have," Jacqueline said.

"No, you're right. He would never have released them. He figured Adonis and his family didn't have any hunter friends here, no one knew anything about them since they were from Florida, so no one would come to their aid. You know how it is. Hunters are territorial just like vampires are. So when they came here looking for a friend who had disappeared and they had gotten involved with Piaras, they hadn't had the local hunters' approval."

"Ahh."

"Anyway, I'm sure Adonis felt the same way about you when he heard what you were going through. Danai also."

"She's dark, and sultry and beautiful," Jacqueline said.

"Yeah, she seems to have come out of her shell for Michael, though she's still cautious about meeting people she doesn't know."

"I can understand that after all they had gone through. Well, I hope she comes to the dance tonight too. I would love to get to know her. Maybe she would come to the therapy sessions too."

"Maybe. Well, I'm going to let you get on with your day. I need to check into some things."

"More vampires on your terminal list?" She wondered why he wouldn't take her with him. Maybe he wasn't comfortable fighting with her as a team on all the cases he was going after.

He shook his head. He looked so serious, she wondered what would be more important than that.

"My parents," she finally said.

"Yeah. I'll let you know how it goes."

"Do you want me to go with you?" she asked.

"No. Unless you insist you have to go. But I would prefer talking to them alone."

"Okay, just don't make them so mad that they'll want to terminate you because they believe *you're* a rogue."

"No one else will believe it and they'll be up on charges of killing an innocent vampire."

"Just don't make them too mad."

"I'll try not to." Then he kissed her and said, "Off I go." And he vanished.

She loved surprising him and rogue vampires by doing that herself, but she realized she didn't like it when he did it with her. But he needed to so that he could protect himself better. Then Princess was meowing, telling her she hadn't fed her yet.

"Demanding kitty, aren't we?"

Princess continued to talk to her until Jacqueline poured some food into her bowl, and she filled up her water dish too. Jacqueline headed into the laundry room to do a load of wash, and prayed Dane didn't really aggravate her parents too much. Though she had to admit a little bit was fine with her.

12

Dane probably should have taken Jacqueline with him to see her parents, but he wanted to get this off his chest. He was afraid they might think he planned to mate her and wanted their permission, which was the furthest thing from his mind. Not that he hadn't totally considered a union between them, but he didn't have any intention of asking her parents' permission after the way they had treated her once she had been turned. It might have helped if he had taken Matt with him to show them that family stuck together. But he figured he had this on his own and he really didn't need to get his family involved. It might cause more tension.

As soon as he arrived home, Matt was waiting for him. Dane frowned at him. "What are you doing here? Did you leave something important behind?" Dane couldn't imagine Matt had any other reason for being here.

"You. I'm going with you to see Jacqueline's parents."

Dane's jaw dropped.

"Come on, Bro. I hadn't gotten very far when Jacqueline called me and said to return to your house where you were planning to drive your truck to see her parents. So I'm going with you to keep you out of trouble."

Dane shook his head. "I *had* considered taking you." But he'd then discounted the notion.

Matt didn't look like he believed him as he dipped his chin down and lifted his brows.

"I'm serious. Come on then."

"We'll take my car," Matt said. Then they left in his car. "Do you miss them?"

"Hmm?" Dane asked.

"Princess and Jacqueline," Matt said as he drove out of the housing development.

Dane smiled. "Yeah, you know it. They both add a lot of warmth and fun in my life."

"I could tell. So you don't want to screw things up with her parents if things work out between you."

"I don't care how her parents feel. They don't care about her."

"They could come around and so you want to keep a civil tongue when you speak to them."

Dane growled under his breath. Matt smiled.

A half hour later, they found her parents' home on the north side of the city and parked in the circular drive, the landscaping featuring majestic old live oaks, green boxwood hedges, and a red rose garden, elegant and pristine.

"Are you ready?" Dane asked.

"They might not be home, you know," Matt said. "Unless you made an appointment with them."

"I'll wait."

Matt sighed. "All right."

They both got out of Matt's car and went to the front door of the house and Dane knocked a little harder than he needed to. Sure, he could have rung the doorbell, but knocking gave him more of a statement of power.

Then a young woman answered the door, but she looked too young to be Jacqueline's mother.

"Yes?" she said.

"We're here to see Mr. and Mrs. Anderson about Jacqueline," Dane said.

"Jacqueline."

"Yes, are they in?" Dane asked.

"Uh, Mrs. Anderson is. Who should I say is calling?" the girl asked.

"Dane and Matt Edmonson." Dane hoped that Mrs. Anderson wouldn't know that he had been turned.

"I'll check and ask if she has time to meet with you." Then the girl shut the door.

Dane said, "She had better."

Matt smiled. "Keep it cool, brother."

"I will." Maybe. It depended on how her mother reacted.

A short while later, the front door opened and a redheaded woman who looked like Jacqueline, only about thirty years older, wearing a flowery dress like she planned to go to a luncheon with friends, frowned at them. "What's this about? Is...is she all right?"

Did Jacqueline's mother even care? "Maybe we should speak inside." Dane wasn't about to have this talk with her out here.

Mrs. Anderson hesitated. Then she said, "All right." She sounded reluctant to speak to them. What if they had news that Jaqueline had been terminated herself? Dane thought she would have been more concerned. Then again, maybe not.

She led them into a formal living area and motioned to a couple of chairs to sit on. "I have a luncheon to attend so make this quick."

"I'm here because of Jacqueline and the fact that she had been turned. This is my brother, Matt. When I was also turned against my will, my three brothers were right there, killing the vampire who had turned me, supporting me, having my back just like a decent hunter family would have should one of their own fall to the teeth of a rogue vampire."

The woman's face fell, and they all hesitated to take any seats. He felt empowered to tower over her, irritated that she had told him she had a luncheon to go to when he had news of her daughter.

"You might want to know, or maybe you don't care, but we terminated the vampire who turned Jaqueline," Dane said.

Matt said, "It was quite a battle. There were several vampires and several hunters. Jacqueline took out two on her own and successfully fought the vampire's commands who had turned her until Dane eliminated him."

"Uh...well, thanks."

"Do you feel it would be better if she had died when she fought with the rogue instead of having been turned?" Dane asked.

The woman glowered at him, her eyes filling with tears.

Dane shrugged. "I know my brothers were mad at me for not having them at my back, but things happen like this. In the past, vampires would just kill a hunter if he could get away with it. But today, there are more rogues turning hunters so they can control them. Is it the hunter's fault? How many times did you go into a fight and—"

Suddenly, Jacqueline entered the living room to Dane and his brother's astonishment. Not to mention Mrs. Anderson had lost all the color in her face. She sat down suddenly on a chair, shaking.

"I didn't tell Dane and his brother to come here to speak on my behalf," Jacqueline said.

"They...they told me they killed the vampire who had turned you," Mrs. Anderson said.

"Yeah, Dane did. He unfortunately ended up in a similar situa-tion as me, overwhelmed and outnumbered. We didn't have a choice. But every one of his brothers have backed him since he was turned," Jacqueline said. "Not so with my family. I can understand Van dumping me because it wouldn't have worked out—"

"Not me," Dane said. "I don't understand it at all. He was supposed to have loved you. He might not have wanted to marry a vampire who would have such a long life after the fact, and that could be understandable, but he should have been your hero anyway, and helped to destroy the vampire. He's a hunter. That's his business. That's the *least* he could have done for you. Especially since he supposedly had loved you just like your family had. He should have asked all his friends to assist him if he hadn't been sure he could manage on his own. There's no call for the way he abandoned you."

Jacqueline smiled at Dane.

Dane hadn't meant to speak to her parents in an effort to earn points with Jacqueline, though that appeared to be a benefit once she showed up and he was glad for that. But he had done it more to tell her mom, and dad—if he had been there—that family should have meant everything to Jacqueline. Most hunter families were close to each other, helping each other out, taking care of each other—no matter the circumstances.

"I...I shouldn't have let you in. I need to go to a luncheon," her mother said, as if that was more important than trying to mend fences with her daughter.

"Go, enjoy your time with your women friends," Jacqueline said to her mother. "Come on, Dane, Matt. You're more family to me than my mother, father, and brother are." Then she left the way she had come, just by vanishing.

Dane saw the frightened look on her mother's face. He shook his head and vanished to reappear outside the house to be with Jacqueline, hoping she wasn't too upset. He hadn't meant to leave his brother behind, but he soon joined them outside, the normal hunter way.

Matt laughed. "I didn't expect both of you to just disappear on me like that. Though Jacqueline's mother didn't either."

"Well, I expected more of a reaction from your mom," Dane said to Jacqueline.

"I didn't. That's the way she has been since this all happened. Both my parents were disappointed in me, and they were especially disappointed about the messed-up mating between Van and me."

"Now that's really screwed up," Dane said. "So they took his side in all this?"

"Yeah, they did."

Dane shook his head and they got into Matt's car. "I still don't believe it's a wasted effort though."

"No, I agree. I'm glad she knows that you took down my 'master,' if that was something that was even bothering my parents. And I'm glad you said all that you did. Sometimes they need to hear it from someone else who's going through the same issues whose family is backing them," she said. Then she paused. "You know, we should go to her luncheon."

Matt glanced at her, and Dane chuckled. "We might get thrown out of the establishment."

"It's human run. She goes to the restaurant in Plano every week with her girlfriends. We don't have to say anything to them, unless we feel the need, but I've been staying away from her since I was turned. Maybe she needs to see that I'm not going to go into hiding and that while we all live in Dallas, she might just run into me from time to time and she'll have to deal with it. We all need to have lunch, right?"

Dane said, "I'm all for it. Should we call on Trey and Ryan to join us?"

"On it," Matt said, getting on Bluetooth and giving them both a call. "We're going to—"

"The Blue Diamond Restaurant in Plano," Jacqueline said.

"Jacqueline is with you?" Ryan sounded intrigued.

"Yep, and Dane. We'll fill you in when you get there," Matt said, then ended the call. "You don't think she'll call the police and say we're stalking her, do you?"

"No. Not if your brothers all show up and we're just there for lunch. We won't speak to them, unless she initiates some conversation. We might not even see them. But if we do, I won't mind glancing at them, and letting them all know I'm still in the area and not going away."

"Are your mom's friends all huntresses?" Dane asked.

"Yes, and they all know what happened to me. Both Lettie's and Van's moms are part of their little clique. They were all looking forward to the wedding. What about you, Dane? How about the hunters who were going to your wedding?"

"Nobody was disappointed. Not on my side of the family. Some of my friends rejected me after I was turned. But my brothers were glad. The thing of it is any of us could end up being turned at any point during our hunter's career. So what if we had been married already?" Dane asked.

"That was exactly my thought," Jacqueline said.

"Okay, but let's turn this around, just for the sake of argument. What if your fiancé and fiancée had been turned instead?" Matt always was good at looking at both sides of a situation. "What would you have done?"

"I would have been there to kill the vampire who turned my fiancée, for one," Dane said with conviction. "Staying together? I don't know. It depends on how it changed her view of things. And whether she had even wanted to stay together."

Jacqueline said, "Okay, I have to be honest here. Like Dane, I would have done everything in my power to kill the vampire who had turned him. But staying with him? I'm sure he would have changed too much for me. I could just imagine him being aggravated, hot-tempered, ill-at-ease, and not the man I had planned to marry."

"That was probably me last week," Dane said.

Matt laughed. "Yeah, I have to agree you were all over the place after you were turned, but then you settled down, got back to the business of taking down rogues, and went to your first therapy session."

"And met Jacqueline."

"I wasn't even giving you the time of day," she said.

"I know. That's what intrigued me so much," Dane said.

She laughed. "It's not that I was trying to play hard to get."

"I know. You've been through a lot. We both have. But I still wanted to get to know you."

"You're not afraid of being on the rebound?" she asked.

"Not where you're concerned."

She smiled.

"Well, you can be a member of our family anytime," Matt said to her.

Then they arrived at the restaurant where Matt and Dane's twin brothers were waiting in the parking lot. Ryan said, "Trey and I were going to have a fast-food burger and now we're going to be at a dress-up kind of place?"

"You deserve it after all we did at the vampire's house," she said.

"Yeah, I can always go for a steak instead," Trey said. "The hamburgers can wait."

"Lobster for me." Jacqueline headed for the front door of the restaurant while Dane hurried to open it for her.

They all went inside, and the hostess set up a table for five. When she returned, she led them to the table, carrying their menus, then she offered them the menus and left so they could decide on want they wanted to order.

"So are they here where we can see them?" Dane asked, picking up his menu.

"Yes, way over there by the windows overlooking the lake," Jacqueline said.

All the guys looked that way, giving the women a hard glower. Not that anyone noticed.

"If we stay long enough and they leave first, they'll have to walk right by our table," Jacqueline said. "You can save your disparaging looks for them then. For now, we're here to celebrate our victory."

The waitresses brought them glasses of water and then took their orders. "Be up with the rolls and salads soon." Then she left.

Dane was watching Jacqueline's mother's table. Jacqueline reached over and squeezed his thigh. He smiled at her. "Just enjoy the comradery we have here," she said. Though she was looking forward to giving her mother and her mother's friends the evil eye when they walked by.

But then one of her mother's friends left the table and headed to the restroom and saw Jacqueline. The woman missed a step, her face turning pale. Her gaze shifted to the hunters with her, and Matt said, "Hey, Mrs. Gifford. How are you doing?"

"Uh, uh, fine." Then she hurried off to the restroom.

"Well, you rattled her," Trey said.

"She deserved it. Any friend of Jacqueline's mother's is in complicity with her, as far as I'm concerned. They're not backing Jacqueline. She didn't say hello to Jacqueline or acknowledge her in any way. She didn't tell her she was sorry for what she had been through," Matt said.

They all watched the bathroom for when Mrs. Gifford left it and she glanced at their table, and they all put on their best glowers. Jacqueline wanted to laugh. She felt bad in a way because she had been friends with all her mother's friends, but now they were treating her like she was bad news. As soon as Mrs. Gifford headed to her table, they observed her sitting down and speaking, then everyone at her table turned to look at them. They just stared at them, and the women quickly turned around to eat their meals.

Good. They got the point that Jacqueline could show up anywhere that they might be, and she wasn't a threat, and she could still share the same space as them. She wasn't a non-entity like they were trying to act like.

"What about your dad and brother?" Dane asked.

"We might see my brother at the club tonight. I don't know how he would react. My father?" Jacqueline shrugged. "It's possible that he might try to have words with you for going to see my mother at their house without my father being there. But you and Matt had my best interests at heart. And if they can't see that, shame on them."

"I agree," Ryan said.

Trey said the same thing.

The women appeared to not want to leave their table though they had been at the restaurant first and had ordered lighter lunches. Even now, Jacqueline, Dane, and his brothers had finished their steaks and her lobster, and they were ready to leave.

"I think they are going to stay until we leave, and I have things to do at home," Jacqueline said.

"Yeah, let's go," Dane said. "If they feel uncomfortable about us, that's their problem."

"I can't wait to see what happens at the club," she said.

"Yeah, I hope that we don't end up in a fight and get kicked out. I just want to dance with you," Dane told Jacqueline.

She sure hoped they would be able to enjoy dancing the whole night through.

13

A fter Jacqueline arrived at home and greeted Princess, she got a call from Lettie, her former best friend who had taken up with her ex-fiancé. "Hello?" She was really surprised to hear from her. What did she want? Jacqueline still felt resentful toward her, but she thought if they could talk it out, maybe she would understand why Lettie had done it.

"I...I didn't expect you to be at the house that was once owned by Piaras," Lettie said.

"Would you have gone there if you had known I would be there hunting rogue vampires?"

"Uh, well, yeah, because we were after Paine. Well, maybe not, if we had known you would be there. You all would have probably gotten to him first, even though Van wanted the bounty."

So all they cared about was the money.

"My friends made it their mission to go after the vampire who had made me." Jacqueline wanted to know how Lettie felt after she'd been her friend since they were little girls and then just dumped her like that.

Lettie didn't say anything for a minute. "Uhm, okay."

"You knew about it, right? That Heskel had turned me?" Jaqueline figured the news would have been all over the hunter community. Especially those closer to her—like Van and Lettie—would have known.

"Uh, yeah."

Jaqueline had figured that or otherwise Lettie wouldn't have started dating Van.

"We didn't know he was in the house though. We were after Paine."

Jacqueline would have felt better if she had known that Van and Lettie had gone there to at least take Heskel down. "Sorry"—not really—"but Paine was on my list and I killed him." Jacqueline smiled a little, glad—if nothing else—that she'd taken the bounty money from Van and Lettie.

"Uhm, I...I guess you're upset with me for hunting with him, with Van, I mean."

Hunting? Yeah, since Van didn't like hunting with Jacqueline. Now he was hunting with Lettie? But she was more annoyed with that than that Lettie was dating Van after she had been such a good friend of Jacqueline's and did it behind her back. She could have at least asked Jacqueline if it was all right with her. Jacqueline would have appreciated the heads-up. But instead, she had done it as if she didn't want to be Jacqueline's friend anymore. Since Lettie hadn't called her once to see how she felt after being turned, that had confirmed it for her. She had felt so isolated from family and friends as soon as it had happened when she had needed them more than ever.

"Did Van give you a reason why he didn't want to go after Heskel? I mean, my new friends tracked down all his blood bonds and his vampire friends to learn where he was staying and to terminate him. That's proof that they're loyal friends even though I had never even met them before." Though she recalled that she'd seen Dane with a woman at one of the hunter clubs, but she hadn't paid much attention to either of them because she'd been engaged to Van at the time.

"I'm sorry."

"Answer the question. Why didn't Van want to go after Heskel?"

"I don't know. We didn't ever discuss it."

"And you? Why didn't you want to go after Heskel? He'd turned me. He was a rogue. There was a bounty on him."

Lettie cleared her throat. "I was dating Van by then and I wanted to go with him on hunts."

"That was damn fast." That's another reason Jacqueline had been so irritated about it because they hadn't let any time pass. It was like she had been turned, Van ended the engagement, and he was dating Lettie.

Lettie didn't respond.

"Have you gone on many hunts with Van?" Jacqueline didn't know why but she was even more pissed off about that than that he was dating her traitorous bestie.

"This was the first time. He brought his brothers also because he thought that Paine would have more rogue vampire friends there."

Jacqueline hoped that Van wouldn't like hunting with Lettie either and wouldn't take her on his hunts. See how Lettie felt about that. "He didn't know Heskel was there or that he owned the house?" She wanted to know the truth.

"No. Van had followed Paine to the house and that's why the four of us went there."

"So why are you calling?" What was the bottom line? Did Lettie want to clear her own conscience? Get Jacqueline to tell her she forgave her? Want to tell her she wanted to be her friend again?

"Van was angry that you were at the estate taking down vampires. I was kind of taken aback."

Jacqueline wasn't surprised. "Believe me, if you were turned, you would suffer the same fate, if I could call it suffering. Though

I'm not glad that it happened, I realized once it had, Van hadn't been the one for me. So I was relieved to be rid of him." Jacqueline felt the same way about Lettie. That there was no sense in being friends with anyone who wouldn't accept what she had become. At first, she thought she wouldn't find anyone who would be there for her until Dane and his brothers showed up in her life. She couldn't have been more grateful for their friendship.

"Yeah, well, I'm sure of that. You really don't mind that I'm dating Van?"

"I don't give a damn if you're dating him." Well, Jacqueline said it, but she hadn't exactly meant to say it in that way. Yeah, she was still mad at her friend for dating him and not caring how she had been faring.

"My mother said you were at the restaurant where she was having lunch with your mother and their other friends."

"Like Van's mother? Yep."

"Why?"

"We were celebrating. Why not?"

"You just happened to go to the same restaurant where you knew they were going to be."

"What of it? If I hadn't been turned, would it have been an issue for me to go to the restaurant at the same time?"

"It...they thought it was like you were trying to make them feel uncomfortable."

Jacqueline scoffed. "Why should they feel uncomfortable? We were just eating and if they were bothered by something, it is their problem."

"All right, well, I just don't want things to get out of hand."

"Why would they? You know, Lettie, I'm going to go where I want, when I want, just like I have always done. I'm not going to worry about whether you or any of my 'old' acquaintances are going to be at some of my old haunts. And I'm not going to stop going to them to appease you or anyone else like you."

"You don't mean you're going to go to the Starlight Club for hunters," Lettie said, as if she had to tell Jacqueline that's who the club was for when she had been going there since she was old enough to legally drink.

Well, even before that if she was with a guy who got carded and not her. "Are you saying that I'm no longer a huntress? Really? Then how am I able to get bounties for taking down rogue vampires?"

"Vampires can take down rogues," Lettie said.

Jacqueline sighed. "All right, that's true. But vampires can't take down hunters, and believe me, if one is a rogue, I can take him or *her* down legally." Which suspected wasn't true, but Lettie wouldn't probably know that.

Lettie didn't say anything in response to that.

"Okay, good talk." Then Jacqueline hung up on her.

She suspected the real reason Lettie had called her was she was feeling guilty about having been her best friend and had started dating Van right away. But also that Lettie wanted to know why Jacqueline had gone to the same restaurant that their mothers had gone to at the same time. She figured she wanted to know if Jacqueline was going to continue showing up where Lettie and their acquaintances, family, and friends would frequent, and that was a big yes. If it made the hunters uncomfortable, so be it.

Though maybe she was pushing things a little bit too far, too soon after being turned. Yet, she wanted to get on with her life, and get back to something that felt more normal.

She saw Princess sitting in the window looking out front. Waiting for Dane to return?

Usually, once Jacqueline had taken care of the rogues on her list, she would go online and sign up for more. But...she needed some time off, she thought. Some time to learn how to cope with her new abilities.

She began to vacuum, and Princess made a hasty retreat to her bedroom. Other things might have changed in her life, but that was one thing that hadn't. She tucked some of her hair behind her ear and said to Dane telepathically, *"Do you think maybe I'm pushing things to go to the hunters' club tonight, possibly too soon after us being turned. Or at least with me being turned?"*

"Jacqueline?"

"Yeah, did I startle you?"

"Hell, yeah. I'm not used to having you speak in my head."

She chuckled. *"Sorry about that. We need to get used to talking this way. It's a great way to talk to each other hands free, even when we're doing something noisy like vacuuming."*

"Oh, I am too."

She laughed. *"Wow, like minds."*

"So why are you having second thoughts about going to the club tonight?"

"Lettie called."

"Hell. What did she want?"

"To know if I was upset with her because she is dating Van, and she didn't like that I was at the restaurant where my mother, hers and Van's, and others were having lunch. Anyway, the final upshot was I told her that I'll go where I please anywhere that I've been before."

"Which is the way you should feel. No one should have the ability to dictate where you go or don't go."

"So you don't think it's too early to go to the hunters' club? Or maybe we could go to one further away?"

"No. At least I feel we're going in the right direction—if you want to call it that—in our recovery. Or at least trying to normalize the changes in our lives."

"Okay, that's what I was thinking, until I got the call from her. And then I thought maybe I wasn't looking at this clearly."

"Everyone's coming tonight. We won't be alone," Dane said.

"Everyone would probably be disappointed that we didn't go, don't you think?"

"*I'm sure they would understand if we didn't go,*" Dane said.

"*Yeah, I agree. I think Lettie just made me feel unsure of myself.*"

"*Don't let her, or anyone else like her, make you feel that way.*"

"*Okay, I'll see you at five then.*"

"*See you then.*"

She finished vacuuming, then put away the vacuum. She loved teleporting from place to place, but it sure confused Princess. She would see Jacqueline disappear in front of her and then she went looking all over the house for her. Jacqueline appeared in the bedroom where Princess had been sleeping on the bed, startling her. She meowed at her as if telling her not to do that to her, and then she came over and rubbed against Jacqueline's legs to show her all was forgiven.

She petted Princess's head and then began looking through her fancier club outfits. Because of her red hair, she preferred wearing black, emerald green to teal, any shade of blue, red, royal purple, and crisp white—like the wedding gown she had chosen to be married in.

But which of her dressy dresses were the best to wear to show off in tonight? Long? Short? Something in between? Lacy? Sequined? Velvety? Or satiny?

She decided to go with the long teal gown that had a lacey bodice, fitted waist and gown, showing off her curves, and a long slit up the side that would make it easy to dance.

14

Dane had been so irritated that Lettie had called Jacqueline and had made her self-doubt her intentions when she had every right to go anywhere that she wanted to, just like anyone else did. Technically, they could also go to vampire clubs, but he wasn't sure they would be welcome there. He had never really talked to Adonis about whether he and Zachary and the others went to vampire clubs after they had been turned. He wondered if they did so as a group, would the vampires feel threatened as in the hunter part of them was looking for rogue vampires at the club?

Dane suspected it would be hard to turn off that part of their nature, if they spotted someone in a vampire club who was on one of their termination lists. He still thought it would be easier to fit in with the hunters at a hunters' club since they'd been born hunters and knew so many of them.

He finally dressed in black dress trousers, black dress shoes, and a black button-down collared shirt. But then he wondered what Jacqueline was wearing. Wouldn't it make a relationship statement if he wore a shirt that matched her dress? As long as she wasn't wearing peach. He didn't have that color in his wardrobe.

Pink, yes. No purple either, though. Lots of different shades of blue because of his blue eyes.

"Hey, I hope I'm not interrupting anything," he telepathically said to Jacqueline.

She said she was laughing. *"Are you practicing your telepathic communication with me or are you—"*

"Okay, you might think this is silly, so feel free to say so, but I could wear a shirt to match the color of your dress if I have one."

She didn't say anything for a moment, and he figured maybe he was going a little overboard with wanting to show they were a couple. But he thought it would help her feel that he had her back while they were at the hunters' club no matter what happened tonight.

"Do you have a teal shirt? Aqua? Turquoise? Or you could wear another shade of blue that would work."

"I have a dark teal shirt."

"Oh, perfect. That will be so much fun."

He sighed with relief. He was glad she sounded like he had made her night. *"All right. As soon as I pull on my shirt, I'll be on my way over."*

"See you soon. I'm just putting my hair up."

"You can keep it down, if you would like."

"Okay, that makes it even easier."

"Great. I love your hair. See you in a few." Once he finished dressing, he drove over to pick up Jacqueline, trying to anticipate how she would look. She looked fabulous in everything he'd seen her in while hunting rogue vampires or at the therapy meeting. No matter what she wore, he knew she would look sexy. He wasn't disappointed as he knocked at the door, and she let him in.

"Princess is waiting to see you."

He laughed. "Hey, Princess. I'll have to give you another good brushing one of these days."

"She would love it."

"Man, you look gorgeous. I mean, you always do, no matter what you're wearing but dressed like this? I can't imagine any man not wanting to call you his date. My brothers are going to be in seventh heaven when they get to dance with you."

She blushed a pretty shade of red. "Thanks. You're pretty dashing yourself. I can't believe our teals are almost the same shade."

"Yep. We definitely look like we are together."

"Yeah, that's nice."

"See you later, Princess," Dane said, then he shut the door and walked Jacqueline to his truck, opened the door for her, and once she had climbed in, shut the door for her. He climbed into the driver's seat and buckled in. "Well, are you ready for this? My brothers said they would meet us there."

"Yeah, I'm ready for this. Though I would be lying if I said I wasn't somewhat nervous about this. What about you?"

"Oh, yeah, I think I wouldn't be honest with myself if I said I was feeling totally fine about this. In the past, it would be just a fun outing. Now? It's a whole other story. I keep anticipating a fight from some of the hotheads who might want to keep the club patronage strictly to hunters who haven't been turned."

"Then what do we do?"

"We'll play it by ear. If push comes to shove, and we don't want to make a scene, we can disappear and drive off into the sunset. Or we can stay and force the issue. But I really don't think we can plan what will happen until we see what happens. I kind of doubt Zachary or Adonis would back down if any hunter gave them issues."

"Why would you?"

Dane glanced at Jacqueline. To protect her.

"Don't you back down on account of protecting me. I'm just as likely to stay and make them eat their words."

He smiled. He could see her doing it too.

"Oh, I was thinking about Stacey and how she said her brother had come to her aid when she had been turned. I wonder if he'll be there to back her up on this."

"Maybe, since my brothers are. But you never know. For him, taking down the rogue that had turned her was really important. Allowing a bunch of half vampire, half hunters into an all-hunter club might be another story. He might even feel pressured by his hunter friends to go along with keeping us out." Then Dane pulled into the club parking lot and saw his brothers there. To his surprise, so were Stacey and her brother, Richard. Zachary and his mate Pasha were there. Danai and Michael were also there, along with Adonis, and his mate Rachael.

Dane smiled. He was glad they had such a nice turn out. The club wasn't really busy at this time of night, so they would grab seats in a section of it, claiming their bit of territory, and have the wall to their backs.

Then they went inside. Five hunters were there, all male, all sitting up at the bar, three of them there on their own, two sitting together talking. They didn't pay any attention to Dane and his friends' arrival as they took their seats at the perfect spot. They could watch everyone coming into the establishment. A window was situated on their right side. They weren't going to be sitting hidden in the back because they wanted everyone to know they were there, and they had every right to be.

Through the window, Dane saw two more cars roll up into the parking lot, and Zachary said to Stacey and Jacqueline, "The blue Cadillac is my dad's. Tobias's brothers, my uncles, Brent and Curt, are with him. In the other car, that's my cousin Ferris and his mate, Mary, and his twin, Ned, and his mate, Trish."

"Wow, this is a great turnout," Jacqueline said, taking hold of Dane's hand and squeezing it. He leaned down and kissed her mouth.

He was glad to see her so cheerful when she had been so apprehensive before. Of course, it didn't mean that they wouldn't have trouble from some of the hunters when they arrived. But it felt good to be at the club like he was still a hunter and belonged here just as much as anyone else.

Everyone greeted everyone and more introductions were made to let everyone know who Stacey and Jacqueline were.

Tobias said, "You ladies must not have gone to this hunters' club much or I would have noticed you."

Stacey said, "I usually go to one that's a little closer to my home, so this one is new to me."

"I've been with my ex-fiancé here a few times. We probably just were here on nights that you weren't," Jacqueline said. "I had seen Zachary here before, but I didn't know him at the time."

"With a huntress?" Pasha asked, looking askance at Zachary.

Jacqueline smiled. "No, with Michael, I believe, though I didn't know his name either at the time. And I had seen Dane once."

"With my ex-fiancée?" Dane asked.

"Yeah."

"How did I not notice you?" Dane asked.

She chuckled. "You were with your fiancée at the time."

Everyone seemed of good cheer, dressed to the nines, happy, smiling, ordering cocktails except for Rachael who just got flavored water.

"Have any of you been to a hunters' club since you were turned?" Jacqueline asked.

"No," Zachary said, all the others in their family who had been turned agreeing.

Zachary's uncles and other cousins hadn't been turned, but they had backed the family once the changes had occurred. It had been hard for them to deal with it at first, but necessary. And their family was family, still the same personalities, but just having vampiric abilities that made them stand out from the rest. At least that's how Tobias and his brothers had finally come to view it.

"Are we doing the right thing?" Jacqueline asked, looking at Rachael who had recently had a baby.

Rachael smiled. "Oh, absolutely. This is a long time in coming. We've been busy hunting, well, until I couldn't hunt any longer, but yeah, it's something that we had talked about doing and the family finally is home from Florida for a little while, so…it's perfect. If we have any trouble, we'll take care of it as we see fit. If worse comes to worst, we can vanish and reappear somewhere safe."

"Which is the only reason I said it was okay for Rachael to come, since she had our baby not that long ago," Adonis said.

Rachael laughed a little. "As if you could keep me away from having fun dancing with you."

The music was playing, no live band yet, but after they all ordered their drinks, the mated couples began to dance, joined by others as Trey took Stacey to the floor, and Dane took Jacqueline.

When she was dancing with Dane she felt as if she were dancing on air, he was such a smooth dancer, completely in control. She loved how gracefully he moved.

"I don't know about you, but I swear I've never danced so well in my life," Dane said.

"Oh, me too. Is it because we are vampires also now?"

"Or maybe we just gel because we're meant to be together. I feel like I've been taking lessons for years."

"Me also. This is so nice. I want to dance all night long," she said.

He did too, but they still had to worry that they were going to have trouble with some of the hunters once the club began to fill up. But the distance between them soon changed and he was holding her close, the dancing become much more intimate, sexy, turning her on. God, was he a hottie. She swore when he looked at her with his heated gaze, he was seducing her with his piercing eyes.

More than that, she felt his arousal growing and he pulled

away a little in a gentlemanly gesture, but she wanted the heat between them and dragged him close again, telling him she was enjoying that part of the dance and not to distance himself from her.

He smiled with that sexy smile of his that bordered on total seduction. "You're a captivating dancer, so sexual, so beautiful."

She smiled at him and wrapped her arms around his neck. "You make it easy to feel that way—and believe me, I've never felt this way while dancing with any other guy."

"The same with me with any other woman, and I don't believe it all has to do with being vampires."

"I agree. I'm just so...I don't know, attuned to you," she said.

"I feel that way about you and feel so much more spontaneous. I normally wouldn't be this...forward with a woman I had just met, but with you..."

"No holds barred."

He smiled and leaned down to kiss her. "Yeah, no holds barred."

Their lips were nearly touching again, their eyes focused on each other's mouth and then they were kissing again.

THEN LETTIE and Van walked into the club with two other couples. Jacqueline pulled her mouth from Dane's, and he felt Jacqueline tense in his arms. He ran his hand down her back, and she quickly relaxed.

"Sorry about that," she said.

"Don't be sorry about it. If my ex walked in with a new guy on her arm, I would be tensing too."

"You're so good for me. I never thought I would be dancing with anyone, or spending the night in his bed, any of this, so soon after being turned and after the breakup," she said.

"Ditto for me. But spending time with you has been great. I

wouldn't have wanted it any other way. You have really opened my eyes to what being with someone as special as you is like."

"Thanks so much. I really feel the same way about you. Not at first when you came into the meeting half dressed, but I overcame that pretty quickly."

He laughed. "I had gotten that impression."

"I couldn't believe you would ask me if I thought you should remove your bloody shirt at the meeting."

He smiled. "I couldn't help but want to get your reaction. All I've got to say is that you are so beautiful. This gown on you, the color and style, are just gorgeous."

"We look good together."

"I agree."

"I love your teal shirt. You look very dashing."

"Thanks." Dane glanced at Van sitting with Lettie and their friends at one of the tables. They were drinking their cocktails and watching him dancing so intimately with Jacqueline.

"I want to tell them to get a life," Jacqueline said. "I mean, we can't be all that interesting to them, can we?"

Dane leaned down and kissed her. "Apparently so. Maybe your ex is not so over you." But as soon as Jacqueline gave him a deep kiss back, her hands cupping his face, he felt his teeth extending. He tried to pull his mouth from hers, not wanting to worry her that he was losing control, but she held him tight and caressed his fangs with her tongue. When he deepened the kiss, he felt her own canines had extended and he measured them with his tongue, intrigued. Maybe she was just as fascinated with his as he was with hers.

Then they pulled their mouths away from each other, smiled a little, their hearts pumping hard, their breathing fast. The song ended and she cleared her throat. "Would you like to get another drink and cool down a bit?"

He nodded, afraid to show off his extended canines further. As soon as they returned to their table, Adonis and Rachael smiled at them. The others were still dancing.

"Fang trouble?" Rachael asked.

They chuckled.

"Yeah, when do you get control over your fangs when you're kissing?" Jacqueline asked.

"I still don't have control over it," Rachael said. "You know it just happens when you're...really happy to be with someone."

"Or angry with someone," Adonis said.

"Sometimes even if you're startled," Rachael said.

Dane had to admit that he loved stroking Jacqueline's extended canines with his tongue. There was something totally erotic about it and another part of him was seriously becoming engaged also, which had just made them extend even further.

They ordered margaritas and the cocktail waitress leaned over the table and said, "So you are all vampires?"

The music was loud and only they heard her words.

"Yeah," Adonis said, "but we're also hunters and have been for much longer than vampires."

"That's sooo...well, cool." She smiled and then left to put in their drink orders.

"Well, that's one vote for us," Adonis said.

"I think there are more who aren't happy with us being here." Rachael sipped on her chilled glass of strawberry-flavored water.

"Aww, hell." Dane hadn't expected *his* ex-fiancée to show up at the club with a date. And she was with a guy Dane had never liked —to top that off.

"Oh, that's your ex," Jacqueline said, sounding surprised.

"Yeah, and that's a hunter I never got along with. He was always a bully. Moose Warner. I can't believe Wendy would go out with him."

"Maybe she didn't think he was a bully."

"She always agreed with me, but I guess things have changed for her."

"Or maybe no one else would go out with her," Jacqueline said.

Dane smiled. He wished. Not that he wanted Moose to bully her, but he wouldn't be bothered if no one wanted to date his ex-fiancée right away. He could understand why Jacqueline would be upset that her ex ended up with her best friend. That was a real low blow.

Then Jacqueline took a deep breath and let it out. "There's my brother with his girlfriend." She scoffed. "He wanted me to go to therapy, but he didn't say anything about taking down Heskel. He never asked me how I was feeling. We were close before that. Giving each other a hard time in a fun way, going on hunts together on several occasions. When I was turned and except for telling me to go to therapy—so that I could be with others like me!—he hasn't had anything to do with me."

Dane shook his head.

"I love your brothers. They are so wonderful."

Dane agreed. "Yeah, I never had any doubt that they would back me, after of course giving me hell for not calling them sooner."

She laughed. "That's better than the silent treatment." She finished her drink and reached out her hand. "Let's do some more of our hunter-vampire dance moves."

"Yeah, I'm so ready." He took her hand and led her back to the dance floor. They began dancing hot and close again.

That's when their fangs extended. But instead of being shocked, they embraced this new change, getting all worked up.

She finally broke free of the kiss and said, "You're staying over at my place tonight."

He smiled, showing off his fabulous canines. "Yeah, I'm ready."

"Good. But more of this first. Your dance moves are wickedly fine. Did you dance this well before?" she asked.

"With you, I just feel it. I swear you really bring it out in me."

"That's good. You do that with me too. Van always said I was out of step with him half of the time, but he would throw me off balance. With you, I have no problem."

Then five hunters came into the club, glanced at those of the hunters who had been turned, and immediately voices were raised. "Hell, who let *them* in?"

Dane and Jacqueline immediately glanced at the five men. But Dane noticed the other hunter-turned vampires were also observing the men.

Not only them though. Even Stacey's brother had seen her dancing and then was watching the men who had made the comment. The tension was palpable. Things had been fine until those men had shown up. Even Moose hadn't said anything, and Dane suspected he was glad Dane had been turned so that Moose had a chance to be with Dane's fiancée.

The five men got a bunch of beers and got a table as close to Dane and his friends' table as they could. They were itching to start a fight and drinking would certainly help to get that going.

Dane thought about taking Jacqueline home, but he hated to look like he was afraid of a little confrontation. Plus, the whole business of showing his fangs off if he got riled wouldn't be tolerated in a hunters' club or anywhere else, unless he was fighting a rogue vampire, he figured.

Jacqueline slid her hand over his shoulder. "Ignore them."

"Do you want to stay?"

"We came to enjoy the company of our friends while having drinks and dancing. Are you worried they'll start real trouble?"

"I'm worried I'll show off my fangs and then cause real trouble."

She sighed. "Yeah, that could be an issue. I hadn't thought of that. How about we stay here unless they really become a problem?"

"All right. But the first sign of real danger to you, I'm whisking you out of here."

She chuckled. "Unless I do it to you first."

"I'll go along with that." He kissed her again.

They heard a couple of taunts from the men at the table next to theirs. "Go suck blood somewhere else." "Man, when a hunter club turns into a vampire club, it's time to find a real hunters-only club."

Then go somewhere else, Dane wanted to say.

Tobias glanced at the men, and Dane was afraid he would walk over there and start a real scene. Tobias had a lot of clout in the city since he was the head of the League of Hunter's Council. Ever since his son Zachary, his son Michael's fiancée, Danai, and his niece Rachael's mate, Adonis, had been forcibly turned against their will by rogue vampires on hunters' terminal lists, he had advocated for the hunters. Tobias had realized that it could happen to any hunter on a case. And Rachael had asked Adonis to turn her, and their baby was a hunter-vampire mix. So far, the baby didn't need to drink blood, but she wasn't affected by sunlight at all. They wouldn't know whether she would have telepathic communication until she was older and could really speak to them as a human to begin with. It was all such a new phenomenon.

Tobias and his brothers, Brent and Curt, were all glowering at the five hostile hunters.

15

"If one of us forces a vampire to show his or her fangs, we can terminate them," one of the five hunter rabble-rousers said, which so irritated Jacqueline, mainly because she was afraid it could be true.

"Who are these hunters? Do you know them?" Jacqueline asked Dane.

"Yeah. Friends of Gregory Devine, a hunter who wanted to marry Rachael until Adonis fell in love with her and she wanted Adonis to turn her. Gregory attempted to kill Adonis. Gregory was banned from here, but then he helped Adonis and his family to eliminate the rogue vampire threat to the rest of his family in Florida, where he made some amends. Still, some of Gregory's friends are still here and itching to cause trouble," Dane said.

"Why weren't they banished also?" she asked.

"They hadn't done anything like Gregory had with trying to kill Adonis. The other hunters that had stood by Gregory, left with him, looking for places that they could still work as hunters and ended up in Florida. They didn't realize they would end up fighting for Adonis and his family at first. But a few of Gregory's friends, who had kept their noses clean until *now,* stayed behind."

"Hmm. It appears that they still feel like Gregory had felt about hunters who have been turned," Jacqueline said.

"Yeah. Sore heads. I would like to see how they would feel if they were in our situation."

Then one of the hunters rose from his chair and started across the dance floor with a beer bottle in his hand. Immediately, Van jumped out of his chair at the table he was sitting with Lettie and Michael released Danai while dancing with her as they both headed for the beer bottle wielding hunter.

"If you know what's good for you, you'll return to your seat with your friends or even better, you should leave before you get hurt," Michael said, his voice dark with threat.

"Or what?" the guy said.

"Or we'll make you," Van said, to Jacqueline's surprise. His voice was hard and brooked no argument.

She couldn't believe her ex would get behind hunters who were friends of the hunters who had been turned. Maybe he was feeling badly about what had happened to her and he'd felt guilty about not showing some compassion after what had happened. She hadn't been turned on purpose and what if it had happened to him? She would have been there for him, and she would have immediately gone after the vampire who had turned him. He might be rethinking his actions regarding her. But it was a little too late for that.

Then the guy's friends came up to join him, all wielding bottles. Not good. The hunters weren't allowed to wear their swords in the club, because alcohol and deadly fights could erupt. So Jacqueline figured they were planning on using the beer bottles in the fight, which could have dangerous and even deadly consequences.

Then to everyone's surprise, a couple of big club bouncers, both hunters who were at least six-five and brawny, wearing tank tops to show off their muscles, stalked onto the dance floor and the music finally stopped, all the dancers turning to observe the unfolding drama.

"Okay, you five, set your bottles down on your table and leave, now. If we have any further trouble with you, you'll be banned from the club for a month—longer, if necessary," the one bouncer said.

"You can't take all of us," the one guy said, shaking his bottle at him.

"Yeah," one of his friends said.

Not a good idea. The guys definitely had too much to drink. They had probably been drinking before they had even arrived at this club.

That's when several other hunters, including Van, came to the dance floor to help mediate the situation. Between the bodyguards and their other "volunteer" help, they removed the beer bottles from the five men and then escorted them outside.

The five belligerent men were forced out, throwing punches, cursing the bouncers and everyone who had assisted them. The bouncers gave them a three-month ban from the club.

Dane said to Van, "Thanks, man."

Van glanced at Jacqueline. "Sorry."

She shrugged. "It wouldn't have worked out after I was turned, so no hard feelings."

"It doesn't excuse the way I deserted you, that I didn't go after the rogue vampire who had turned you, or..." Van glanced back at Lettie, still sitting at their table. He didn't say anything more, the look he'd given Jacqueline's bestie told Jacqueline all she needed to "hear."

Jacqueline realized Van hadn't danced with Lettie once tonight, but Lettie loved to dance, so did he. So what was up with that? Jacqueline had been halfway watching to see if they would approach the dance floor, curious if they would dance together as well as she did with Dane. She had hoped they wouldn't have a confrontation. That was before Van apologized to her, which she still couldn't believe.

"No problem," Jacqueline said to Van, not sure what else to say. She was so unprepared for his comment.

"Okay, thanks for understanding." Van looked like he wanted to take a step forward, the way he was leaning in that direction, and his gaze shifted to focus on her lips as if he wanted to kiss her even.

But then Dane moved in that direction, possessively, and she didn't want him to extend his fangs to get Van to back off. Van immediately got the point though, inclined his head to the both of them, then turned and headed back to his table.

The dance music began again, and Dane leaned down and kissed her in his very seductive way. "Do you want to dance further, or do you want to leave?

She smiled up at him and kissed his mouth, amused that he was trying to convince her that she should leave with him and do more of this—privately. But she loved being with him like this too. "More dancing." She wanted to dance with him until the club closed. They might not have another chance like this with a bunch of hunters who would be there with them if they needed them.

Adonis telepathically said to the group, *"When we go, we leave here together just in case we have trouble outside of the club."*

"Absolutely," Dane said.

Then they continued to dance with each other like they were the only ones there for each other, loving the music that thrummed through them, the way they pressed their bodies hotly together, the feel of his hardness—she was definitely making love to him tonight —the way he kissed her, and their fangs extended, and they shared the touching experience in a hot and sexy way. Being with Dane was just magical. She wanted to hold him like this forever. Everything about him made her heart beat in an excited way. This was her fairy tale. The best feeling ever. Dancing would never be as good with anyone else. When she was with him, they were synced.

Was that why Van had wanted to apologize? That he realized what he had lost in giving her up? And what she'd gained in having Dane in her life? She wondered if Van had thought she would have been just pining away at home without him in her life any longer, and then realized now that he was easily replaced. Too bad.

Then she saw Van and Lettie get up and leave the club with their friends. *Wow*.

Dane kissed Jacqueline's ear. "Looks like he still has some feelings for you."

"Yeah, but it would never have worked out between us. Once I met you, I realized even if we had all still been hunters, he didn't have what it takes to make me feel like you do. I believe he could see that. So it kind of hurts his ego."

Dane chuckled. "Good, because he doesn't deserve you."

"Neither does your ex deserve you."

"Yeah, you can't believe how shocked I am that she's here with Moose," Dane said.

"They haven't danced once together."

"I didn't dance like this with her, to tell you the truth."

"Oh, me either with Van." She rubbed against Dane to make her point, eliciting a groan from him.

He gave her a sinister smile. "You will pay for that."

"I can't wait."

When it was late and nearly time to close the club, the friends all gathered together to leave. Dane's ex and Moose had left a couple of hours earlier too. She realized, maybe when she had only eyes for Dane, her brother and his girlfriend had left the club too.

Then the friends all exited the club together to ensure no one was waiting in the parking lot to give them grief. The rabble-rousing hunters who had been kicked out had left the area, thankfully.

"We'll have to do this again," Adonis said, "though it might be much later. We're visiting with the Bremertons, but we will be returning to Florida to run the hunter group out there in about two weeks."

"That's understandable," Dane said. "After what happened the last time with rogue vampires taking over your hunter territory when you left, I don't blame you."

"Michael and I will be returning to Florida also," Danai said, "but Zachary and Pasha are hanging around here to help out his father and uncles."

"With visits back home to Florida a few times a year," Pasha said, "to see my family. We didn't want to have all of us abandoning the Bremertons."

"We will be swapping out too," Danai said. "Michael and I need to spend time in both places."

"The same with us," Adonis said.

That made it hard, Jacqueline was thinking. Three of the Bremertons had mated with three of the Cameron family and their homes were so far apart. If she and Dane ended up mating, at least both their families were here. That was only important if her parents and her brother came around to accepting her. Otherwise, she was glad to be around Dane's brothers.

Jacqueline had hoped they would have more time to practice telepathically communicating with all the Bremertons. Still, they had their therapy group members—Anne and Stacey—to also talk to. And maybe more if some others showed up at the meeting.

"It was great meeting you ladies," Tobias and his brothers said.

Everyone else who had just met them said the same.

"Thanks, it was nice meeting all of you," Jacqueline said.

"I'll see you at our group meeting in a few days," Stacey said to Dane and Jacqueline. "I don't have anyone on my list to hunt, and I'm not looking for any for a while. I have enough money saved and I think I need a break."

"I feel the same way. See you there," Jacqueline said, thinking how much she had changed with the way she viewed going to the meetings. Instead of resenting them, Jacqueline was actually looking forward to them now and even meeting other hunters like them, especially since she would be going with Dane.

Stacey left, and Matt said to Dane, "You know, you said we would all be able to dance with Jacqueline. But you never once gave any indication that you were okay with any of us dancing with her once you took her to the floor."

Dane smiled.

Jacqueline laughed. "Yeah, did you see Van approach me? Dane gave him a growly look that made Van take a step back."

Trey said, "We knew that would happen, despite Dane saying he was fine with you dancing with us."

Ryan agreed. "We didn't even bother taking bets on it. Unless you had come and asked one of us to dance, Dane wasn't going along with it."

"I noticed. But none of you approached us either on the dance floor to cut in," she said.

The brothers laughed.

"We didn't want him to show off his fangs to us and get himself in trouble," Matt said. "He still doesn't have perfect control over them."

Both Jacqueline and Dane chuckled. She actually loved that he was showing how possessive he could be with her. Van had never demonstrated those feelings toward her, and she had always wondered if there was something wrong with their relationship because of it.

Then everyone said their good nights, got into their vehicles, and headed out.

"If you had wanted to dance with my brothers—" Dane said, driving in the direction of his house so he could grab a bag.

"After the way you were dancing with me? No way. If you hadn't been such a suave dancer, then maybe."

He smiled and parked in his garage. "You wouldn't have wanted to dance with anyone else even if I hadn't been such a suave dancer."

"You know, you're right."

~

DANE KISSED JACQUELINE, then said, "I'll be right back." He vanished and reappeared in his bedroom and threw a change of clothes and his toiletry kit into it. Then in no time at all, he reappeared in the car, startling her.

"That was quick."

"Yeah," he said, "that's one of my favorite tricks as a vampire. Using all that speed to get things done." But when it came to making love to her, he was much more for slowing things down.

When they finally reached her place, he parked in her garage, grabbed his bag, and he and Jacqueline headed inside. Princess greeted them and they both petted her. Despite having an important mission at hand, they had to show Jacqueline's cat some affection too as she purred away with content.

Then with his bag strap over his shoulder, Dane swept Jacqueline up in his arms and vanished and reappeared in her bedroom, setting her down on the bed, and dumping his bag on the carpeted floor.

"Hmm, you're getting good at teleporting yourself."

"Yeah, it really can have its advantages." He slipped her dressy pumps off her feet, rubbed the soles of her feet for a moment, and she purred like her cat.

Then he slid his hands up her legs underneath her long gown, her skin soft and warm and smooth. He reached the waistband of her panties and slid them down her legs and off, tossing them to the floor. Taking hold of her hand, he pulled her up from the bed, then turned her around so he could unfasten her dress in the back, kissing her bare shoulders, the fragrance of roses in her hair and on her skin making him take another deep breath. He pushed her silky, red hair aside, kissed her back and neck with passionate kisses, and listened to her heart beating wildly, just like it had when he'd been dancing with her. The same as his was beating out of bounds both then and now.

Then he helped her out of her teal gown and set it on one of the chairs in the bedroom. She turned around and started to unfasten his belt while he reached down to untie one of his dress shoes and dropped it on the floor. She was unzipping his dress trousers when he removed his other shoe. Afterwards, she pulled his pants down and he stepped out of them, but she quickly pressed a kiss on his cheek and then his throat before she proceeded. She put his trousers on top of her dress on the chair, while he reached behind her to unfasten her bra while she unbuttoned his shirt.

He licked her breastbone, and she licked his collarbone, tickling him, making him smile.

He slid her bra straps down her arms and once he dropped it, she pulled his shirt off his shoulders and tossed it on top of the chair. He cupped her breasts, enjoying the feel of the soft mounds in his hands, and she reached down and cupped his arousal. He would not be able to hold off and slowly seduce her when she did that. When he massaged her breasts, she did the same with his erection. He groaned. She smiled and slid his boxer briefs off, releasing him. He was beyond ready to make love to her.

JACQUELINE TOSSED the covers aside and climbed onto the bed, ready for Dane to make love to her. He didn't make her wait any longer but quickly moved over her body like a sleek big cat and kissed her mouth with a passion that reached all the way to her toes. Their tongues stroked each other's as he pressed his hard body against hers, and they rubbed their intimate parts together.

Instantly, their fangs extended, and they enjoyed that part of them that was vampire now. Tongues touching, teasing their elongated canines. There was something hot and sexy about it that she couldn't exactly describe.

"Hmm." She licked his lips and then gently bit his lower lip and pulled it toward her, not breaking the skin, enjoying the moment.

With Dane, she felt everything was an adventure and dancing with him had just made their relationship so fiercely sexual. His mouth was hot and needy on hers again, deepening the kiss, hard and thorough. Then they were stroking each other's tongues this time.

She felt his erection pulse while she rubbed her body against him and she breathed in his scent—spicy male, testosterone, pheromones going through the roof. She heard his heart beating hard, the blood rushing through his veins, just like she could hear hers beating just as wildly, like they were both running a marathon.

He moved his heavenly lips to feather kisses on her neck, then licked her, and mouthed her, as if getting ready to bite her. She often felt the urge when they were this intimate. He scraped his elongated teeth on her neck with a deliberate, sexy caress. And then she pulled his head to the side so she could do the same erotic thing to him. His erection jumped, his nipples fully erect, and he groaned. "Bite me."

She wanted to. She really, really wanted to. It wasn't a case of needing his blood, it was just part of their vampire experience— part of who they were now, and part of their new sexual need. But she was afraid to hurt him.

He rubbed her arm with a reassuring touch. "You can do it. Vampires and blood bonds do it all the time and they get extreme pleasure from it. I want you to do it."

She licked her lips, kissed his mouth, and then turned her head to nuzzle his neck again. Her teeth itched to cut into him. "Okay." Then she dipped her teeth into his neck, but that wasn't enough.

She realized she had to taste his blood. It wasn't a matter of want. It was a desire so powerful, she had to. She just hoped she didn't drink too much of his blood.

Her teeth sank slowly into his neck, and she tasted his blood. He moaned in a satisfied way and after she drank a little bit of his blood, she licked the puncture marks, and sealed the wounds.

"Oh, man..." he said.

"Good huh? Okay, I'll go with it. Bite me."

"Are you sure?"

"Yeah, you can't have all the fun. Though I have to admit, that was so intensely erogenous."

"It was for me too." Then he licked her neck, blew on it, and kissed her before he touched her skin with his teeth. Then he gently sank his teeth into her neck, and she arched against him and groaned. "Okay?" he asked.

"Don't stop."

He sucked from her blood, and she wrapped her legs around his hips, pressing her body harder against his arousal. He was right. This was incredible. No wonder blood bonds were eager to find a vampire who would give them this kind of pleasure.

He finally sealed her wounds and kissed her. "Now that was incredible."

"Yeah." She knew they would do it eventually, but every time they were intimate, the urge had become more overwhelming.

Then he reached in between them and began stroking her clit, but just the blood exchange and sucking action had worked her up to a near climax. She was so ready for him, her blood on fire as he stroked her until she couldn't hold on any longer and cried out with joy. Then he was shifting his body so that he could fill her with his erection and began to thrust.

She had her legs around his hips and was moving against him hard, wanting him as deep as he could go. He leaned over and kissed her mouth and she cupped his head and kissed him, her tongue lathing his in a stimulating way. She admired his strength as he maneuvered and lifted her onto his lap and began thrusting that way, his hand free to coax another climax from her. Ohmigod, she had found her hunter vampire for life. He was the one. No other huntress was going to have him, she was thinking. Right before she had another orgasm that took her to the moon.

And he groaned with release. "Man, you're the only one for me."

She smiled. "I was feeling the same thing about you."

Then they took a shower together and when they finished, dried off, and headed for the bedroom. They found Princess on Dane's side of the bed. Jacqueline laughed. "At least I can still climb into bed."

"So you think." He made her move to the center and climbed in on her side of the bed so Princess was on his usual side, but at least she wasn't in between them.

"That was a great maneuver," she said.

"You bet. Nothing was separating me from you tonight."

16

E arly the next morning, Dane and Jacqueline woke to Princess purring and pawing at him. He chuckled. "I take it she wants to eat."

"Yeah, sorry. I'll get her food for her." Princess would do the same thing to Jacqueline when she didn't get up early enough for her liking. She hadn't thought she would bug Dane since he didn't usually feed Princess. She hoped Dane didn't mind that Princess was plaguing him to get her food instead of Jacqueline. From the very beginning, Princess had bonded so much with Dane.

Dane leaned over and kissed Jacqueline. "No, I'll get it. That way she likes me better."

She laughed. "As if she doesn't already. Go for it." But she wouldn't let Dane go until she gave him another deep, toe-tingling kiss.

Princess was insistent that she got fed, but Dane was totally locked into the kiss with Jacqueline, and it took him a few minutes to finally let go. "Damn, Princess, I hope you know how much of an inconvenience this is to your momma and me."

"Nope," Jacqueline said, stretching in bed. "She's all about wanting you to herself, as a means to an end."

"Food."

"Yes."

"After I feed her, I'll make us breakfast."

"Add bloody Mary cocktails to the meal." She was so tired. She felt she didn't have any energy at all. Sure, she'd been up all hours of the night and several hours during the day fighting vampires or dancing with a hot and sexy one, but she wondered if it was due to not taking in enough blood over too long a period. It was something she had to remember to do. She would feel fine, and then suddenly, not. It was just hard getting used to that part of the business of being a vampire.

"Gotcha." Dane had been feeling like he needed some blood, and he was glad he could share that need with Jacqueline. He couldn't imagine being with a huntress who wasn't a vampire like him. And with them both being more newly turned, they had the same needs. He reached into his bag and pulled out a pair of boxers, then put them on, all the while Princess was rubbing her furry body against Dane's legs.

"She's persistent."

Dane agreed. "See you in a bit."

"Wait. Take Princess with you if you're going to teleport or she'll bother me mercilessly, believing you abandoned her and now *I* have to feed her."

Dane laughed and finished dressing. He lifted Princess off the floor and held her close to his chest. "Okay, your royal highness. Ready for a trip out of this world?" Then he teleported.

In the kitchen, Dane put food out for Princess, and then she was happily chowing down. Dane made ham and cheese omelets, toast, and bloody cocktails. When Jacqueline didn't join him by the time he had finished making breakfast, he took the tray up to the bedroom using his vampiric transportation.

When he reached the room, he believed she looked pale, and he realized she really did need her cocktail. She must not have had much blood during the last couple of days, if any. "Hey, are you okay?"

"Yeah, just feeling really tired." She perked up when she saw the Bloody Mary.

He helped her sit up and then gave her the drink, but steadied her hands until she was able to take a couple of good sips from her glass. "You must not have been drinking enough."

"I forget about it," she said.

He drank from some of his too then. "I was too, until my brothers found me passed out on the floor of my living room when they couldn't get hold of me. When I have a craving for blood, I often ignore it. I want to have control over my life like I was used to." He sat next to her on the bed and stroked her pretty red hair.

"Oh, yeah, don't I know it. I just can't stand feeling that it controls me."

"But it doesn't. Not all the way."

She finished her cocktail. "Thanks so much. I feel so much better already."

"Yeah, me too."

"So what happened when your brothers found you passed out in your home?"

He chuckled. "Well, of course they were truly upset. They thought I had died! So they made me drink some blood and I was doing great, but they also made me set up regular feedings on a phone app so that I wouldn't miss them. Of course, sometimes I'm in the middle of a fight or—" He winked at her.

"Dancing with a huntress and making love to her?"

He smiled. "Exactly. So that means drinking earlier before we're off to do some new adventure, or right after. It's hard to think of it when—"

She leaned over and kissed his lips. "When we're in the moment."

"Absolutely. So we'll have to make sure that we don't neglect that."

"If we had been at a vampires' club, we could have ordered bloody cocktails," she said. "But of course not at a hunters' club."

"Yeah, so before we go to the hunters' club, we'll have to have a refreshment. Otherwise, my brothers—should they find us both passed out—will give us both hell."

She laughed. "At least they care about us. My family would never even know that I was blacked out at my home."

"Yeah, that's scary. You know we should probably mention that in the therapy group, especially for those who don't have any family or friends' support." He began eating some of his omelets.

She was eating some of hers and smiled. "You are a great cook."

"Thanks. My mother always said it was important for all her sons to cook well so they could prepare meals for their huntress mates also. Dad loved to cook too. His mother hadn't insisted on him learning to do so, but our mother did."

She smiled. "Even breakfasts in bed?"

"Absolutely. After having four sons, she needed a break, and he was proud of her for being a great huntress too. They fought together on hunts and trained all of us. Some hunters and huntresses have private instructors, but my parents wanted to teach us. Plus, my brothers and I had each other to practice fighting."

"My brother felt I wasn't enough of a challenge when practice fighting. He wanted to fight with all his male friends. So I understand that. On the other hand, I needed to fight males too so that I could fight male vampires. Though females can be just as powerful and difficult to fight. That's why I like practice fighting with males in addition to females."

"Well, you've got four of us males to do workouts with."

She ate some of her strawberry-coated toast. "I will take all of you up on it."

"I might have to fight them just so I get in enough time to play-fight with you," Dane said.

She laughed.

Then Princess jumped up on the bed and Dane grabbed the tray of their empty dishes and left the bed. "I forgot about her."

"I know. She's not used to me eating in bed. She'll think this is a regular routine."

"It could be."

She smiled. "We'll have to shut her out of the bedroom then when we do it, or she'll think that she can join us for a second breakfast."

Dane smiled. "Yeah, I agree with that. I'll take our dishes downstairs."

"I'll join you in a moment."

Holding onto the tray, he vanished. He really liked that part where he could move like this with a tray of food and not spill anything. He didn't think he could have managed the stairs otherwise. Not with two full glasses of bloody cocktails when he carried them to the bedroom in the first place.

He ended up in the kitchen and was cleaning up the dishes when she suddenly wrapped her arms around his waist and kissed his back, his neck, and he loved it. He dropped the pan and scrubber in the sink. And turned around in her arms, leaned down, and kissed her mouth, his hands cupping her face. "You are not conducive to cleaning up the kitchen."

"Hmm, neither are you," she said, kissing him again. But then she pulled away and started putting the dishes in the dishwasher. "It feels so strange to be doing such normal things as vampires, when we did all these same things as hunters."

"Yeah. Some vampires have staffs to do the minimal tasks. I

haven't felt any need to hire anyone to do housework or anything else."

"Me either. But then I'm not interested in having blood bonds."

"I don't want blood bonds either. Picking up blood at blood banks works for me." He finished scrubbing the pan he'd cooked the omelets in. "What do you want to do today?"

"We could check for some postings for rogue vampires. Then we can sign up for one of them and do some research to find where he or she is located. But I was thinking for tonight we could take a moonlit walk in the park?"

"I should have suggested it first."

"No way. We can both plan intimate outings," she said.

They finished cleaning up the kitchen and for the first time ever, he and she got on her computer to search for rogue vampires the police had posted for elimination. They found listings for all of Texas and the nearby states, though they could search for anywhere in the event they wanted to travel that far or had trips planned and wanted to eliminate a rogue while on a vacation.

Before they could pick a viable rogue, she said, "On second thought, let's go to your pool and swim."

Now he hadn't expected that. He was glad she wanted to just spend some more time with him and not just go on another hunt. He enjoyed the time he was spending with her.

"Yeah, that sounds great to me."

"Good. I'll change into a bathing suit and be right down."

"What about Princess?"

"She can stay at home. We can return home for lunch and feed her."

"All right."

Then she vanished and he found a furry mouse toy and pulled it along the floor. Princess immediately started to chase it. Princess was too fast and caught it with her claws extended. "You are quite the hunter," Dane said.

"She is," Jacqueline said, appearing near him wearing a teal bikini, and carrying a beach bag that probably had her change of clothes in it.

"Man, you look great. I'm so glad Van is history with you."

She smiled. "Yeah, he's the past." Then she pulled Dane into her arms, and they were suddenly in his living room.

"I'll be right back," he said, needing to change into his swim trunks.

"I'll be in the pool."

"Meet you there."

He was in his bedroom, tearing off his clothes as fast as he could, and then he threw on his swim trunks and appeared in the swimming pool room. She was in the middle of the pool swimming a lap. He dove into the pool and swam to her as fast as he could. She was smiling at him and that encouraged him to enfold her in his arms.

"You are the light of my life when I thought I was living in darkness once I had been turned," she said, wrapping her arms around his neck and kissing him.

He loved this with her. His ex-fiancée didn't care for swimming in the pool. She didn't like getting her hair messed up. With Jacqueline, she was like a water sprite, diving under the water, coming up, swinging her hair like a wet whip, and smiling. He loved the water too so this was a fun way to enjoy the day with her when they weren't working.

He chased her in the pool and just when he was about to grab her, she vanished. Holy shit! That was cheating!

Then she was behind him and grabbing his hips. He twisted around and wrapped his arms around her. "You tricked me."

She laughed and kissed him. "We're different people now that we are vampires. We can do numerous things. We can experiment and have fun doing it."

"Yes, I love being with you. I love that you are always challenging me with your vampire moves, surprising me, but in a fun way. I love it. You're always a step ahead of me when you're using your vampire abilities."

"I'm glad you're not annoyed with me."

"With you in my arms like this, no way." Even now the intensity between them was through the roof blazing hot.

They kissed each other, but then the rain began pouring down heavily on the top of the roof of the pool room and she said, "Ohmigod, I didn't know it was supposed to rain. I wonder how long that's going to last."

"Knowing Texas, it could be over any second. Or last for days." He smiled at her.

"Then we'll have to do something else if it's raining tonight when we planned to walk in the park."

"I'm sure we'll come up with something." Then he began kissing her again because this was what he really wanted to think about for now.

But then they heard a noise in the house. That was the thing with their hunter and vampiric hearing. It really was greatly enhanced. They didn't say anything to each other for a moment.

Then they remembered they could talk to each other telepathically. *"Did you hear someone in the house?"* he asked.

"I...I thought I heard voices."

"I'm going to check it out," he said.

"I'm going with you."

They got out of the pool, and he grabbed towels for the both of them. As soon as she was standing on the pool patio, he wrapped her in a towel. She quickly dried herself off as they heard drawers opening in the upstairs bedroom.

"Break-in," she said.

"Yeah. I have a couple of swords behind the pool bar. I have them everywhere in the house."

"In case a vampire or his or her minions break in," she said.

"*Right.*" He vanished and reappeared behind the bar.

She joined him. "*Me too.*"

"*Let's go.*" He handed her a sword. "*If they're armed with guns, vanish. Nothing I have in the house is worth getting shot over.*" If she had been human, he wouldn't have wanted her with him, but she was a skilled huntress, so he knew she would do great.

Then he took her hand, because he wanted her with him even so and not off on her own. "*My bedroom.*"

"*Yes.*"

Then they transported there and found two young men dressed in jeans, sneakers, one in a gray hoodie, the other one's was black. But they could hear a couple more people in the guest room, looking through the drawers. "Hell, nothing in here," one of the guys in the other room said.

Dane wanted to tear into them like a vampire, scare them to pieces and change their mind about doing crime. Permanently.

17

Dane was angry that anyone would be foolish enough to break into his house and try to steal from him. His teeth immediately extended, and he hissed. Okay, so that had never happened to him since he'd been turned.

The two guys were intent on trying to find something of value, and then one found a sword under the bed and pulled it out. "Hey, Jimmy, look at this. Here's one of them. What if this isn't a collector's sword though?"

"Shit, you mean what if that's a—"

"Hunter's sword?" Dane asked. "Like these?" He showed his sword to the men.

The two men hadn't even been watching the doorway where Dane and Jacqueline were standing and observing them. But as soon as Dane spoke, the two guys whipped around. He swore they nearly peed their pants as their eyes widened, their jaws dropped, and their skin drained of color. Their hearts were beating triple time.

"It doesn't pay to break into homes when you don't know who owns them. Just a clue. Many of the homes in this development are owned by hunters. And some are even vampires." Dane showed off his canines.

Then the other two guys came out of the guest room. Dane figured they had heard what he had said, and they raced down the stairs. Forget helping out their friends. They were on their own.

The two in Dane's bedroom were just standing there, frozen in place, smelling of fear. Dane and Jacqueline were blocking the doorway, until Jacqueline wasn't. Damn, he wished she had stayed with him, even though he felt confident in her abilities. But he was worried now too.

"Okay...okay, we'll...we'll leave," the one guy finally managed to say, his voice shaking, his knees knocking.

"You can't turn us, or you'll be a rogue and hunters can terminate you," the other guy said, defiant, all knowing, threatening.

The nerve of the bastard! "We're hunters. Sit on the floor." He said it in a way that controlled a human's actions. He'd never tried doing that before, but both men immediately sat down on the floor. "Stay." He hoped this worked like that and then he vanished to see what had happened with Jacqueline with the other two men, wanting to provide backup for her.

She had the other two men lying on the floor in the living room with their hands behind their backs while she was making a call on Dane's home line. *"I've called the police. They're on their way."*

He loved her and was glad she had the same thought of doing the same thing as he did. *"Another ability we haven't used, eh?"*

She smiled at him. *"I've used it before."*

Now that had surprised him. *"Oh?"* She was such an open book, but also such a mystery.

She kissed him. *"Yeah, I told the driver of the big pickup truck following behind mine, hugging my bumper, to back off on the highway one day and he did it! I couldn't believe it."*

Dane laughed. He was glad it wasn't something that was, well, rather roguish. He had never thought of trying to do that with someone who was tailgating him.

"How did you get through the security gate?" Dane asked the two men.

"A guy gave us the code," the one man said.

"What guy?"

"The guy who sent us to this house."

"Who is he?" Dane had thought this was just a random robbery.

"I don't know, man. He gave us each fifty dollars to steal all the swords in the house. He said that you're a sword enthusiast and he was supposed to sell the swords. He was going to give us another two-hundred-dollars each after he sold the swords."

"And you believed that he would really come through with the money? Was he a hunter or a vampire? You didn't figure that maybe I am one or the other since I 'collect' swords?" Dane was skeptical, but these guys looked a little strung out on drugs so they might have believed about anything the guy told them.

"No. He said you just collect them. We figured he was going to resell them on the hunters' market or maybe they're collectables and rarer, worth a lot more."

"And you were meeting him where?"

"We're supposed to call him once we have the swords, and he would pick them up."

"Call him then."

The guy called the number he had, but no one answered.

"Give me your phone and the number," Dane told him.

The man did both.

Then the police arrived, and Dane let them in. "There are two more upstairs. They're sitting in the master bedroom on the floor."

One of the officers, Murphy, had been at the scene where they had taken down Mabon and recognized them. "I can't believe how compliant these guys are."

"Yeah, once they realized whose house they were in, they came around pretty quickly. Uh, I might need to release the guys upstairs to go with your officers." Not to freak the police out, Dane dashed up the stairs instead of disappearing and reappearing in the room. A couple of officers couldn't get the two men to leave their sitting position on the bedroom floor as if they were staging a sit-in. "Go with the police officers," Dane said.

They instantly stood up and the officers handcuffed them and took them into custody. They headed them downstairs.

"Are you going to file charges?" the officer downstairs asked.

"Yeah. If we don't, they'll just break into someone else's home. At least we can have a clear conscious that we tried to do something about it," Dane said.

"You do a lot for the community by taking down rogue vampires, and we really appreciate it. Taking in a bunch of would-be thieves is the least we can do for you," Officer Murphy said.

Dane and Jacqueline gave their statements to the officer.

"Hey, we found a car filled with stolen merchandise just down the street," another officer said, coming inside. "It belongs to one of these guys."

The housebreakers looked like their gooses were cooked now. Good. Dane hoped they would serve some time for this.

"Oh, how did they get inside your house?" Murphy asked. "Were the doors all locked?"

"They were," Dane said.

"We found where they had torn off a window screen on one of the windows on the back of the house. They broke the window and climbed in that way," the other officer said.

"I'll need to have that fixed." Dane noticed that Jacqueline was talking to the four would-be thieves outside on the covered front porch before the officers carted them off to a holding cell and he wondered if she was telling them never to steal from anyone again. He hadn't thought of it at the time, but he could have done that himself. That was one neat vampire trick—

persuading humans to do something—he needed to use more often.

Then the officers put the would-be thieves in some patrol cars and Jacqueline walked inside the house. Dane closed the door and locked it.

"I'm glad the doors were all locked when they broke in," she said.

"Yeah, so it proved they had actually broken in. I'm surprised we didn't hear them."

"That's probably what alerted us, though we hadn't known what it was."

"Yeah, true. I guess that's it for swimming. Do you want some lunch? After we get dressed."

"Sure."

They both vanished and appeared in his bedroom.

"So I told the men not to ask for lawyers and to confess everything illegal they've ever done, and where all the stolen merchandise is now," Jacqueline said, peeling off her wet bikini and putting it in the bathroom over the tub to dry.

Dane laughed. "I'm sure the police appreciated that." He set his swim trunks next to hers.

"Yeah, they began recording their confessions as soon as they got them into the vehicles because they were starting to list all the crimes they'd committed from when they were kids—stealing from stores and even their mom's purses. It's going to be a long list." She started to fasten her bra and Dane quickly took over and fastened it for her. "Why thank you, sir."

"You're so welcome." Then he began getting dressed too. "I thought you were going to tell them never to steal again."

"Oh, I did that too. But I also wanted them to reveal all the crimes they had done in the past so that they might bring some closure to others that they had stolen from—crimes that they had gotten away with."

He smiled. "Great thinking. I had never thought of using vampiric persuasion to get someone to do something. But it comes in handy."

"I rarely think of it either. It's just one of those things we need to practice at for it to come more naturally."

"The next time we want a better table at a restaurant..."

"Oh, can you see us saying that to a hostess, and she makes someone who is in the middle of eating their meal move to another table?" she asked.

"We would be outed for sure," Dane agreed.

"Yeah. We can only do it when it's for the good of a situation." She wrapped her arms around his neck and kissed his mouth, slowly, eagerly, passionately, and he matched her delicious moves. "We handled this matter well."

"We did. I was thinking we would have to use our swords to intimidate them to hold still until we could get hold of the police and they arrived. I realized then that I could make them comply with a vampire's persuasion and get the police there, but I have to admit as much as I know you are great at fighting, I still worried about you."

"I had the same thing in mind and immediately scared them to pieces when I showed up in front of them before they could reach the front door. It looked like you were handling things fine, or I wouldn't have left you."

"I'm glad to hear it. Did you show them your fangs?"

"No, I just told them to lie down on their stomachs and put their hands being their backs until I released them. Then I called the police."

"That worked great. I've got to get a hold of someone to replace the window." Dane got on his phone and called the man he'd used for house repairs before, and he said he would come over to measure the window. "I've got someone coming over to take a look at the window frame."

"That's quick."

"I killed a rogue vampire who was after his teenaged daughter. The vampire wanted her for his own, and I went after him right away. The girl was only fourteen. So Howard really appreciated my help and whenever I need some handywork done, he's there for me get it done."

"That's great, especially since you need that window replaced as soon as you can."

"Right. What appeals to you for lunch?" he asked.

"I could make grilled cheese sandwiches if you have cheese and bread," she said.

"Yep, that would be great."

They both transported downstairs. "You didn't transport like that in front of the officers," she said.

"No. I figured I would startle them too much if I suddenly appeared upstairs and the officers might have shot me."

"Oh, true."

He brought out the extra sharp cheddar cheese and the butter while she found a frying pan. Then he set the bread out for her. She started grilling the sandwiches and he brought out plates, dill pickles, and potato chips.

She glanced at the bag of chips. "Oh, sour cream and onion chips. My favorite."

"Great. Mine too."

Within a few minutes, she flipped the sandwiches over and grilled the other side. Then she served them up and he got glasses of water for them. "Do you need any more blood?"

"No, thanks, I'm good."

They ate their sandwiches and pickles and then she sighed. "I'll see you tonight then?" She glanced out the window. "If the rain settles down."

"We can see each other anyway. We can do something different. Like watch a movie, or something."

"Yeah, sure."

"I'll clean things up."

"Okay, see you at..." She glanced at her phone. "Okay, rain is stopping soon. Five?"

"Yeah, see you then. And we can have dinner and then go for our walk."

"Yeah, I would love to do that."

Then the man came to replace Dane's window, and she kissed Dane and said, "I'll see you soon."

He kissed her back. "See you too."

Jacqueline went home while the handyman went into the back room to take measurements on the broken window. She had barely arrived home when someone knocked on the door. She wasn't expecting anyone, so when she went to the door, she was surprised to see her brother. "Robert, what are you doing here?"

"Dad was furious that you and your hunter friends arrived at their house and gave Mom grief. And to make things worse, you and even more of your new friends showed up at the luncheon Mom and her friends were having at the restaurant."

"Do you want to come in?" She wasn't about to put up with her brother's scolding, but she sure didn't want to air their grievances on the front porch.

"Uh, yeah, of course." Robert stepped into her house and shut and locked the door.

"So, do you want to ask me how I'm doing now that I've been turned? Or are you going to continue to act like nothing happened?" She got him a glass of ice water and they sat down in the living room. Princess immediately came to sit on her lap to be brushed. She picked up Princess's brush and began working on her coat. Jacqueline was ready to clear the air with her brother. If he didn't want to be part of her life any longer, or at least until he got over this, she was prepared for it.

"Yeah, okay, you're right. I apologize to you for not coming to see you."

"Or going after the vampire who had turned me." She began brushing Princess's tummy as she stretched out on her back on Jacqueline's lap.

"I had a full load of cases to deal with."

"All right, so a rogue vampire who could control me wasn't as much of a priority to you or our parents as other vampire rogues on your list."

Robert didn't say anything in response. She figured he would try and talk his way out of feeling guilty about it, but then it seemed he thought better of it.

He ran his hands through his hair. "I'm sorry. You're right. You are always so together. You fight and don't need anyone. Even from a young age, you were like that."

"You don't think this whole business would have turned my world upside down? That I might have needed my family to act like they cared and not like I'm carrying a communicable disease?" At least she had gotten him off the topic of Dane and his brother seeing Mom at the house when Dad wasn't there.

"Yeah, I..." Robert let out his breath and shoved his hands in his pockets. "Okay, you're right. I didn't know what to say to you. I felt bad that you'd been turned. Mom said to leave you alone for a while until you got over the newness."

"You've got to be kidding."

"No. She said that we all know how you are when you're faced with change in your life. You need time to sort out how you are feeling."

"I needed my family to be there for me. A change like this is life altering. How would you feel if the roles had been reversed? If you had been turned and none of us had checked to see how you were feeling? If you needed anything? Not only had I been turned, but

Van had dumped me, never asking how I was feeling, and he wouldn't fight Heskel either."

"And then he started courting your best friend. We all felt that was going too far. I'm sorry, really, Jacqueline. When I think about all the stuff you went through, I realize that we should have been there for you. I want you to know that I want what's best for you. I'll do whatever I can to make it up to you and be the brother I've always been."

"Or better."

He raised his brows.

"An even *better* brother."

Robert smiled. "Okay, that's the sister I knew."

She frowned at him. "Were you worried I would be a rogue? That I might attack you?"

He shook his head. "No. Even if Heskel had tried to convince you of it, we knew you wouldn't. Truly, we know when you need your space. We really felt you needed some time after all that had happened, but we should have at least made sure, and I sincerely apologize for that."

"At least I had Dane there for me."

"Okay, so what's the deal with him?" Robert asked.

"I met him at the therapy session for hunters turned, and you know what? Not only did he step in to be my hero and take down Heskel, his brothers stood by the both of us too."

Robert lowered his eyes to the floor, and she knew he was feeling guilty about it. Then his blue eyes caught her gaze and he said, "I told you Van wasn't the right one for you. As soon as he went hunting with you and then said he preferred fighting with his brothers but then here he is off hunting with Lettie now."

"I know. I think that irritated me more than his dating her."

"Knowing you, I'm not surprised."

Then there was a knock at the door and Jacqueline wondered who that would be now. She set Princess on the couch and walked to the door, though if her brother hadn't been here, she would have just used the vampire way to get there. Not that she was afraid to show what she was in front of her brother, but—she felt maybe it would be like showing off? She wasn't sure why she was feeling that way.

"Are you expecting someone?" Robert sounded concerned.

"No, but I hadn't been expecting *you* either."

18

J acqueline looked through the peephole in her front door and saw four men she didn't know, standing on the porch, looking a little wet from the rain, all wearing rain jackets.

"Trouble?" Robert asked, coming up beside her.

"I don't know. I don't recognize any of them. What do you think?"

Robert looked through the peephole. "They're armed. You can see the tip of their swords tucked under their rain jackets."

"I'll be right back." This time she vanished and grabbed two swords from a sword stand near the living room since her brother hadn't come armed when he came to see her, which she had appreciated. It meant he really hadn't felt that she was a threat to him.

"Okay, now that's a cool ability to have," Robert admitted, watching her.

She was glad she hadn't freaked him out and rejoined him in the vampire's way. "Yeah, one of the coolest. Telepathic communication is too." She was relieved he didn't seem to be bothered by her new ability because she didn't want to have to guard against using it around her family. She opened the front door, her sword in hand, resting by her side.

"Hey, uhm, I'm Zeek Weatherby and my friends and I were hired to, uhm, take down a rogue vampire." Zeek was a strawberry blond, longish hair, a madcap of freckles sprinkled across his cheeks and over the bridge of his nose and was staring at her red hair, before he noticed the sword in her hand. But he didn't look too worried about it. Maybe because he had three friends with him when there was only one of her, but of course her brother was with her, so she wasn't totally alone.

"I'm not a rogue, if you are talking about me." This was the weirdest situation she swore she'd ever been in. If these guys were here to terminate her, why were they standing on her front porch and weren't doing anything but being honest with her? It was as though they were waiting for her to give them permission to kill her.

"Yes, ma'am."

Shut up! They were the politest would-be hunters she had ever met.

"Well, what are you? You can't be real hunters. None of them would ever talk to the rogue vampire they were supposed to take down. They would just get on with business."

"Uh, yeah, we're humans who work as hunters," Zeke explained.

"Okay, Van Helsing hunters." A lot of hunters didn't care for humans who worked in that field because they felt that was a hunter's job and though humans could be well trained, they still were weaker than hunters. Too many human hunters were killed each year compared to the number of hunters who were born that way who fought rogue vampires.

"Uh, well, sure, if that's what you want to call us," Zeke said. "You're not the last one who will."

"Are you new at this?" She just couldn't figure them out. Why hadn't they forced their way into the house and tried to kill her. They hadn't moved to pull out their swords at all.

"Well, no."

"Then you should know better than to knock on a vampire's door, who you believe is a rogue, and then tell him or her that you're there to eliminate him, right?" She felt like she needed to teach them a thing or two so they wouldn't get themselves killed so quickly in a future fight with a vampire. If she'd been a rogue, they would have been dead already.

"Yeah, of course."

The other guys with him were nodding their heads in agreement.

"So then, why are you here? It can't be to eliminate me." She figured they must be having second thoughts. Maybe they realized she wasn't a rogue. If they killed a vampire who wasn't, they would be up on charges of murder.

"We were hired to eliminate you," Zeke repeated.

"I'm not a rogue. The police haven't sanctioned it, have they?" That was a scary thought.

"No. Hunters hired us."

Her jaw dropped. "Hunters?"

"Shit," Robert said. "What are their names?"

She knew from the intensity of her brother's voice he was ready to take out some hunters. Hunters who tried to eliminate hunters who had been turned if they weren't rogues would be considered rogue hunters and then hunters could terminate *them*.

"The only one who actually talked to us was a dude called X. At least that's the name he gave to us. But the others were there as well. My friends and I said we would do it, because we wanted to warn you and if we didn't take the job, we were sure they would have hired someone else. They might have also figured we were a liability at that point and killed us."

"Come inside," Jacqueline said. "Would you like anything to drink? Sodas? Tea? Water?" Since they said they weren't here to try to terminate her, she figured they needed to move this indoors and she needed to learn as much as she could about the hunters who had hired them.

"Water would be good," Zeke said.

She got everyone some water to drink, and they eyed hers, as if they were surprised to see her drinking it too instead of blood. Blood was important, of course, but staying hydrated by drinking water was too. They all sat down in the living room. Princess greeted them, breaking the ice. "I'm going to call on a hunter-vampire friend of mine who was turned also to come join us."

They all looked at Robert.

"That's Robert, my brother, a hunter who hasn't been turned."

The guys were all petting Princess, the cat setting them more at ease.

Then she said, *"Dane, I'm visiting with some Van Helsing hunters who were hired by hunters to eliminate me. If you're not busy doing anything, I would like you to join me to see what they have to say."*

Immediately, Dane was standing in her living room with a sword in hand.

The men all jumped up from their seats on the sofa. Even Robert did, but he was concentrating on the humans, not on Dane, in the event the humans tried to fight Dane and Jacqueline, which she so appreciated.

"They warned me that some hunters had contracted them to terminate me," Jacqueline said. "They're not about to do it."

"It's too bad we couldn't have them return to the hunters and kill them, but they can't do that without going to jail for it," Dane said privately to Jacqueline.

"Right. We need to learn who the hunters are and then out them to the head of the League of Hunter's Council."

"Tobias."

"Yes."

"Take a seat, gentlemen," Dane said, sitting down next to Jacqueline while Robert sat on a chair nearby and the humans sat back down on the sofa. As soon as Dane was sitting down, Princess jumped on his lap, and Dane smiled, then began petting her.

That seemed to set the humans even more at ease as if they felt the cat wouldn't go to Dane if he was dangerous and they relaxed a little.

"All right, tell us everything you can about the hunters," Dane said.

"One was called X, but we were sure that wasn't his name," Zeke said.

"That's Zeke," Jacqueline said to Dane, "and this is Dane. Like me, he went to take down a rogue vampire and lost the battle."

"He might be one of the ones they wanted to have eliminated," Zeke said, motioning to Dane.

"I thought you had only come for me," she said, worried this was more a case of taking out all hunter-turned vampires.

"Yes, but they said there would be more jobs for us, if we did this one without getting caught. That there was a rogue hunter-vampire male who was a friend of yours," Zeke said. "Since he came to your defense, I would say that's a good bet. And by the way, we always check the records to see if a vampire has committed certain crimes and it can all be verified. We have our own private investigator."

A skinny, mousy-brown-haired guy raised his hand. "That's me. I'm Timothy. I did a lot of research on you and found you were an excellent fighter, always took down rogue vampires, never targeted anyone who was innocent, and saved some humans from being turned by rogues. Even after you were turned by Heskel, you were fighting the rogues. There's not one thing that showed up that would indicate you had turned rogue. So we figure, for whatever reason, the hunters have a beef against you. Or that it's just a general hatred for hunters who have been turned. What if one of them was turned? That's what we wanted to know."

The blond guy of the group said, "I'm the IT guy, Callaway, and

I did a lot of digging, trying to learn who these guys were before we came here. We wanted you to have as much intel as we could gather so that you could ensure your own safety. No way were we going to take money for the job and try to eliminate you. Then those guys would have their way, and if anyone discovered we had done the job, we would end up with sentences of life without a chance for parole. Even if we didn't talk, the hunters would have gotten away with your murder. I found where they had been last night, via the GPS on their phones—the Starlight Club. And Timothy learned the bouncers and some hunters threw them out of the bar over an incident with some hunter-turned vampires who were dancing."

"The five rabble-rousers we had to deal with at the club," Dane said, glancing at Jacqueline.

She couldn't believe it! It was one thing to hassle them in a club and not want them to be there but to hire a hit on them?

"Who are they, do you know?" Robert asked.

"Sorry, Dane, I should have introduced you to Robert, my brother," Jacqueline said, so wrapped up in what was going on, she realized her mistake in not introducing the two of them to each other.

"Good to meet you," Dane said, but he didn't really sound like he was too pleased with her brother.

She didn't blame him. She hadn't been either.

"Yeah, I know them. They're friends of Gregory Devine," Dane said.

"Hell, the hunter who stabbed Adonis? If the Bremerton family had wanted to charge Gregory, he could have been in prison for life for attempted murder," Robert said. "I thought he was banished from here, and his friends followed him to wherever they ended up."

"In Florida, but it appears some of his friends remained behind," Dane said. "Two are cousins, Flynn and Felix. Ralph, Manning, and Samuel are the others. Felix would most likely be X.

He's really a leader. But we'll need proof that they hired you to eliminate Jacqueline."

The IT guy, Calloway, rose from his seat and pulled a recorder out of his pocket and handed it to Dane. "We always record the conversations when we take on a job. That way we have proof that someone actually hired us to do it. Of course the hunters didn't know it."

Dane smiled and said to Jacqueline. "I like these guys. They're on the ball."

The guys gave him tentative smiles and she thought he had kind of won them over. Otherwise, he looked like a hunter/vampire that could do some serious harm to them. The same with her brother. She could too, but some thought she didn't look that capable to win in a fight—which gave her an advantage sometimes.

Then Dane looked at the other two guys in the Van Helsing group of human hunters. Both men were dark haired, and they held their hands up to say they didn't know anything. Both were well-muscled and probably worked out to fight vampires. The other three might too, though they didn't look like they were that strong, but sometimes looks could be deceiving.

"So if you don't do the job, then what? Would the hunters want to terminate you because you know too much?" Dane asked.

"Yeah, we figure that would be the case. That's why we're hoping that you can take them down before that happens. No matter what, we want no part in eliminating good vampires," Zeke said, all his friends agreeing.

"How was this supposed to go down? You kill Jacqueline, then report back to X?" Dane asked.

"Yeah, they said she would look like, uh, a regular dead body when we killed her. Not turn to a wizened-up form since she was so newly turned. So we were supposed to take a photo of her after we killed her and send it to X. Then he would tell us what our next job is and would wire us the money. He only wanted the one meeting face-to-face. After that, he wants to do this without physically seeing us to limit his connection to the crime. He let on that this was just a job. If it was just a legal job, there was no reason to keep his connection to the hit a secret. Though of course he told us she was a rogue. But we knew better," Zeke said. "And the other thing is —if she was a rogue—the hunters would be paid a bounty. They wouldn't be paying anyone to take down a rogue vampire."

"Exactly. What was the timeline on the hit?" Jacqueline asked.

"We told him we would get it done by midnight tonight. X said that worked for him, but that if it wasn't done by then, he would contract someone else to do the job," Zeke said.

"Yet they don't have the balls to do it themselves," the IT guy said.

Everyone agreed with him.

"I'll contact Adonis and tell him what's going on. Adonis, Rachael, Zachary, Pasha, Michael, and Danai, all are hunters turned and they could be next on these hunters' list," Dane said. "Adonis will relay this information to the rest of the family, especially to Tobias and his brothers. These hunters won't stand a chance."

The human hunters visibly sighed in unison, looking vastly relieved.

Dane got quiet after that and she realized he was talking to Adonis telepathically since he wasn't getting on his phone.

"In the meantime, I'm sure we can make some kind of arrangement to keep you safe. Kind of like a Witness Protection Program only it will be handled by the League of Hunters. Probably Tobias and his kin will be in charge of it, so that no one else in the league will hear of it in case some of the members are friends of these hunters," Jacqueline said.

"Thanks. We appreciate it," Zeke said. "We figured we would be in trouble no matter which way we went. I mean, with the hunters or your people."

"Well, thanks for coming to our aid. We had no idea this was going on," Jacqueline said.

"You're welcome. We count ourselves as good guys and don't want to change that," Zeke said.

"The same with us." Jacqueline relayed the information to Stacey because she'd been at the hunter club dancing with them too last night and she wanted to make her aware of the danger to them.

"Thanks. I'll tell Anne also," Stacey said.

Dane joined the conversation with Zeke and his team. "Danai and Michael are coming to escort you to a safe place. Tobias and his kin own the land and homes, and they'll take you to one of them they use for guest quarters. No one will dare come there who isn't good friends of the Bremertons."

"Great," Zeke said. "We want to get back to work as soon as we can."

"We'll have to take care of the hunters first, but you'll have free food and lodging, and you won't want for anything. If you have family or friends who might be looking for you, let them know you're going out of state on a job, and you'll communicate with them when you're done. We don't want the hunters to learn where you are," Dane said.

"Yeah, thanks. We'll do that," Zeke said.

"So, uh, I guess I need to thank you," Robert said to Dane, "for getting rid of the vampire who turned Jacqueline."

"You don't need to thank me for anything," Dane said. "I did it for her. I would have done it for anyone who was in that situation."

"Well, I should have been there for her," Robert said.

"Yeah, you should have been. You and your family *and* her ex-fiancé." Dane went to the kitchen and got some water to drink.

"So I guess you all had something to prove by going to the hunters' club last night," Robert said.

"That we're still hunters? Yeah," Dane said. "We could go to a vampire club, but I believe we would be less welcome there." He retook his seat next to Jacqueline.

"Uh, probably," Robert said. "They might think you were there to hunt a rogue."

"Exactly."

"What about human clubs?" Zeke suggested. "I mean, I don't see that anyone would even know what you are if you went to one of them."

"We've actually been to one and really enjoyed it," Jacqueline said, "but like Dane commented, we don't feel that we should be shunned from a hunters' club when we had only been doing our jobs and ended up getting turned. Though I guess it counts for those hunters who fall in love with a vampire and then are turned also. They still fight the rogues." She realized that she hadn't really thought about them because they were in a different category. Just like babies born of hunters turned would be even another category of hunter-vampire combos.

Then they heard someone park in the driveway and Jacqueline vanished, reappeared, and peered out the peephole in the front door. "It's Danai and Michael." She got the door for them.

"Hey," Michael said, "Tobias is so pissed off about the hunters who are friends of Gregory who are planning to eliminate hunters turned. Aren't there enough rogue vampires to get rid of? Asses."

Danai was quiet but came inside the house and petted Princess that eagerly greeted all the newcomers.

"Okay, so Tobias is coming to get your statement and the recording you had made," Michael said. "After that, we'll move you to our compound. It won't take long before the word gets out that the hunters have been added to a list to arrest and be dealt with."

"Dealt with," Zeke said. "I hope that means they'll be terminated because that's the only way any of you will be safe, well, and us included."

"We'll deal with it," Michael said. "Rest assured. We can't afford to have them come after one of our own, or honest citizens like yourselves who are working on the side of good."

Then someone knocked at the door and Michael hurried to get it. "It's Tobias. Come in, Dad."

After Tobias discussed the matter with Zeke and his friends, he asked Jacqueline if she had someplace private that he could use to talk to the league council members.

"Yes, in the den." She led him in there.

"Thanks."

Then she left him alone so that he could conduct his business.

Once he contacted the other council members concerning the matter, he returned to the living room. The human hunters seemed a little on edge, shuffling in their seats, and she was sure it was because they worried about what the upshot of all this would be.

"We're taking care of it," Tobias said.

"We have a little problem with time." Dane explained about what Zeke and his team of hunters were supposed to do.

"Then we stage it. Probably somewhere that we can easily mop up the blood from the scene afterwards," Tobias said.

"Maybe the back patio?" Jacqueline suggested. "That way I can hose off the patio after we spill some blood there." Though she hated to waste the precious commodity that she had purchased.

"What about your clothes? Do you want to change into something that you don't mind ruining if we can't get the blood out?" Tobias asked.

"Yeah, I'll be right back."

"But it needs to be light-colored enough that they can recognize the blood on you in the photo," Tobias called after her.

To her surprise, when she appeared in her bedroom, Dane followed and took her into his arms and kissed her. "I'm so sorry about this."

"You needn't be. I was the one who wanted so badly to go to the hunters' club to prove we had a right to be there."

"Well, you were right, and we deserved to be there. I'm just sorry that the hunters have decided to try and terminate you, but I want you to know I'll always be there for you."

"If you're proposing to me…"

He smiled.

"Okay, yes, I'll marry you. Do you have a ring?"

He laughed.

She sighed. "First I'm engaged to a hunter who deserts me and now one who doesn't even want to give me a ring."

"First chance we have to get one, I'll take you to a jewelry store, but first, we have to stage your death and keep you out of the public eye." Then he kissed her soundly.

And she kissed him back. "You are so the one for me."

"That's the way I feel about you."

"Okay, let's get my death over with." She rummaged through her clothes, found a white shirt that she'd worn that had speckles of yellow and blue paint on it when she had been trying to paint some garden decorations and splattered a bit of paint on it. She pulled it out and yanked off her shirt and replaced it with her painted shirt. Then she found a pair of green jeans she had never liked. They were too tight in the waist, too baggy in the legs, and too short. She should have gotten rid of them a long time ago.

She stepped out of her jeans and then pulled on the green ones. "Let's do this."

They both vanished and ended up on the ground floor in the living room. No one was in there, but then they heard voices on the back patio and went out there. It was still storming out, so much for the weather report saying it was going to end, but she had a large-covered patio and so they were protected from the rain.

Everyone watched while Dane helped Jacqueline lie down on the patio, making sure she was in a position that looked natural for a huntress who had just been felled by a hunter. "What do you think?" Dane asked.

"Just have her clutching her sword," Zeke said.

"But wouldn't it be more realistic if she hadn't been able to grab her sword?" Dane asked. "Otherwise, she might have killed the human hunters."

"No sword then. She was defenseless. But we need to show what she was doing out on the patio when it's raining," Tobias said.

"I could be watering my potted plants over there." Jacqueline motioned to a watering pitcher. "They like the patio shade, but it means I need to water them."

"I got this," Zeke said, grabbing the water pitcher and filling it with water from the hose next to the patio. Then he returned with it. "How do you want me to do this?"

"I'm right-handed. You can put it next to me on the patio, but maybe throw up your arm like I might have and let the water rain down on me, then lay it down on the patio where I might have dropped it and let the water spill out."

"I'll drop it from the height you probably would have been holding it when we startled you," Zeke said.

Michael moved the plant stand near where she was lying so they could capture the picture of both. "You could have grabbed the plant stand or knocked it over and—"

"No. I'm not destroying one of my plants for them," she said.

They all smiled at her. She figured they were thinking that she was more important than her beautiful bougainvillea was.

19

"I have a better idea." Dane helped Jacqueline up off the patio floor and handed her the water pitcher. "You're watering your plant, and I come at you with a sword to your heart. React like you normally would and Michael will catch you when I pretend to cut you and set you gently down on the patio."

"Okay got it." She began watering the plant, and Dane pretended to thrust his sword at her. She threw her arms up in defense, the water splashing on her shirt and pants, getting them wet, and then she fell. Michael caught her and laid her out on the patio.

Tobias poured some blood on her chest, letting it spread naturally across her shirt and it mixed with some of the water on the fabric. She'd dropped the water pitcher nearby and the contents were spilling out, puddling next to her shoulder.

"How about some blood under her head, like she cracked her skull when she fell?" Zeke asked.

"Yeah, that's a good idea, or that one of the other hunters hit her in the back of the head at the same time the other came at her from the front. That would make it seem more doable for them to take her out without having a fight on their hands," Michael said. "And a reason for her not having time to disappear and arm herself."

Then Dane lifted her head and Tobias spilled some blood on her head and underneath it.

"How does that look?" Dane asked, stepping back from the scene. He hated having to stage this because to him it looked too damn real, though he could hear her heart beating, which grounded him in the moment.

"It looks good to me," Tobias said.

Danai agreed.

"I think we're ready for pictures before everything dries," Michael said.

Zeke pulled out his phone and took several photos from different angles. Then he showed them to the hunters while Jacqueline waited for them to decide if everything looked realistic enough.

"That looks good to me," Dane said, though he waited for everyone to agree before he helped Jacqueline up. He knew she had to be uncomfortable while lying on the hard, cement patio.

"Yeah," Tobias said. "This should be perfect."

Everyone thought it looked real.

"Which photo do you want me to send to X?" Zeke asked.

Dane pointed to the one that showed the spilled water can and all the other details. "This one."

Then Zeke sent the message, and everyone waited. It seemed like forever before X responded.

X texted: *Take out Dane...now. The money for the hit on Jacqueline Anderson is being wired to your account.*

Zeke texted: *On it.* Then he checked his bank account. "The money is in the account. What should I do about it?"

"It's your money. Share it with your hunter partners," Tobias said.

"What if Dane went to her place and finds her like this and we killed him? Well, for pretend," Zeke said.

"It's not a bad plan," Tobias said, "but it might look a little suspicious. I say we wait on the second hit to stage it and do it at Dane's home."

"Can I get up now?" Jacqueline asked, sounding like she didn't want to mess up the scene if they needed her to stay there.

Dane helped Jacqueline up and she said, "I'm going to wash up and get changed."

"We'll get this cleaned up for you," Zeke said.

"Thanks." Then she vanished.

Dane got her a bloody cocktail from the kitchen and took it to her bedroom in a flash. "Just in case you had the need after being soaked in blood."

"How did you know?" She drank the cocktail, then handed it back to him, removed her clothes in the bathroom, and turned the shower on.

"I was feeling like that. I'll go back and get one for myself."

"Thanks. I'll be down soon." She stepped into the shower and closed the door.

Then he returned to the kitchen to fix himself a glass and drank it before anyone returned to the house. He still didn't like having to drink it in front of hunters or humans if he didn't need to.

He went out to the back patio to see if he could help with the cleanup, but nobody had done anything yet.

"So I was going to have Michael and Danai take the men to the hunter compound to protect them until X and the others are captured, but I guess we need you for a while longer to stage another killing," Tobias said.

"Do you think X and his friends will come here to see if Jacqueline's dead on the patio?" Zeke asked.

"Hell, I hope not," Jacqueline said, coming out to the back patio, her hair freshly washed and wet.

"We need to move our cars, unless," Tobias said, "*we* learned that she was dead."

"Okay, that works. How about a scenario where I went to see her," Dane said. "I can get into her house freely."

"I can too, though I always knock first. Maybe I was worried when she didn't answer because we were supposed to be getting together. We have keys to each other's homes, Mom and Dad, mine, Jacqueline's," Robert said.

"The way we'll handle this is Robert came to see his sister for a prearranged get together and Robert called Dane and me to tell us that Jacqueline had been murdered," Tobias said. "Then Dane and I arrived at her home."

"What about killing Dane?" Zeke asked.

"You can tell X that you can try to locate Dane at his home later tonight because he wasn't at his home when you last checked," Tobias said. "Speaking of which, if you have any idea that they are tracking your vehicle, you might want to drop by Dane's house first before you call him."

"Wait. We killed Jacqueline on her back porch. How will we be able to explain how we reached the backyard if X asks?" Zeke asked.

"The gate isn't locked. I have a yard service so I never lock the gate," Jacqueline said. "But how did you get in through the security gate at the entrance to the development?"

"X gave us the code."

"Then he might know someone in the development. What if he has the friend or associate, most likely a hunter, watching my place?" Jacqueline asked.

This was getting more complicated by the minute, Dane was thinking.

Everyone was quiet.

"That could be a problem." Tobias rubbed his chin in thought.

Michael said, "Zeke, you and your friends go to Dane's house, pretend to gain entry into his home, then leave and go to the compound. But before you do, leave your phones off somewhere."

"At home. We'll go there after we drop by Dane's house as a ruse first, then go home to pack the stuff we'll need and leave our phones, then go to your place. Oh, and we'll make sure we don't have any tracking devices on the car," Zeke said.

Michael said, "Other hunters in the group can shop for you if you need anything else that you might forget to get once you are settled in at the compound." He gave them the address.

"Okay, thanks," Zeke said.

"I'll join you all at the compound later. I need to meet personally with the members of the council about all this," Tobias said.

Then Michael and the others left the house, and they heard them drive off. Dane sure hoped all of this worked out like they had planned, as much as they kept having to improvise.

"What about the police? Wouldn't you and or Tobias call the police when you found me dead?" Jacqueline asked.

"Uh, yeah," Tobias said.

"I have a police detective friend who often handles these cases. I can call him, and we can see if he will keep our secret," Dane said.

"Hopefully that will work," Tobias said. "After we speak to the detective, if the two of you think you'll be all right until these scumbags are picked up, I'll leave. But if you believe you would be better off at the compound, you're welcome to join us."

Dane and Jacqueline shared glances. "I'm good here or with Dane," Jacqueline said, "if he feels the same way."

"Yeah, we'll stick together," Dane said, assuring her he was going to be there for her. "We can call Adonis, who can be here in a flash."

"And Stacey and Anne," she said.

"Zachary, Pasha, Michael, and Danai too. They've been on standby all this time. If you change your mind about joining us, just let us know and we'll have a house set up to accommodate you. We don't want to lose any of you. And we don't want you to get yourself into trouble because they come after you and you have to terminate them," Tobias said.

"Right, but if they do, we will. It will be self-defense," Jacqueline said.

"I totally understand. But we would prefer it if hunters who haven't been turned take them down should they come after you, just to keep you safe," Tobias said.

"But they're going on a list, right?" Dane asked, frowning.

"Yes, with a warning to apprehend them at all costs to begin with. We want them for questioning. If they fight any of our hunters—"

"Who haven't been turned?" Jacqueline asked, irritated. She understood why Tobias and the council would want to handle it this way, but she was used to being a huntress who could terminate a hunter who went rogue.

"Yes. But if we go to arrest them and they fight us, we eliminate them. That way the two of you, and any other hunters who have been turned, will be in the clear," Tobias said.

Dane agreed. "All right. Thanks, Tobias. If we get into trouble here, we can always use our vampire skills to vanish and leave and not fight them."

Jacqueline pushed her hair behind her ear and scoffed. That wasn't the way of a hunter, but to keep themselves from getting put on a rogue's list... Then she frowned. "The ruling needs to be changed. I mean, the one where vampires can't eliminate rogue hunters. It should be that hunters turned vampire can still kill a rogue hunter, if a rogue puts him or her on his list for no reason."

"It's something we're discussing," Tobias said, surprising her. "It has been in the works since Adonis, Danai, and Zachary were turned against their will and Gregory tried to kill Adonis. Also because Michael, Pasha, and Rachael chose to become vampires to be with their mates. There was a lot of resistance to the idea at first, but the council members are slowly coming around. When they see all the good you are doing, all of you, and that you're not suddenly becoming rogues, the hunters on the council will come around given time, though we hope it will be sooner than later."

"Well, at least that's something," she said.

"Yeah, I agree," Dane said, rubbing Jacqueline's back and she instantly felt a little calmer, a little more relaxed.

"Those of us who want the ruling changed continue to work on getting it amended. The thing of it is, if the holdouts had kin who were turned, I'm sure they would feel differently and it would be approved right away," Tobias said.

"We could do it," Jacqueline said, just kidding because she knew that if they did something like that, they would automatically be branded rogues.

Tobias and Dane both smiled at her, and she was glad they got her dark humor.

"I'm going to call the police detective," Dane said.

Dane called Patrick, put it on speakerphone, and said, "Jacqueline and I have a situation that needs a delicate touch. Human hunters came here to warn us that they were hired by hunters to kill Jacqueline."

"Hell," Patrick said. "You didn't kill the human hunters, did you?"

"No, they're good guys and going to the Bremerton compound to stay safe. But we staged a scene where Jacqueline appeared dead, and they sent the photo to the hunter in charge. Now he has hired them to kill me."

"Why?" Patrick asked.

"They hate hunters who have been turned. Tobias has put them on an arrest-on-sight order. But hunters will have to take them in."

"Do you know who they are?"

"Yeah, we do."

"So what do you need me to do to help you out?" Patrick asked.

"We need you to come here like you are handling a dead body. We take care of our own when they're our guys normally, but when it's murder, you all get involved. At least as far as coming to the crime scene," Dane said. "Well, even when it's a case of us taking down a rogue vampire."

"Okay, I'll be there with a select group of officers who can keep a secret."

"Thanks," Dane said. "Also, the human hunters were given the key code to come into the development. It's possible that the hunters are friends of someone here and they might be watching the whole thing."

"We'll make this look good," Patrick said.

"Thanks. We'll see you soon." Dane knew they would come through for them.

"I'll stay here with the two of you until after the police take the 'body.' And then I'll leave," Tobias said.

POLICE CARS ARRIVED and they were surprised to see that five cars had been dispatched. "Oh, man, I hope all these guys can keep a secret," Jacqueline said, worried that the more people that knew, the harder it would be to keep the truth from coming out until they could capture the hunters.

Patrick came to the door with two other men. "The county coroner is on his way. He knows the situation. We thought of just having a fake coroner come, but he said he knows you and he's thankful for the job that you both do."

"Great," Jacqueline said, surprised to get such a great response from everyone who was dedicated to helping them stay alive.

Then the coroner and a couple of EMTs arrived. Patrick and other officers went inside the house.

"The back patio is where I 'died.' We were going to clean it up, but you might need to see the 'crime scene' before we do." She sure hoped the blood wouldn't stain her patio. She'd wanted to clean it up right away until they worried someone could be watching the house.

They all headed through the house and outside onto the patio where the police officers and the coroner saw the blood on the cement.

"This is one case of a 'dead person' that I don't mind 'seeing,'" the coroner said.

The police officers smiled.

"Okay, we'll hang around for a bit. We have a mannequin we'll bring in and place in the body bag," the coroner said.

"Can one of you bring the mannequin in as a vampire?" Tobias asked.

"I will," Dane said.

Then he vanished and reappeared in the ambulance. He grabbed the mannequin, then vanished and appeared inside the house. The EMTs brought the gurney in, and they put the mannequin in a body bag, then finally removed it from the house. The coroner left, but the police officers all had cups of coffee while they waited it out and talked about what was going on.

"So you're going to handle the hunters hiring hitmen?" Patrick asked.

"Yeah," Tobias said. "The hunters will have to take them down."

"Okay. But you know if you have any trouble with this further, call on me," Patrick said.

"We sure will," Dane said. "And thanks so much for helping us to keep Jacqueline safe."

"You too. What are you going to do about yourself?" Patrick asked. "Are you going to stage another murder?"

"We're thinking of it, but if we can put these hunters away, that would work even better. So we hope that we can do that first and not have to stage any more murders," Tobias said.

Once the officers felt they had been at the house long enough to pretend they were doing a thorough investigation, the police finally started to leave the house, all shaking their hands, telling them good luck.

Patrick said one last time, "Call me if you need my help in any situation."

"Yes, thanks," Dane said.

Then Patrick left with the others.

"Are you sure you don't want to come with me?" Tobias asked Jacqueline and Dane.

"No, we'll stay here, or at Dane's house, I guess," Jacqueline said.

"We need to pack up your clothes, the cat and her things, and move to my place."

"Right, because I can't be coming and going from my house," she said. "This is such a hassle. I want to just get this over and...I mean, we're just going through all this turmoil already, so I hate that hunters are really messing with us."

"Do you think I should take Princess instead?" Robert asked.

"No. She has really bonded with Dane. Unless you're worried that the hunters will hit Dane's house and Princess will be safer at your house," she said.

"I was just thinking if anyone wondered why Dane took the cat instead of me," Robert said, "it might look suspicious."

"If anyone has been watching us, they've seen us take Princess over to Dane's house already. So I don't think any questions will be raised about it," she said.

"Okay," Robert said.

"Well, if that's all we needed to discuss, I'm going to leave here and go meet with the council members. This is just why we need a change in our rules." Then Tobias said goodbye and Jacqueline locked the door.

"Now what?" she asked Dane.

"I'll go home and get my truck to pack up your things. If anyone is watching, they'll see me taking your cat because he needs to be taken care of after you had been murdered. But rather than ride back with me, you'll need to just transport over there, Jacqueline," Dane said.

"Can I help with anything?" Robert asked. "I'm so sorry all of this has happened to you."

"You can tell Mom and Dad what is up, just in case they hear on the news that a hunter—me—has been murdered. Oh, I wonder if this case will be reported in the news."

"Probably so to make it more official sounding and hopefully prove to the hunters that you are really dead, if they aren't having the house watched," Dane said. "Though Patrick might have to get the police chief's approval."

"Okay, well, while you get your car, I'll pack up my things and Robert, can you clean up the patio? If you're up to it."

"I am." Then Robert got a bucket, soap, and a mop and carried them out to the back patio.

Jacqueline kissed and hugged Dane. "I never expected anything like this to happen."

"I know. It's unreal. I sure didn't either." He gave her a heartfelt hug back and kissed her thoroughly. "Are you going to be all right if the hunters send someone else here to investigate your place in the meantime?"

"Yes. Robert's here with me and you're only a telepathic call away. Besides, I can just leave and join you also. I'm off to pack then."

"I'll return soon." Then Dane and Jacqueline shared another kiss and he vanished.

She was so glad she had met him. She loved the way he wanted to take care of her. Since leaving home, she had never felt that way. Certainly not with Van. She realized how truly self-absorbed he was.

She finished packing some bags and Robert came up to her bedroom to help her take them downstairs.

"For whatever difference it will make, I got a call from a friend of Van's who said he was no longer dating anyone," Robert told her as he carried two of her heaviest suitcases downstairs.

She beat him downstairs by reappearing there with her laptop and a couple of smaller bags in hand.

Robert smiled. "I will never get used to you doing that."

"Yeah. It's a pretty neat ability. So Van's not dating...for sure?"

"That's what he said. He said Van feels he can't be with another huntress for a while."

"Maybe later?"

"Who knows? I haven't had anything to do with him since he ditched you."

Jacqueline was surprised to hear it. Robert had been friends with Van, and they'd been like brothers really.

Robert gave her a hug. "Yeah, really, I'm sorry for being such a jerk."

"Thanks for admitting that to me." She gave him a warm hug back. She loved her brother, but once she had been turned, it was like her whole family had abandoned her. "Oh, I have to see if you cleaned up the patio enough."

He snorted.

She laughed. "Hey, I know you."

"I've gotten better about it."

But she wasn't taking his word for it. She went out and he followed her. When she found how clean it was, she was surprised. "Wow, you did a great job."

"Thanks. Coming from you, that's a big deal."

She laughed. "Well, maybe you've changed."

"I know how much you like to keep things clean, so I worked extra hard on it. Particularly so you wouldn't have to be reminded what the blood was there for."

"Well, I appreciate it."

Then Dane was in the living room, calling out, "I'm here."

Jacqueline and her brother joined him there.

"She was inspecting my clean up," Robert said.

"Did all the blood come off? I was worried we'd left it too long," Dane said.

"Yeah. It didn't look like anything had spilled out there at all," Jacqueline said. "Okay, we need to move your car into the garage so that no one can see you loading up stuff like my suitcases. Moving the cat and her belongings wouldn't be a problem. We just don't want anyone to witness Dane carrying my suitcases out to his pickup truck. What would be up with that?"

"I agree," Dane said, and headed back outside.

Robert opened the garage door.

Jacqueline stayed in the house while the guys packed up her bags and Princess and her things. Then Dane and Robert returned to the house.

"Okay, you call me if you need my help, just any time day or night," Robert said, giving Jacqueline another hug. Dane smiled as he watched her and her brother coming together in friendship. Then Robert shook Dane's hand. "You take care of her."

"I'm taking care of him too," she said.

"That's a given," Robert said.

Then she said to Dane, "I'll meet you at your house."

"I'll lock things up here after you leave, Dane," Robert said.

"Okay, we'll talk later."

Then Jacqueline vanished and arrived at Dane's home. This wasn't her home, and yet she felt good about being here. Maybe not one hundred percent because she didn't have anything of her own here, but when Dane arrived with Princess and her clothes and personal items, she would feel more like she belonged here.

And then she remembered he had wanted to make this a permanent situation. She couldn't have been more thrilled.

20

Dane was so glad Jacqueline's brother had come around. Hunter families were important in a hunter's fight against rogue vampires and rogue hunters. But Dane was also glad Jacqueline was going to stay with him while they were trying to sort out the issue with these hunters. He drove into his garage and shut the door, and immediately, she was there, hugging him and he laughed. "I hope you feel totally at home here. I feel this is where you belong—with me, protecting me as I protect you." He just held onto her, loving their connection, both emotionally and physically.

"I do. And when I'm wearing a ring, I guess we'll have to put my house up for sale."

"Yeah. If we want to live here."

"Your house is bigger and has a pool, so definitely. It's the party house."

"With you staying here it, it is."

Princess was standing in the driver's seat, looking like she was being neglected. Jacqueline opened the driver's door, took hold of Princess, and carried her into the house while Dane got Jacqueline's bigger bags.

"You've already explored his whole house," Jacqueline said to Princess.

Dane vanished and reappeared in his master bedroom carrying her bags. Then he was back to the car to get more of her things. She was already carrying Princess's food and dishes into the house.

"What about our walk? Or do you think it's too dangerous until the league members take those hunters into custody?" Jacqueline asked.

"I think it would be best if we stay here and give the hunters a chance to round up 'X' and his buddies. On the other hand, if we're walking in the woods and encounter hunters who plan to eliminate us, we can just vanish," Dane said.

"Unless one of them is an archer."

"Hmm, okay, then we stay at the house. But we don't have to feel cooped up here. We can visit the Bremertons at their compound. And we could even go walking through their woods there," he said.

"I hate feeling like the hunters are putting restrictions on us, more so than they already have," she said, putting her clothes away in his closet where he had quickly made room for her.

"Yeah, I agree. It sucks. I'll get all of Princess's stuff sorted."

"Thanks. I'll be right down."

Then he reappeared downstairs, startling Princess, who quickly greeted him with a rub against his legs. Dane wondered what it would be like to have a dog. Would their sudden vampiric appearances in a new place make the dog bark?

Dane began putting the cat food in the pantry and filled her water dish up. He set up her litter box out in the mudroom off the foyer. Then Dane got on his phone to call Matt. "Hey, brother, we have a new development." He explained the situation to his oldest brother.

"Ah, hell. You should have called us right away."

"We weren't in any danger since Jacqueline's brother and Tobias were here," Dane said.

"What about tonight? I mean, if the hunters are after you and the Bremertons, how safe are you at your house?" Matt asked.

"They'll think I'm alone, but I won't be."

"And if they outnumber you?"

"We can vanish, reappear at your home even."

"Ahh, hell, no. I'm having a date with Marissa. She would have a heart attack at first. Then pull her sword out next."

Dane smiled. "You're finally going out with her. Well…if things even get serious between the two of you, she's going to have to know what she's getting herself into with regard to one of your brothers."

"She's sympathetic to your cause."

"Being sympathetic and really experiencing being around us, are two different scenarios."

"True. But really, all of us will land in on your place to protect your backs if you need us to," Matt said.

"Even Marissa?"

"I'll talk to her."

"Maybe this will be the perfect way to break her in," Dane said. "She might just decide it's too much to deal with."

"Then she won't be the one for me."

"That's true," Dane said. "But she could come around if she got to know us and came to love us."

His brother laughed. "Well, we're only on our first date."

"Well, she might be fine with it. So right now, we're okay, but if we need to, we'll call you and get hold of Adonis and he and the others like us can come help us a lot faster and then you can join us."

"You and Jacqueline want to spend the time together alone," Matt guessed.

"Yeah, we need it."

"Yeah, you do. But we don't want the two of you to be at risk. I mean it," Matt said.

"I agree. If they don't get these guys soon and we're afraid the hunters have hired someone else to take us out, either we'll move onto the Bremerton compound, or we'll have you stay with us," Dane said. Sure, he wanted to have the time to spend alone with Jacqueline, but more importantly, he wanted to make sure she stayed safe.

"Okay, I'll let you go."

"Have fun on your date."

"I will."

Then they ended the call and he smiled when he saw Jacqueline joining him wearing her bathing suit. "This is what I love about your house," she said, running her hands over his chest. "Your swimming pool."

He chuckled. "I knew there was a reason you were so taken with me."

"For sure." Then she vanished and he heard a splash in the pool. He chuckled and appeared in his bedroom, changed into his swim trunks, then ended up at the pool room. He quickly jumped into the pool to join her.

She paused swimming laps, and he swam toward her. She began swimming away from him and he cornered her at the end of the pool, and she laughed.

"I heard you speaking with your brother."

"Yeah, he's pretty upset about what we're going through. Don't be surprised if he and the twins show up to watch the house."

"Well, if they do, we can invite them in. We'll still have our alone time. And there's no reason for them to sit outside the house."

He smiled and kissed her. "I have to say swimming with you has been a real joy."

"I love being here with you like this." She kissed his wet shoulder and then his lips.

Then they began to race each other across the pool. But he was listening for any sign anyone was trying to break into the house again like when the thieves did it. He was also aware someone else might show up—of the hunter persuasion. He heard his phone ringing in the house, and he sighed. "I'll be right back." He left the pool and ended up on the patio, grabbed a towel, and transported to the living room. He really was getting great at this.

When he reached his phone, he found it was his brother Trey. "Hell, Dane, I can't believe you're in the middle of trouble again. Except now as a vampire. Is Jacqueline all right?"

"Yeah, but we worry someone will come after me now, since that's what the human hunters told us."

"Then you shouldn't be staying at your house, Dane! Tobias said you could stay at the Bremertons' compound, or any one of our homes."

"If we need help, we'll call."

"And that will take how long for us to get there? I wanted to see how you were, but I also wanted to tell you to look at the TV. Jacqueline's death is on the news. I hope her family knows she's okay," Trey said.

"Robert said he would tell them." Dane hoped he would before they heard the news on the TV, unless Patrick gave them the news himself already that the whole thing was staged. He probably did to let them know not to panic. Dane turned on the TV to watch the news. Princess came over and rubbed against Dane's wet legs and got her fur all over him.

Then Jacqueline showed up, wrapped in a towel, probably to see who was calling and what was taking him so long to return. She sat next to Dane and watched the newscast.

He put the phone on speaker. "It's my brother Trey," Dane said. "Well, it looks real. I'm glad we got out of there before the reporters converged on Jacqueline's house. They don't know I was seeing her, hopefully, so they won't be coming here next."

"If they do, why don't you both come to my place?" Trey asked.

"If they know about me, they'll know about all of my brothers," Dane said.

"True."

Dane thought about it for a moment, then said, "If the reporters come here, we'll ignore them. Hell, if they're sitting outside, it will make it harder for hunters to break in and try to eliminate me." At least he hoped that was true.

"Are you going to stay put? I mean, no clubbing, no moonlit walks, no going out at all?"

"Yeah. No rogue vampire missions." Then Dane smiled and leaned down and kissed Jacqueline.

"I already know that look on your face, Dane. You have something in mind," she said.

"What are you considering?" Trey asked.

"Clubbing."

"No way in hell," Trey said.

"A vampire club." Dane shrugged. "I mean, hunters wouldn't go there."

"Exactly. And you're hunters."

"And vampires. It might be time for us to try a vampire club out and see if we get better reception there," Dane said.

"You can't even consider taking Jacqueline with you on that suicide mission," Trey said.

"I wouldn't let him go without me," Jacqueline said. "If they see us together, they'll realize we're a couple just out on the town for the night."

"A hunter couple who is a team who hunt down rogue vampires and if any of them are in the club you go to?"

"We'll leave in a flash." Jacqueline smiled at Dane.

"You're both playing with fire," Trey said. "Besides, Jacqueline is supposed to be dead."

"We wouldn't do it until the rogue hunters are taken down. It's just an idea, not that we have to do it," Dane said.

"I would tell you to take Adonis and more of their family, if you go to a vampire club, but that might be too much of a show of force. I'll let you go. And tell us for certain if you decide to go and we'll try and talk you out of it," Trey said.

"All right. Talk to you later." Dane said.

"Are you done swimming?" she asked, watching the police chief talking about her death.

"Yeah. That was fun."

"Did you ever consider the idea that you might be turned when you had to fight a rogue?" she asked.

"No. I always figured that if I lost a fight with a vampire, he would just kill me. It used to be that we all thought that vampires drinking a hunter's blood would kill them. When they realized it wouldn't, and they could actually turn a powerful hunter, some of them decided to do that, rather than just eliminate the hunter. Not only did they eliminate the hunter threat to them, but they had a minion to control."

"But hunters can't be controlled as well as a human, and their hunter friends will seek out the master vampire and terminate him," she said.

"Exactly."

The talking heads on some talk show were trying to second guess what the police were doing with regard to Jacqueline's murder.

"The police are keeping really hush-hush about this," the one commentator said on the TV news show. "Do you think that it's a vampire hit? Or maybe the murderer is someone closer to home?"

"A hunter friend or family member, you mean? That happens with humans for sure, but not with hunters so much. Not that it *can't* happen. Or maybe Ms. Anderson terminated a vampire and one of his or her family members wanted revenge. That has been known to happen."

"Why don't they wait to see what really happens with the investigation?" Jacqueline asked Dane.

He smiled at her.

"I mean, if there really was a murder. They talk these situations to death, and they don't know anything. Just to have more TV views. And often they make conjectures that are totally off base. Sometimes that puts some innocent person under the gun and their lives are ruined."

Dane agreed.

They showed a picture of her home with yellow security tape across the front of the house and reporters converged on the sidewalk in front of her home. "I bet my next-door neighbors are thrilled about this."

"Are they hunters?"

"No. Just humans. The one on the right is owned by a doctor family, both family physicians. The one on the left—he's a home developer and she's a nurse. But look—as soon as one of them drives their vehicle out of their garage, the media is swarming them to question them about me—probably if they heard anything or saw anything."

"Yeah, I'm glad I don't live next door to you."

She laughed. "Who would ever have thought! But if we have trouble, we might have to stage another murder and then your neighbors will have all the issues from that."

"You know if that happens, it's possible that the hunters living here might really ban together to catch the rogue hunters," Dane said.

"That could be."

Then someone was knocking on Dane's door, and he grabbed his sword. "You probably should stay out of sight because your photo has been all over the news."

"I will, but I'll be listening in." Then Jacqueline stayed in the kitchen where no one at the front door could see her.

He looked out the peephole and said to her telepathically, *"One of my hunter neighbors."* He opened the door and said, "Hey, how are you doing, George?"

"Hey, man, we heard what had happened to you," George Bridges said. "Sorry that we didn't come by sooner. But when we heard about Jacqueline Anderson being terminated by human hunters, we wanted to make sure that you know that we have your back. If anyone comes for you, let me know and we'll be over here in a heartbeat."

"Thanks, George. I sure am glad to have you as a neighbor and hunter friend."

"Well, one other thing. I heard you were seeing Jacqueline. She was a great huntress. I'm so sorry to hear it. We also have gotten together to do a neighborhood watch, something we've never done before. After humans broke into your place to steal, and then with what happened to Jacqueline, we figured it was time. We assume you'll be watching out for anyone who doesn't belong in our neighborhood too."

"You know that the police believe it is a conspiracy of a few hunters who paid human hunters to kill her, don't you?"

"Hell, no. They didn't mention it on the news. Is it a working theory? Or do they have something to back up the notion?" George asked.

"I don't know. I've heard through the grapevine that they were hunters." Even though Dane liked George and whenever he and his family had a barbecue, he was invited, Dane didn't know who all of Georger's friends were. What if he was friends with the ones who were wanted for questioning? Then if Dane told him what he knew, it could get right back to the rogue hunters.

"Well, just know that we don't feel that way," George said.

"Thanks, that means a lot to me."

"You're welcome. Talk to you later, bro."

"Talk later."

Then George left and Dane shut the door.

Jacqueline came out of the kitchen. "Do you trust George?"

"He and his wife are nice people, but I really don't know how they feel deep down about hunters who have been turned. They've been busy, I'm sure, but they haven't once come over and told me that they're sorry for what had happened to me. Maybe they didn't know how to approach me about it because they were worried about how I was feeling. I suspect that they finally figured they had to talk to me, considering what had happened with this business with the hunters putting a hit out on you. And I could be next. But I still don't know if he's a friend of the hunters we need to have taken into custody," Dane said.

"That's what I was thinking. Right now, all I trust are your family and mine, and the Bremertons, and the two ladies in the therapy session. I heard your neighbor say that they were starting a neighborhood watch," Jacqueline said.

"Yeah, who would have ever thought they would do something like that. Being a community of hunters, we've never really worried about break-ins, or anything," Dane said.

Then there was another knock at the door.

Jacqueline kissed him. "I'm ready, if you have any more trouble."

"Okay. I've never had visitors like this unless they're family or friends that I know are coming here." Dane checked the peephole. "It's five more people that live in our neighborhood—all hunters."

"As long as they're good guys and not wanting your head."

"Yeah, agreed."

Then she vanished.

He answered the door. "Hey, I guess you heard the news."

"Can we come in?" Dillion Johnson asked.

"Yeah, sure." Dane hoped he wasn't making a mistake by letting them in.

They all came inside, and he offered them sodas.

"We're good," Dillion said, and they took seats in the living room. "Your next-door neighbor, George, called us about the earlier break-in at your house, which of course concerns us as a whole. But this business with Jacqueline is horrifying. George said human hunters were involved in her death but that there's a possibility that our kind might have been behind it."

"Yeah, we're sure of it," Dane said.

"Damn," Dillion said. "Does anyone have any idea who they might be?"

"The League of Hunters might," Dane said. "And if so, they'll have warrants out for them."

"That's good, but I would sure like to know who they are, and I'll help take them down," Dillion said.

"Yeah, me too," Josh said.

"I'm with you," Phillip said.

"Even if you are friends with those hunters?" Dane asked, wanting to see how they would react.

"Hell, yeah," Dillion said. "If any of us are turned—and we all know it can happen—we can't become targets of our own kind. No matter who they are, we need to take them down."

"I agree," Phillip said. "Friendships are one thing, but we can't lose sight of the fact that we're all hunters at heart. Becoming a vampire doesn't change that. I'm sorry that it happened to you, brother, but I guess you have some cool abilities now."

"Yeah. Drinking the blood isn't something I had signed up for, but I'll tell you, having the other abilities is damn great," Dane said.

"Can you communicate with other vampires telepathically?" Phillip asked.

"Yes." Even communicating with the dead. Dane was thinking of Jacqueline.

"Okay, well, we're here for you. Other than doing a neighborhood watch and making sure people who don't live here are checked out, what else can we do to watch your back?" Josh asked.

Then there was another knock at the door. Dane laughed. "More neighbors or—"

"More hired hunters," Josh said.

21

When Dane went to the door, he smiled to see his brothers had arrived. He should have known they would pop in even though he hadn't called them to come to his aid. "Come in, brothers. I'm having a neighborhood meeting."

Everyone got up to welcome the brothers. Hell, Dane wondered how poor Jacqueline was doing. He hated that she had to hide from their neighbors. If his brothers were the only ones here, she could join them.

"They've implemented a neighborhood watch," Dane said as his brothers took their seats in his living room.

"That's great. If you wondered, Dane's on that hunters' list also and that's why we're here even though he said he felt he could handle it," Matt said.

All heads turned in his direction. "I hadn't exactly told them that part," Dane said to his brothers. "Yeah, the League figures since I was courting Jacqueline, I'm the next one on their hit list."

"But we don't know who they are, do we?" Josh asked. "We're taking them on if they do."

"You would have to ask them. They're not telling us anything."

Not that it was a total fabrication on Dane's part. The *League* hadn't told them about the hunters. The Van Helsing hunters had told them instead.

"If you need any of us to drop by and even stay over, let us know," Phillip said.

"Thanks so much, man," Dane said.

"That goes for all of us," Josh said, affirming Phillip spoke for all of them there.

"Thanks," Dane said again, then walked them to the door. As soon as they left, he closed it and found Jacqueline had joined his brothers in the living room. He was glad to see her smiling and giving them all hugs.

"We're damn glad you're all right," Matt said. "Those hunters have a death wish."

"We were lucky the human hunters were willing to warn us and not just take the money for the job. If they had been successful, I mean," Jacqueline said.

"It's horrible being dead, isn't it?" Matt asked. "I really think the two of you should go to Bremerton's compound. Jacqueline won't have to hide, and we don't have to worry about hitmen coming for you. We would stay here and take care of them if anyone showed up."

"You just want to enjoy the swimming pool," Dane said.

"Yeah, really. But if you're completely against leaving, we want to stay with you as a contingency force," Matt said.

"We'll need to park your car in the garage then." Dane knew his brothers were dead set on watching his back. If anyone thought to terminate him tonight, they most likely wouldn't be prepared for Dane's brothers to be there unless they saw their vehicle sitting out front.

Trey hopped up from the couch. "I'll do it." Once he had parked in the garage, he and the other brothers went out to grab their bags.

Jacqueline squeezed Dane's hand. "They are so sweet to do this."

"You know they're doing this mostly for you, to show you how chivalrous they are."

She laughed.

Then the brothers entered the house from the garage and headed up the stairs to the rooms they had stayed in before.

"They seem to be used to staying at your place," she said.

"Yeah. We have pool parties, and they bring the steaks, we take turns grilling and preparing the meals and drinks. Then they just stay the night. We do it for holidays, but also after successful multiple vampire hunts to let off some steam."

"And tonight?"

"If they brought extra steaks with them..." Dane said.

Matt returned to his car and brought in bags of groceries. "We've got it covered."

"What happened with your date?" Dane asked.

"Uhm, well, I told her you were in danger, and I needed to be there for you. She totally understood, I think," Matt told him.

"You could have had your date first and just let Trey and Ryan join us first" Dane was glad they had brought some more food. He was certain he didn't have enough for all of them to eat for an extended period of time.

"No, family comes first. We can go on grocery runs for us," Matt said.

"We can grab some food from my house too," Jacqueline said. "I should have thought of it when you picked up Princess and my clothes."

"You and I can do it as vampires whenever we want to." Dane knew they couldn't just drive over there in case anyone was watching. To get the cat, sure. But once that was done, that was it.

Tobias called Dane then and he put the call on speakerphone. "Hey, what's up?"

"The hunters are either on the run, hiding out, or doing a job somewhere. But they are not at their homes or anywhere that they regularly hang out," Tobias said.

"So they could have gotten the word that hunters are closing in on them to take them in for questioning," Dane said.

"Yeah. They'll have friends who aren't part of the plan to terminate you and Jacqueline, but they'll still give them a place to hide if that's what they're doing. I suspect they're not out hunting."

"Can you learn who they have on their lists to hunt?" Dane asked.

"We found the police departments they were working for," Tobias said. "It will take a while to learn where the rogue vampires are that they're supposed to be targeting but—hold on, got another call." Then he continued. "So two of the vampires they were supposed to be after have been terminated. Eight others are on their lists."

"When did they terminate the other two vampires?" Jacqueline asked.

"Four days ago. So it was before they targeted you, Jacqueline," Tobias said.

"Well, my brothers are here to stay with us for the time being," Dane told him, wanting Tobias to know they had backup just in case.

"Good. I'm glad to hear it. Adonis, Zachary, Pasha, Michael, and Danai were planning to join you if you didn't have anyone there with you. The human hunters have settled in here, so everything's good as far as that goes."

Then Jacqueline got a call on her phone and fumbled with it. As soon as she looked at the caller ID, she saw it was Anne from the therapy group. "I'm supposed to be dead. You answer it," she said, handing the phone to Dane. But then the call ended.

Then Dane got a call from Anne. "Hey, I've been out of state and just saw what happened to Jacqueline. I called her, just not believing she could be dead. But since she didn't answer, I guess I have to realize it's the truth. We have more problems though. I'm calling for a meeting tonight to discuss this. The Bremertons are back in town, and I called them to come to the meeting. Do you know Adonis, Danai, and Zachary?"

"Yeah, they're friends of mine. Same location? What time?" Dane asked.

"Fifteen minutes, same location. I believe all of us are targets. I've called Stacey and the others who didn't come to the last meeting that we had."

"See you in a few minutes, Anne," Dane said.

"Okay, two of us are staying here with Jacqueline and one of us is going with you, Dane," Matt said.

"All right by me," Dane said.

Jacqueline sighed. "I wish I could be there with you all."

"Yeah, me too, alive and kicking. I want to get these hunters taken down so you can be yourself again." Then Dane hugged and kissed her and said to his brothers, "Keep Jacqueline safe." But he wondered what was going on that Anne thought that all the hunters turned were now on a hit list. He figured just the ones who had been at the hunters' club that night were. Then he and Ryan left in Matt's car.

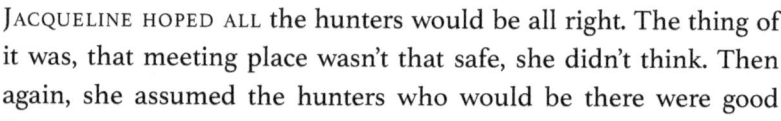

JACQUELINE HOPED ALL the hunters would be all right. The thing of it was, that meeting place wasn't that safe, she didn't think. Then again, she assumed the hunters who would be there were good fighters.

Not long after Dane and Ryan left the house to go to the meeting, they heard a noise at a window in back of Dane's place. "Someone's breaking in," Jacqueline said, her voice low. Then she grabbed her sword and vanished.

"Hell," Matt said.

Then she was in Dane's office, saw the window broken, but nobody inside yet. Matt and Trey came running up behind her, and she put her finger to her lips, and they all backed out, waiting for whoever it was to enter the office.

But no one tried to come in. Then another window broke, this one in the laundry room. "Laundry room," she whispered. "One of you watch this window. I'm afraid they're coming in from different directions."

"They must have been watching Dane leave the house and probably think no one is here right now. Then they would ambush him when he returned," Trey said, his voice hushed.

"Brother, you stay here and watch this window. Let us know if someone comes in. We're going to check out the laundry room," Matt said to Trey.

But Jacqueline wanted to get an eye on who was outside breaking the windows in the first place. She vanished and reappeared outside and was near a shed that would give her some shelter from whomever was breaking the windows. Then she saw them. All five hunters that had hassled them at the hunters' club. They weren't bothering to hire someone to do the job this time. She wondered how their neighborhood watch had missed seeing them. But then she saw four more hunters in addition to the five original men! All of them were dressed in black, but they weren't wearing anything to cover their faces.

Then one of the hunters saw her and made a mad dash to fight her. "What the hell. You were supposed to be dead. Well, you will be now."

Not this time either, if she could help it. She told Dane, *"The hunters are here! I'm in the backyard by your shed fighting one of them."*

"Where the hell are my brothers?"

"In the house where the bastards broke the windows into your house. Laundry room and your office."

Then she took on the hunter, a hefty blond-haired guy. She knew Dane would be there momentarily. But then two of the other hunters saw her fighting the one guy, and they raced toward her to kill her.

She was going to vanish because she couldn't fight that many hunters when Matt and Trey rushed out through the back door once they realized she was outside in a fight.

But then the other hunters turned who had been at the meeting —Anne, Stacey, Dane were there, right in the middle of it. Right after that Adonis, Danai, Pasha, Michael, and Zachary joined them, swords swinging, striking metal.

No one had any time to say anything, but Zachary and Danai terminated one of the hunters while Dane and Jacqueline fought another. Adonis killed another hunter, who was not giving up for anything. Anne and Stacey worked to finish off another. Some were just not going to allow themselves to be taken prisoner. The goal really was to turn the hunters over to the League so they could deal with them but terminate them if the hunters were determined to kill the hunters turned.

Matt took out another hunter. Trey pulled out some zip ties for the hunters they'd been able to take down without killing them.

Another hunter fell, wounded, but still alive and Dane zip tied his wrists. "You're a disgrace to our kind, Felix."

"You are, as a vampire. You should have died rather than have been turned," Felix said.

As if they'd had any choice, Jacqueline thought.

Four of the nine rogue hunters were dead. Two were injured, but their wounds would heal faster than a human's would. The other three hunters finally dropped their swords and gave up, raising their hands above their heads.

Ryan showed up in his car and hurried to join them. "Hell, I missed helping out."

Dane slapped his back. "Sorry we had to leave you behind."

That was the great thing about moving in the vampiric way. The vampires had all arrived instantly, while poor Ryan had to drive from the meeting place to get there.

Adonis was on his phone to call Tobias, who would notify the League that they had caught all the rogue hunters. There was no doubt in anyone's mind that these men were rogues, but now the League would take care of them in their own way.

Then Jacqueline took Dane into her arms and held him tight, never wanting to let go. She couldn't believe there had been so many hunters who had wanted them dead. What was wrong with them? The hunters turned had only been after rogue vampires. They hadn't once hurt a hunter. Not even one who was a rogue. Not until now.

They had no worry about killing the ones here that they did. Not when they were defending themselves against the threat on Dane's property and they had other hunters who had witnessed the fight.

This would hopefully prove that hunters and those who were turned would stick together to fight against the hunters who thought to kill those who were now vampires.

The police were also called. Ambulances arrived, and the EMTs took care of the two injured hunters. Tobias finally arrived. "Has everyone been identified?"

"Yeah," Matt said. "We have their IDs."

"All right. We'll take the ones still alive in for questioning to learn if there are any others that have the same mission as these hunters," Tobias said.

"I can't believe you didn't kill me or the others who you gained the upper hand on," Felix said.

"We didn't want you dead," Dane said. "We wanted you to be held accountable for your actions."

Jacqueline said, "It will be up to the League to decide your fate."

More hunters arrived, some of them who were neighbors in the neighborhood. One of them inclined his head to Felix and immediately, Adonis grabbed him and took him into custody.

"Get your filthy hands off me," the guy said.

"You were in collusion with Felix. You were the one who allowed these men to come into the neighborhood. And you're here now to try and see what happened to the hunters you were working with to take us down," Adonis accused.

"Hell, I wasn't. I just live here. And like the others here, I wanted to know what was going on."

"You signaled to Felix. Don't lie."

"Yeah, I saw it too," Dane said.

"Me too," Zachary said. "You can try to dig yourself out of the situation, but the League will uncover the truth."

Then the police cuffed the neighbor and took him with the others.

In the meantime, Dane's good neighbors congratulated them for exposing the rogue hunters. "We can't have murdering hunters like them among us. Any of us could face what you already had to," George said. "None of you deserve this kind of treatment from our kind or from anyone else."

The hunter neighbors all looked at Jacqueline, smiling. Josh said, "We're glad you're fine."

"Yeah, it was the only way we could think of to make sure they wouldn't try another hit on me. Then the human hunters told us they were going to eliminate Dane also," Jacqueline said.

"Thanks to everyone. We appreciate it," Dane said.

The hunters from the neighborhood there gave them hugs, wished them well, then walked back to their homes.

"I guess we can leave the two of you alone to take care of your own business," Matt said to Dane and Jacqueline.

"Thanks so much for coming to help us," Jacqueline said.

"Moving like you do as vampires sure is a great ability," Ryan said. "When we were at the therapy meeting place, Dane told me the news. All the hunters turned left me, and I ended up jumping into our car to return here, but man, I wished I could have traveled like you did and gotten here a lot quicker."

"Yeah, I was so glad to do that since Jacqueline and our brothers were in such a dire situation," Dane said.

"We felt the same way," Matt said. "We were in the house when she ended up fighting them. Hell, we didn't know there were so many of them."

"I didn't either. I saw the one who suddenly observed me. The others were spread out at different locations on Dane's property. I saw two others suddenly coming toward me, but I was trying to concentrate on the one I was fighting. But I also let Dane know I was fighting one at his home. I really thought there were only five of them, the same five hunters at the hunters' club. I never expected them to gather more hunters who had gone rogue," Jacqueline said.

"Two of them were already rogue hunters on an elimination list for hunting down vampires who aren't rogues. I guess Felix knew them so they could do this hit with them," Dane said.

Then everyone helped to make the steak dinner they had planned on making before all the craziness began, except that they had a few more guests and a couple of the guests brought more steaks to their place.

"I guess we'll be packing up our things again," Matt said.

Jacqueline and Dane laughed. "Well, thanks for coming to stay with us," Dane said.

"We're glad we were here for you when you needed us," Trey said.

They all enjoyed their steaks, asparagus, and rice.

After they finished eating, Dane's brothers packed up their bags and gave them hugs, then they left the house.

With promises to see them at the next meeting, Stacey and Anne left. The Bremertons said they would also attend the next meeting and they all vanished.

Then Dane and Jacqueline cuddled on the sofa together as Princess sat on their laps. "Love you, Dane."

Dane said, "I love you, Jacqueline. I'm so glad this is all behind us."

"I would say we could go for a moonlit walk now finally, but I'm more interested in joining you in bed. What about you?"

"Oh, yeah, absolutely."

Then they vanished and ended up in the bedroom, poor Princess left back on the couch. But she didn't need to participate in their next activity.

"We need to get your handyman in to replace the windows," Jacqueline said, as they began removing each other's clothes. "And we need to know if you were setup before Lucilla ambushed you."

"Absolutely, but first things first."

She smiled as she ran her hand over his chest. "Naturally."

22

After the fight with the hunters, the adrenaline was still flooding Jacqueline and Dane's systems and making love was a great way to use that adrenaline up. He lifted her off the couch and they reappeared in the bedroom, and he left her on the bed. He removed her boots before she barely was aware that he was doing it. He'd used his vampiric speed to remove them. Now she had never done that to dress or undress. That was nifty.

So she tried it too and quickly jerked his shirt off him with her vampiric ability and she heard it rip. She stared at the two pieces in her hands in shock.

He laughed, kissed her, and started to remove her pants, at a normal pace. Removing clothes with vampiric speed might take some practice. She started to unfasten his belt and then unzipped his pants and began to pull them off. Once they had their pants off, he pulled off her shirt—at least hers was intact! She owed him a new shirt.

Her panties and bra were ditched, and she tugged his boxer briefs off. She realized he had used his speed to remove his boots and socks and she hadn't even seen him do it.

But now they were naked together and were kissing and moving against each other in a lovers' embrace. Then they were kissing deeply and teasing each other's canines, which was such a turn on. Not only because of the sexual nature of being a vampire and the eroticism she felt from their pheromones kicking into high gear, just stroking each other's canines made her wet with anticipation.

She was so ready to have his erection deep inside her. He changed things up by pulling her with her back against his chest and pulled her left leg over his. Then he pressed his arousal deep inside her, but he reached over her hip and started to stroke her between her legs. Then he brushed his warm lips over her shoulder, sending shivers of pleasure through her. She turned her head to meet his lips and he pressed his mouth against hers, still stroking her, still thrusting into her.

So hot! Their blood was pumping, and she realized she wanted to do the vampire bite with him again. But she wasn't stopping what they were doing right now for anything. He was pushing her closer to the top and she was soaking in the sheer pleasure of his touch.

She couldn't believe how far they had come in such a short time, yet he uplifted her and fulfilled her in life-changing ways. The physical attraction, though important, wasn't all that made her feel such a strong, unbreakable bond with him. He was there for her through all life's ordeals, as she was for him. This was just the cherry on top.

"Oh, yeah," she moaned as he continued to stroke her, dipping a finger into her, and swirling it around and then poking in and out, sending her racing to the heavens above.

He was still thrusting into her as he nibbled on her ear, then licked it. She wanted to roll around in his arms to kiss him, but she didn't want to lose the connection between them while he thrust into her. Nor did she want him to stop stroking her. This was just too perfect. His hot, muscular body coveting hers and giving her the utmost enjoyment. Then she felt the climax coming and she came in a burst of pleasure and cried out with exaltation. She felt him groan and fill her at the same time, making her even wetter.

He continued to pump into her while she turned her head to meet his mouth with hers and he deeply kissed her, their tongues toying with each other's until they stroked their elongated canines.

"Have I mentioned how much I love you?" she rasped out.

"I feel the same way about you. You are the only one for me. Love you, honey."

DANE PULLED OUT OF JACQUELINE, and she rolled over into his arms. They just held each other tight for several minutes, just loving the closeness and the satisfaction he had felt when they had climaxed. The adrenaline was still running through their veins, their hearts still beating fast. Before they fell asleep in each other's arms, he asked, "Do you want to take a shower?"

"Yeah, I sure do."

Then he carried her into the bathroom vampirically. She turned on the water, and then they began kissing and washing up. But the next thing he knew, she was scraping her teeth on his neck. And he quickly realized she needed to bond in the vampire way, and he was all for it.

"Bite me," he said.

And she did. Then she sucked a little and he felt the intense pleasure racing through his whole body. He had to admit that ability was something he had never thought he would experience in his lifetime. She sealed the bite marks with a stimulating lick and then she offered her neck to him. He was so ready to make love to her again! He licked her neck before he sank his teeth in and then he drew about the same amount of blood from her. She moaned with delight. He sealed her wounds, then he lifted her up, she wrapped her legs around his hips, and he penetrated her with his full arousal.

"You light my fire," she mouthed against his lips.

"With you, once is never enough." Then he was thrusting inside of her, enjoying the close connection they had when they were making love under the hot water. Princess purred outside the shower as if she finally realized where they had gone to.

He rocked into her until he finally climaxed again and for a moment, he just held her tight. He loved how when they were through, they still kept the connection, proving it was more than just sex.

He set her on the floor of the shower, and they soaped up, kissing other. Being with her was like being in heaven. Once they left the shower, they dried each other off, which added to the intimacy between them. Princess hurried off.

He was glad Jacqueline had said yes to marrying him. They kissed and he could have let her walk on her own, but he loved lifting her in his arms and carrying her to bed. Especially after all they had been through.

"You are the most romantic man I've ever known," Jacqueline said, cuddling with him in bed.

"You are the sexiest woman I've ever known and the love of my life."

Suddenly, Princess hopped on the bed at Dane's back and they both chuckled.

"It appears she was waiting for everything to get quiet so she could join us in bed," Jacqueline said.

"At least I have you in my arms for the night."

"For sure."

THE NEXT MORNING, Dane and Jacqueline just laid in bed, snuggling, loving being together. Princess left the mattress when she got too hot. "Okay, we need to learn if you were set up when that vampire turned you. Whoever it was, he needs to face the consequences. Maybe it's someone else you haven't considered. Or even informant Green was just loyal to Lucilla, or she might have even ordered him to do it. Wouldn't that make more sense?"

"Yeah, it does."

She ran her hand over Dane's bare chest. "What if this has to do with a completely different situation than you're thinking of? I mean, what would anyone hope to gain if they set you up for the ambush? You ended up being turned into a vampire. What was the worst thing you lost?"

"Being a full hunter."

"And? Your brothers stuck by you, but my family hadn't. But we both lost the people we were engaged to."

He snapped his fingers. "Moose had always wanted to date my fiancée. He was so angry when I asked her to marry me, she said yes, and her family was all behind our marriage. Until I was turned. Hell. He wouldn't have dared do that. If they learn he was behind that, he would be putting his own life in danger."

"Yeah, but maybe he didn't realize Lucilla was going to turn you and keep her for her own. Maybe he thought she would just kill you with her vampire minions and then no one would ever know that was the deal."

"Hell."

"But that's just conjecture. How can we prove something like that? I mean, other than the fact he is dating your ex. Talk to him? Or, wait, what about talking to informant Green?"

"That's it!" Dane said. "We can make him tell us what was really going on. I always forget we can make humans do what we want."

"I know. It seems like it's something illegal that we're doing. But really, we're not. It's like giving them a truth serum and then they just tell us the truth about the situation."

"Yeah. I agree, though it's hard to remember that we can do that sometimes."

"Too bad we can't control a *hunter's* mind to learn the truth from the proverbial horse's mouth," Jacqueline said.

"True. But if Green will tell us the truth, that's all we need."

"Do you know how to get in touch with him?" she asked.

"Yeah, I've got his cell number, though usually he calls me to tell me what's going on. I'll give him a call." Dane pulled out his cell phone and called Green, but he didn't answer the call. He left a message.

"What if Moose is afraid that Green might tell on him, especially now that you're a vampire and can get Green to tell you the truth?" Jacqueline asked. "If he had anything to do with this."

"Moose probably doesn't believe I would ever think that he was the one who set me up if he was."

"Hmm, that's probably so. And Green probably wouldn't just come clean with you, afraid of what Moose or you might do to him. Unless maybe you point-blank ask him, but in any event, your vampiric persuasion should get to the truth," Jacqueline said. "We just need to get to him."

"I hope nothing bad has happened to him." Then Dane got a call from Green, and he put it on speakerphone, "Yeah, Green?"

Green said, "Hey, I just saw your message. If you want to see me, I'll be at the vampire club, the Blue Moon at three."

Dane glanced at Jacqueline to see if she wanted to do it.

"I'm game," she said.

"My girlfriend and I will be there," Dane said, then ended the call. "We slept so late that we can have lunch and then go shopping for your engagement ring."

"Oh, yes!"

They made tuna fish salads, and then they headed over to a

nearby jewelry store. Jacqueline was so excited. When they reached the store, they began looking at all the engagement rings. She loved a gold ring that had a half-carat diamond.

"How about this one?" Dane asked, showing her a one-carat diamond.

"Are you sure?" She loved it but she didn't want him to pay so much for it.

"I want everyone to know you're mine."

She smiled. "I love it. That's the one I want. Thank you so much, Dane. I love you."

"I love you. You are the best thing that has ever happened to me in my life." Dane paid for the ring.

Then the jeweler resized it for her, but Dane took the ring, got on one knee, and asked her, "Will you marry me?"

She had never expected him to do it at the jewelry store. She loved him for his spontaneity. "Of course I will. I love you."

"That's what I wanted to hear. I love you too." Then Dane slipped the beautiful ring on her finger and kissed her.

The jeweler and store clerks all cheered and clapped. She figured nobody had probably ever proposed in the store. She was so happy. Then they left the store, the beautiful ring sparkling on her finger. She couldn't believe she would be engaged to another hunter ever.

Then he drove her to her place. "We'll need to dress up a bit. Are you sure you want to do this? We could go together, but you could stay out in the truck, and I'll go in and speak to Green, or ask him to come outside to speak to both of us."

"Nope. We're in this together."

～

DANE WAS SO glad Jacqueline was marrying him. She was the perfect mate for him. "Okay. I'll drop you off at your place and be back in a few minutes to pick you up." Then they kissed and hugged, and she vanished. He really wanted to know if they would be accepted in the vampire club, but no matter what, he wanted to speak with Green and learn the truth. Had a hunter set him up or not? And if so, who had done it?

He returned home and Princess purred and greeted him. "Sorry, Princess. Your momma and I have more business to take care of." Then he vanished and ended up in his bedroom, thinking about moving Jacqueline into his place now and not waiting5, if she was agreeable, and selling hers. There wasn't any reason for them to live apart any further. He just hoped she wanted to do it.

He quickly dressed in a white shirt, black trousers, and black dress shoes, and glanced at his tie rack. But he thought he didn't really need to wear a tie.

He hoped going to the vampire club wasn't a big mistake. No matter what, he didn't want Jacqueline to be in harm's way for anything.

MAYBE JACQUELINE WAS CRAZY, but she really had wanted to go to the vampire club to see what it was like. To see if they could fit in, or would the vampires know they were both hunters and not just vampires. Though it would be hard not to just go and enjoy themselves without looking for rogue vampires while they were at it. Or being self-conscious about not belonging and listening to the conversations all around them about the hunters who shouldn't be there.

She dressed in a black cocktail dress with a flouncy skirt and spaghetti straps, her red hair the perfect contrast. She wore high heeled black shoes too, even though fighting in them could be more difficult. But she had to think that she wouldn't be in a fight. If she and Dane stirred up trouble, they would just need to leave. She eyed her sparkling diamond ring and was thrilled that she could say she was engaged to Dane, whom she loved with all her heart.

Then she heard Dane's truck pull up and she headed outside. He was already out of his truck wearing black trousers and a white shirt, dress shoes, no tie, so he looked dressy but not overly so. He smiled appreciatively at her, kissed her, and opened her door for her. "Man, am I glad you're with me."

She loved that about him. One minute, they were in a vampire or a hunter fight, trying to take down a rogue, watching each other's backs, the next, dressed and glamorous, ready to enjoy the nightlife. Well, at least they looked like it. She wasn't sure they would be doing much more than speaking with Green, not dancing until the place closed down. But she was glad Dane was so free with his compliments where she was concerned. Van had always been stingy with them, as if he thought telling her she looked nice might go to her head.

Dane fastened his seat belt, and they were on their way.

"Well, I'm so glad you're with me. I wouldn't want it any other way. Not only as a fighter companion, but also as my lover, loyal friend, and fiancé. And you dress up nice."

He chuckled. "You are the same for me. Not that I would have wished this on either of us, but it really was a wakeup call as far as who we were engaged to be married to."

"Yes! Even little things like dancing. Van and I loved to dance, but he would dance with other women friends, like being with me wasn't enough. And of course the hunting business. Oftentimes, hunter mates hunt together. They're always there for each other. They can have different hobbies or interests or friends, but their mate comes first."

"Precisely. Why bother mating each other otherwise?"

"That's just what I was thinking." She realized she had a lot more negative things to say about Van than Dane had about Wendy. Maybe they were more compatible than she had been with Van.

Maybe the only thing that was wrong between them was the business with him being turned and her parents being unhappy about it. Then again, Dane did say that he didn't like hunting with her.

"Okay, contingency plans?" Dane asked Jacqueline as they neared the vampire club.

She appreciated that he wanted to hear what she wanted to do first. "We look for Green and try to convince him to go outside with us. If he's afraid of us and feels more comfortable in the club, he can stay in there with us. Though I keep forgetting that you can tell him that he wants to go outside and then we'll discuss the situation. If other vampires try to interfere, then we play it by ear. If they're just trying to give us grief but not really threatening us, we can go about our business. If the vampires begin to get hostile, we'll leave, get into your truck, and depart the area."

"And make a later date with Green?" he asked.

"No way. We take him with us when we leave."

Dane smiled. "I like the way you think."

"We have a mission, and if we can accomplish it without getting ourselves killed, I'm all for doing it in any way that we can go about it."

"I agree."

When they finally arrived at the club, it was in full swing, cars filling the parking lot, a man and a woman talking to each other outside near the door. He was wearing blue jeans and a T-shirt and sneakers, not the look of a vampire at a fancy club. The woman was likewise dressed in jeans and sneakers, her T-shirt featuring a green luna moth. They didn't even give Dane or Jacqueline a second glance.

"*They look a little underdressed,*" Dane said telepathically to Jacqueline.

"*Which may be the reason they're standing outside the club instead of inside of it. Maybe they aren't vampires.*"

"*Blood bonds,*" Dane guessed.

"Right. And without the appropriate attire, they're just on the side-lines, looking for a vampire to pay them for their blood, I suspect," Jacqueline said. This was all so new to her. She hunted down vampires. She didn't really get into their social customs that much as far as blood bonds went unless she needed to learn more to follow and eliminate a rogue.

"Yeah. So far so good."

23

The music at the Blue Moon was playing so loudly, they could hear it all the way out into the parking lot. As soon as Dane opened the door to the club for Jacqueline, a big, burly man with a shaved head said, "I haven't ever seen you in here before."

"We're new," Dane said, sharing the telepathic communications with both the bouncer and Jacqueline.

That was a smart move. If the bouncer thought they were blood bonds, they would have given the name of a vampire who had invited them, most likely. As vampires, they could have shown their fangs, but that could be a sign of aggression in any circle. Telepathic communication was perfect because rarely did a hunter have that ability, so in a non-aggressive way, they *were* able to confirm that they should be allowed to be there. And technically, they *were* new in more ways than one.

The bouncer just jerked his head for them to enter.

Vampires were talking, drinking, and dancing, wearing a variety of clothes from tuxes and full-length gowns to cocktail dresses and dress shirts and dress pants. A few blood bonds were standing at various places in the club—visiting with each other, waiting for a vampire to approach, wanting a drink from them instead of buying bloody cocktails.

The ceiling was covered in blue lights and stars and a bright white moon. Lights flashed across the dance floor and the people in the club. It was interesting to see the different decors and ambience in the various clubs. Despite the dancing and music, it seemed more subdued in certain areas where vampires and blood bonds were seeking a sexually charged blood-bonding experience.

"Do you see Green?" Jacqueline asked.

"No. So we kind of blend in, though no one seems to really notice us yet. We could get a drink," Dane said.

"Sure." But she really wanted to dance. She loved dancing with Dane and listening to the music. She just felt like moving to the beat.

Dane smiled at her. "Come on, honey." He took her hand and pulled her into his arms, forgetting about a drink. He began to dance with her, and she loved it.

"This is so nice."

"Even if we're not at one of our clubs," he said.

"When dancing with you," she said, "anywhere is super good." She ran her hands over his buttocks, and he smiled at her.

"If Green doesn't show up soon, we're going to have to go home and finish this up." He kissed her, and she tongued him, finding his canines elongated.

She smiled, loving how that happened to him. Not only that, but she could feel his arousal pressed against her body. "Oh, I'm all for it." Then she began hearing some conversations at tables near the dance floor.

"Isn't...isn't he a hunter?" a guy said.

"I don't know. I haven't seen him before. What about her?" the woman next to him asked.

"I think she's a hunter," another woman at their table said. "I don't know anything about him."

Then they got quiet and the next thing they knew, a male vampire approached, and Jacqueline was afraid this was going to go south. But then he asked Dane if he could cut in and dance with her. Ohmigod, no way did she want to dance with a vampire that wasn't a hunter turned.

Dane looked like he didn't like the idea. His teeth had already extended just from dancing close to her and she was afraid he was going to expose them to the vampire and get them in real trouble.

She squeezed Dane's hand, curious what the vampire had to say to her. "I'll dance with him and see what he wants."

"All right." But Dane didn't seem happy about it.

She didn't blame him. She would have felt the same way if he started dancing with a female vampire and left her to fend for herself. But then it happened. A female approached Dane and asked him to dance with her.

Jacqueline started to dance with the male vampire, keeping her distance from him, unlike how she danced with Dane, while a vampiress, black hair, blue eyes, long red gown, looking hot and sexy, danced with Dane. Jacqueline felt somewhat unnerved dancing with a vampire she didn't know.

The blond male vampire dancing with Jacqueline said, "We haven't seen you here before—the two of you. But my girlfriend thinks you're a huntress."

"I am. And I'm a vampire." So they were curious about Dane and Jacqueline.

The vampire raised his brows, then it looked like the light dawned as his jaw dropped. "You were turned."

"Right."

"Oh." Then he frowned. "Against your will?"

"Yes."

"Oh. We don't see any of your kind in here ever."

"We're looking for Green, a blood bond we believe might have some information about a hunter who set up my fiancé to be terminated by a rogue vampire."

"What if I was a rogue vampire?" The blond guy smiled a little at her, his expression somewhat dark.

"Then I would have to terminate you."

He laughed. She smiled. She was serious and she was sure he realized it.

"This Green, was he supposed to be here?" the vampire asked.

"Yes, he told us to meet him here."

"I believe he's in a backroom then, offering sustenance to a vampire—willingly, of course."

"Of course." She really wasn't here looking for rogue vampires. They had to learn if a hunter was the reason for Lucilla getting the best of Dane.

"Your name is?" the vampire asked.

"Jacqueline."

"Jacqueline...?" the vampire persisted.

"Anderson. And you are?"

"One of the good guys. Reese Butler. We don't like to see rogue vampires get away with crimes against anyone—hunters, humans, and vampires alike. If we can, we take them down ourselves. But sometimes they have friends who help to protect them. Then they're considered rogues also. They give us a bad name, you do understand? We can't have that."

"Just like we can't have hunters turning on other hunters, or humans or law-abiding vampires," Jacqueline said.

"I like you. If you weren't already with a hunter turned, I would make an effort to get to know you better." Reese gave her a genuine, rather devilish smile.

She was thinking Dane might want to put him on *his* terminal list, whether Reese was a rogue or not. "Can you tell us where Green is exactly so we can talk to him briefly?"

"He's busy. Believe me, when a powerful—friendly—vampire is

busy with a blood bond, you don't want to interrupt things. Now that you're one of us, you'll have to learn how to live by our rules too," Reese said. "I would be willing to teach you more about us."

"Thanks, but we're good." Not really. It would be nice, she realized, to make acquaintances with a few decent vampires to learn what they could about their ways. She also was now aware that though she still thought of herself as a hunter, she and Dane were also vampires and there were another set of rules to navigate by as such. "Wait, I have an idea. I would have to ask the others in the group what they thought about it, but maybe a couple of vampires who have always been vampires, or at least early on, centuries ago, could come to a couple of our...uhm, meetings." She didn't want to say therapy sessions because it might sound like they were weak. But she thought having vampires speak to them about doing things their way might help the newly turned deal with the changes better.

"Meetings," Reese said.

She glanced at Dane, and he looked like he was ready to take her back in his arms, though the music was still playing, and he was still dancing with the vampiress. "Okay, a few of us who have been turned by vampires are meeting to talk about how we feel about the changes."

"When we were turned centuries ago, we could have used such sessions," Reese said, sounding truthful.

She knew it had been awful for them because they hadn't had blood banks to draw from and everyone wanted to hunt them down and eliminate them. The situation had improved so much for them and most lived by the rest of society's rules like anyone else who just worked, had families, friends, socialized, and were fairly normal in every other way.

"I'll ask a couple of my friends and get a hold of you. In the meantime, you can ask your group if they would be willing to have us talk about what you might have to deal with." Then Reese glanced at Dane. "I believe your fiancé wants to dance with you again. I thank you for your honesty."

"You're welcome. And I thank you for yours." She had never socialized with vampires before and was so used to going after the bad ones, that she never really gave the decent ones any thought. But she could see here at the club, everyone was having a good time and they looked just like the hunters at a hunters' club, or the humans at the human clubs.

Then he kissed her hand and moved off to ask the woman dancing with Dane to join him in a dance. Dane quickly rejoined Jacqueline and they decided to get a drink.

She explained what Reese had said to her about Green being in a back room, and even about maybe coming to one of their therapy sessions.

"We would have to talk to the whole group about it," Dane said.

"Yes, of course. We might even be able to come to a club like this more often, if we can have a bloody cocktail and dance and the other vampires don't mind that we're also hunters," Jacqueline said. "Did you learn anything from the woman?"

"Only that she knew I was a hunter, then she saw my fangs, not that I meant to show them off to her, and I told her why we were here. She said the same as Reese. That Green is with a vampire in a back room."

They got their cocktails and stood at one of the tables, watching the other vampires. But many of them were watching Jacqueline and Dane now. "I think we've been found out," she said.

"I think Reese and Eleanor came to speak to us while we were dancing to learn who we are and then shared the information with the rest of the patrons at the club," Dane said.

"I think you're right. I wonder how long it takes for a blood bond to be with a vampire? It seems to me if he's with one for this long, he would be drained dry," Jacqueline said, wanting to just talk to him and get on their way.

Then the bouncer approached them, and she figured he was going to make them leave. "You didn't tell me you were hunters."

"We're vampires. Newly turned. We told you we were new. If we were humans newly turned, then we would be welcome, right?" Dane asked the bouncer.

"You're hunters. You still hunt rogue vampires," the bouncer said. "You need to leave. Now."

"We're here to meet a man named Green," Dane said.

"You'll have to meet him elsewhere. If you have business with him, you'll have to go somewhere else." The bouncer folded his meaty arms and stared them down.

They finished their drinks, not about to leave without doing so.

"I guess we can wait in the pickup," Jacqueline said telepathically to Dane.

"Yeah, let's do it."

The two of them vanished. No sense in leaving there any other way. They might as well make the point that they were genuine vampires.

"What if Green doesn't come out of the Blue Moon before it closes?" she asked.

"Then it means the vampire took him home with him...or her," Dane said. "We'll just wait and see."

Vampires were still coming out of the club or going into the building, the place hopping. It was just as well attended as their hunter clubs. Then a man came out of the club and Dane straightened. "That's Green, but he looks a little unsteady on his feet. I'll grab him and we can talk to him."

Dane left the truck, grabbed Green's wrist, and moved him to the truck.

"Okay so what was the deal with a hunter telling you to inform me that Lucilla would be at the location where I was ambushed?" Dane asked Green.

"Hell, man, I don't know what you're talking about."

Maybe he didn't know anything because all of this was just supposition on Dane's part. Dane stared at Green. "Tell me which hunter had you set me up when I went to take down Lucilla and how that had come about."

For a moment, Green didn't say anything. Jacqueline suspected he was weighing his options. If he told them the truth that the hunter hired him to set him up? It was one thing if Lucilla had controlled his mind and forced Green to entrap Dane. But a hunter couldn't do that. So what would the incentive have been? Money? Something else?

She was kind of surprised the hunter, if that was truly the case, hadn't terminated Green to keep him from telling Dane what had happened, either voluntarily or by vampire compulsion. She figured that the hunter didn't realize that Dane was going to learn of it. She didn't think the hunter would let Green live otherwise.

Dane said to Green, "You will tell me everything that had happened before I met with Lucilla."

But Green said something similar to what he had told them already. "I didn't do anything. I...I don't remember anything about Lucilla."

"Did you try to use your vampiric control?" Jacqueline asked.

"Yeah."

"Try it again. Or I can. I'll try." Then Jacqueline said to Green, "Which hunter set Dane up when you told him to eliminate Lucilla?"

Reese came out to their truck with the vampiress he had been with and who had danced with Dane. "What's up?" Reese asked.

"We're trying to learn what Green knows about how I was ambushed by the rogue vampiress Lucilla. But we're not having any luck with our vampiric mind persuasion," Dane said.

"It could be that Lucilla wiped his mind," Reese said.

"Oh, great," Jacqueline said. "We never considered that could be the case."

"I'll try it on him," Reese said. "Green, tell us who hired you to betray Dane."

Green just shook his head. "I don't know anything."

"Who is Lucilla?"

"I...I don't know anyone by that name," Green said.

"I'm an ancient vampire, and I know the man's mind has been wiped. He couldn't fight my questioning. Whatever information you're searching for isn't there any longer."

"Do you know me?" Dane asked Green.

"No. You called me and just left a message for me. I just figured you were a vampire who wanted some blood. But I already gave too much. I was going to tell you that but then the next thing I know, you took me to your truck and began questioning me. Knowing some vampires can get violent if they don't get their way, I was just listening to you and trying to figure out what you were asking me. How could I know if you were set up if I don't even know you?" Green asked, sounding thoroughly confused.

"Hell," Dane said. "And thanks, Reese, for helping us out."

"If I'd been a hunter and was setup like that, and some hunter was behind it, I would want to know the truth too. And do something about it. Take it easy," Reese said, and then he and his girlfriend left.

"Green, good luck out there," Dane said, sounding like he was truly hoping he was going to be okay.

Green headed for a car and wished them well.

"Well, we learned a few things," Jacqueline said. "Number one, I was thinking maybe our vampiric abilities weren't working, but it appears they still are. He just didn't know anything. Number two, I never thought of a vampire blanking out his mind."

"I'm glad our abilities were working. I was afraid maybe we needed to use them more to get better at it. So it's good to know they're adequate like when we used them before with the housebreakers. I'm like you. I never thought a vampire would wipe his mind, and why would she? Unless she had made a deal with a hunter who set this all up."

"Right. And number three, it looks like going to the vampire club was fine with the vampires, as long as we're not hunting rogue vampires in there. And we even seem to have made a couple of vampire friends," Jacqueline said. "We just have to convince the bouncer we can be there."

"He might have thought we were there to find rogue vampires. So the next thing we need to do is talk to Moose. It's too bad we can't use vampiric persuasion to get him to tell us the truth. I doubt he'll talk, but we need to at least try it. He'll know if he lets the truth slip, if he was involved, he will be on a hunter's target list."

"Should we go now to see him?"

"Yes, when he's least expecting it."

"I'm with you on it." Though she was thinking they were over-dressed for the job. "I guess you don't want to change clothes."

He chuckled. "No. I think if we're dressed like this, he won't feel we're as much of a threat."

"Do you have swords in the car, or something else we can arm ourselves with if we need to protect ourselves?"

"A couple of folding swords and daggers. But we won't be able to hide them in our clothes with the way we're dressed," he said.

"Okay, well, we should tell your family that we're going to speak with him just in case he tries to say we were threatening to kill him over some perceived conflict."

Dane thought about it for a few minutes before he spoke. "If we do, my brothers will want to be there."

"That works for me. That way he can't twist our words. We'll have witnesses. Maybe I should call my brother and see if he wants to join us too. I would like to see if he will be there for us when we need him."

"Sure, go ahead. Of course, they might all try to talk us out of it."

"If they do, we go anyway. We need to know the truth. You know Lucilla wouldn't have wiped Green's mind of who you were if something more hadn't been going on behind the scenes."

"Right." Dane called Matt first and told him what had happened with Green and the vampire Reese.

"Damn, brother. You know how to live dangerously, but yeah, I'll get hold of our brothers and we'll meet you at Moose's house."

"Okay, we're calling Jacqueline's brother too, though he might not want to be bothered with helping us. We want to give him the opportunity though."

"Good. We'll see you there then." Matt ended the call.

"I'm so glad your brothers will be witnesses." Then Jacqueline called up her brother. She told him what had happened, and that Dane's brothers were coming to be there for them. "Do you want to meet us there?"

"Yeah. Don't approach him until after we are all there."

"All right. We'll see you in a few minutes then." She felt relief that her brother was willing to help out. "I didn't know what to expect from him, but I think he has really come around."

"I think so too. So when we get married, maybe your family will all be there."

"Yeah, maybe. We haven't even talked about where to go for a honeymoon."

"Someplace where we can still get blood," he said.

She sighed. "Yeah. We don't know about other locations. I mean, probably it's all set up in the States. But around the world? Not sure."

They finally arrived at Moose's house and waited for their brothers to arrive. She sure hoped this worked. Once everyone arrived at the stucco, one-story, ranch-style house that Moose owned, a blue Corvette in the driveway, Dane said, "That's Wendy's car."

"Oh. Do you still want to question him?"

"Yeah, I do." He got out of the truck and Jacqueline joined him.

The brothers got out of their vehicles and walked up to them. Matt asked, "Are you ready?"

"Yeah. Let's do this," Dane said.

Then they all went together. Dane was holding Jacqueline's hand. He knocked at the door.

No one answered, then Matt got a notification on his phone, and he texted someone. "A rogue vampire was just eliminated. I asked who the hunter was, and the police said it was Moose."

"What about Wendy?" Dane asked.

"She's not listed on the paperwork."

"Unless Moose is going out celebrating or he's on another hunt," Dane said.

"Then we hold tight," Matt said.

Everyone agreed to sit around and wait, wanting to get this resolved if they could.

"I wonder where Wendy is," Jacqueline said. "Her car is here, but she didn't get credit for the vampire Moose eliminated."

"Maybe she was there but he killed the vampire and took the money, not giving her any of it," Dane said. "I wouldn't be surprised."

Jacqueline's brother wanted to know what happened when Dane and his sister went to the vampire club, and she said, "We danced, had drinks." But he was shocked when he heard that Dane and Jacqueline had actually danced with other vampires.

"What could they do? Bite us?" Dane asked.

Robert shook his head. "I'm just glad you weren't in trouble."

"We actually were more accepted there than at the hunters' club, though it might not always be the case, depending on who is at the club, just like we might have better luck the next time we're at the hunters' club," Jacqueline said. "The bouncer did make us leave though."

"I can't believe Lucilla wiped out Green's mind of the whole incident," Matt said.

"It sounds like there was collusion between the hunter and the rogue vampire," Robert said. "But what would be the motivation? The hunter has to know if you ever figured it out, he could be outed and put on a termination list."

"That he was able to date Wendy? That's all I can figure," Dane said. "Her parents are really wealthy, and they give her anything she wants. She's an only child and when they're gone, she'll inherit all their wealth. That's not why I was marrying her, but Moose is the kind of person who would. I had my own money, so her parents knew I wasn't marrying her for her money." Then Dane said, "There's Moose's car."

24

M oose pulled up into his driveway, looking a little surprised to see Dane and his brothers, and Jacqueline and hers. Wendy was also riding in the car with him.

He didn't smile and Wendy was frowning. He pulled the vehicle into the garage and then the two left the car and walked out of the garage.

"Hey, what's up?" he asked Matt, since he was Dane's older brother.

"Lucilla told me a hunter set me up so she could take me down. But instead of her killing me like the hunter hoped, she turned me," Dane said.

"Yeah?" Moose said. "What has that got to do with me?"

"You use Green as an informant like me. One good thing about being a vampire is I can question a human and get the truth out of them."

Moose's eyes widened. Wendy stared at Moose, her jaw dropped.

"Yeah, so all we need to know is why you would work with a

rogue vampire and an informant you and I both use to have me ambushed," Dane said.

Jacqueline hoped his bluff would work and Moose would come clean. But he knew he would be eliminated for such an act of sabotage so it behooved him to keep the secret, if he truly had been behind all this.

"Uh, Green must have been confused when he said I had anything to do with it. I mean, like you said, I've worked with him any number of times."

"That's the thing about using vampiric persuasion," Dane said. "The person you question can't lie to you."

Moose glanced at the other hunters. He shoved his hands in his pockets. He looked and smelled uncomfortable. Sweat beaded up on his forehead. His heart was beating like crazy. There wasn't any reason for him to be scared unless it was all true. Though Wendy's reaction mirrored Moose's.

"Well, I didn't do whatever he said, but I want to clear my name. I need to use the bathroom and then we can go to League headquarters," Moose said.

"We're taking you into custody," Matt said. "You can use the bathroom there."

Jacqueline was glad that Matt said that because she was afraid he was going to try and get away if he went into the house.

"I'll take you there," Dane said, then told Jacqueline, *"I'll return for you."*

She knew that Dane was going to take Moose the vampiric way to headquarters. She gave him a hug and kiss and he hugged her back and then kissed her. "See you soon."

Then to everyone but Jacqueline's surprise, Dane grabbed Moose's wrist and vanished. She just hoped that the League would put Moose in custody and wouldn't let him go. And that they weren't upset that Dane had arrived in a vampire's way with Moose in his grasp.

DANE FIGURED the best way to take Moose before the council was to just do it in the vampiric way. It would make a statement. This was what Moose had deliberately done to him. Well, most likely Moose had wanted him dead and that hadn't worked out like he had planned.

He was surprised to see Tobias there and he hurried to meet with them. "Jacqueline told Adonis you were bringing Moose in and what the charges were for, and he notified me. Come on, Moose, we have a cell for you until we sort this all out."

Dane sure hoped the guy wouldn't get away with it. He had to make sure that everyone believed that Green had told them the whole story. From Moose's own comments, he hadn't realized that Lucilla had wiped Green's mind. But when Green would be questioned in court, he would probably tell the hunters that he didn't even know who Dane was.

This would be a bust, but he was certain that Moose was involved. He just needed to get someone to verify it, or some other proof. A confession wouldn't hurt.

Then Dane got a telepathic communication from Adonis. *"Hey, bud, we're looking into this business with Moose. I mean, everyone. We've got your back. No hunter who sabotages another hunter will get away with it."*

"Hell, thanks to everyone. As long as someone is watching out for Jacqueline. I need to swear out a statement to Tobias."

"Yeah, her brother and one of your brothers is with her. She's speaking with Green."

Dane wondered what was up with that. If Green didn't have any memory of Dane, maybe she was filling his mind with knowing all about Dane and what had happened. Dane still would feel better if they had other evidence before they eliminated Moose for the crime.

"*When you say you're looking into it—*"

"*We're checking his cell records, his and Green's bank transactions, Green's cell records, Lucilla's, all of it. If we can find a connection between the three, we've got him. Before this, we didn't know he was involved. But the fact he was saying that Green got the story mixed up and not that Moose hadn't done such a horrendous deed says everything,*" Adonis said.

"*Okay, thanks, man.*"

"*Yeah, we got you.*"

Then Dane sat down with Tobias and told him everything he knew, even Lucilla's taunting him with the notion that a hunter had helped set up the ambush. And he mentioned how she had said someone close to him was also involved. Even though he couldn't rely on Lucilla's comments completely because rogue vampires were notorious liars, he believed she had been telling him the truth.

Tobias said, "We're keeping him in custody."

"Good. I'm going to help Adonis and the others find more evidence against him."

"So who else would be close to you who might target you?"

"Not my brothers. Maybe a hunter friend? I don't know."

"Good luck."

That was the thing about the hunter league. They had different legal rules. If a hunter was suspected to be involved in putting a hit on another hunter, they were taken into custody so that they wouldn't do that to another hunter. Hunters understood that was the way it was, so it wasn't like they would feel their rights were violated. They were well taken care of and paid remuneration if they were detained and were found not guilty.

Then Dane vanished and ended up back at Moose's house. Everyone was gone, including Wendy. He wondered if she had changed her mind about dating Moose. Which would be a good thing if he was found guilty.

"*Hey, where are you?*" he asked Jacqueline, still wanting to be with her and keeping her safe, not sure why he thought she might be in danger.

"*I'm with my brother and your brother Trey, looking into the bank records of Lucilla, Green, and Moose. You wouldn't believe that they all three banked at the same place, and yes, we found a connection between all three of them. Transfers of money were made between Moose and Lucilla and Green. He paid Green a thousand dollars, and Lucilla twenty thousand.*"

"*Which bank?*"

"*First National.*"

"*I'll be there in a minute.*"

"*Is Moose confined?*"

"*Yes, they put him in lockup.*" Then Dane drove to the bank that was also the one he used! He couldn't believe it. He'd seen Moose in there before. He was surprised Green and Lucilla also banked there.

He smiled to see Jacqueline coming out to meet him. He pulled her into his arms and kissed her. He just felt good whenever he reconnected with her. There was no one more special than she was.

"Hey, we're doing great putting together the puzzle pieces and sequence of events," she said. "The dates of the payouts all match up with the time that you were ambushed. Michael and Danai are talking to the phone company about any phone calls that were made."

"You talked to Green."

"I vampirically gave him some memories of you. He was so excited to remember working with you."

"Wow, that's great. What about the money from Moose?"

"Yes. I reminded him that Moose paid him a thousand dollars to send you into an ambush."

"What if he hadn't though?"

"Moose wrote the checks and paid both Lucilla and Green. And then you are ambushed that very night? Too much of a coincidence," Jacqueline said. "Besides, Lucilla was a known rogue vampiress. Moose had no legal reason to be paying her any sum of money."

"Yeah, I agree," Dane said.

Robert and Trey came outside of the bank with all the paperwork from their investigation. Michael called Dane then and when he answered the phone, he put it on speaker so everyone could hear it.

"So what did you learn, Michael?" Dane asked.

"Good news. Well, it's good as far as proving where everyone was at the time of the ambush, and also who was talking to whom. That's one advantage vampires have. They don't have to use phones. But Lucilla couldn't talk to Green or Moose that way. It's bad news for Moose because it proves he was in contact with Lucilla and Green before you were attacked. Moose speaking to Green was one thing, but Moose shouldn't have been talking to Lucilla. He should have been eliminating her. There's no way he can explain that away. Your brothers killed Lucilla before she could tell Moose that she had turned you instead of killing you or that she had wiped Green's mind of you or Moose's involvement in any of this."

"That's good news," Dane said.

"Moose was also near where you were turned. His cell pinged off the cell tower right there," Michael said.

"Damn," Dane said.

"Yeah, the hunter is a bastard," Michael agreed.

"He did this all so he could date Wendy?" Dane couldn't believe anyone would put his life on the line just to date a woman.

"He didn't have any insurance policies on you, did he?" Michael asked.

Dane laughed. "He better not have."

"We'll look into that," Trey said. But then he filled Michael in on the payments that Moose made to Lucilla and Green."

"Hell. Okay, I'm out of here. Tobias and a team of hunters are going to have Moose's house searched for any incriminating evidence," Michael said.

"Good. Jacqueline, do you want to go there to see what they discover?" Dane asked.

"Yes. I sure do. I want this finished, to learn for sure one way or another, though it sounds like there's enough evidence to prove he was involved in your ambush," Jacqueline said. "You don't think Wendy had anything to do with this, do you? Or her parents?"

"I really don't think so. I think she was duped like the rest of us," Dane said. "As for her parents, they were welcoming me into the family until I was turned."

When they arrived at Moose's house, hunters who were investigators, and Tobias were just leaving it.

"Did you find any evidence at his place?" Dane asked.

"Plenty. He had written in a journal how he planned to take you out, but you would never know what hit you. And no one in the hunter community would be the wiser," Tobias said. "He wouldn't confess the crime at the jail, but his journal laid the whole thing out. Later, after you were turned and your brothers killed Lucilla, he wrote that he was glad she was dead, though he planned to terminate her to clean up loose ends, and to get the bounty for her, but he couldn't believe you were still alive. Still, Lucilla was dead and that worked well for him. And you being turned had the same effect—that her parents said Wendy couldn't mate you, and he was free to date her then. Green had either been hanging out with vampires, at vampire clubs, or in general had made himself scarce, or else Moose said he would have terminated him too. The first chance he got, he planned to. Also, his phone had text messages between him, Lucilla and him and Green. He should have deleted them, but he just never thought anyone would believe he had anything to do with the ambush."

"What happens next?" Dane asked.

"He goes on trial, and once they find him guilty, they eliminate him," Tobias said. "We can't allow someone like him to sneakily attack other hunters." Then he sighed. "Okay, so I have other news. Wendy was also text messaging Moose, and he was texting her back."

"Before I was ambushed?"

"Yeah, for two weeks. After that also, but she hadn't been texting him before those two weeks."

"So something had changed."

"Right."

Dane started to think back to the time before he went on the mission to take down Lucilla. "Wendy and I had been having arguments over finances about three weeks before I went after Lucilla. Wendy spent well over what she made on hunting missions, and she was always asking her parents for money. When they cut her off, she expected me to pay for all her extravagances, but I wouldn't do it. But what if she wanted to get rid of me and save face from having to end our marriage plans?"

"She doesn't have a life insurance policy on you, does she?" Tobias asked.

"Hell, I don't know. But that would be a great motivation if she did, I had died, and she got the money for my death."

"We're taking her into custody for questioning and we'll search her financial records and home. We'll see if she has an insurance policy on you," Tobias said.

Jacqueline couldn't believe that Dane's own fiancée might have tried to have him killed. She had thought Van ditching her was bad, but this was way worse. She felt so bad for Dane. She squeezed Dane's hand. "I'm so sorry this happened to you."

"It just goes to prove she wasn't the right one for me. But I hope she gets her just desserts, if she was the one who was responsible for initiating the whole ambush scenario. All I've got to say is Lucilla must have been laughing her head off that two hunters wanted me dead, and she wasn't about to kill me and turned me instead. She would have had the last laugh, if she wasn't dead."

"I'm surprised Wendy and Moose didn't team up to try and kill you in another way to cover their tracks."

"They might have been planning it. Who knows."

About twenty minutes later, one of Tobias's men joined them at Moose's house waving a piece of paper. "This is a signed life insurance policy we found at Wendy's home listing her as the beneficiary in the event of Dane's death."

"In the amount of?" Dane asked as he read the paperwork and Jacqueline was checking it over too.

"One million dollars?" Jacqueline said. "Ohmigod, I'm really surprised they didn't try to have you killed again. Motivation-wise, that's a million reasons to terminate you."

"Yeah, and it says I signed the paperwork but that's not my signature," Dane said.

"They might have been just waiting for another opportunity, but they might have been afraid of coming after you now that you're a vampire and I'm with you so much. Your brothers also," Jacqueline said.

Tobias got a call and said, "All right. I'll be right there." He ended the call. "One of the hunters who came after you, Dane, and gave up before anyone terminated him is speaking out against those who incited the whole battle at your house."

"That's great," Dane said.

"Wendy and Moose were behind it," Tobias said.

"Aww, hell," Dane said. "But it even makes more sense why the other hunters would come after us—maybe Jacqueline first so they didn't have to fight two of us. Or maybe Wendy was jealous that I was seeing Jacqueline. And the hunters already hated us for being hunters turned."

"She might have also offered to pay some of the insurance policy money to whoever killed you and me," Jacqueline said.

"She did," Tobias said.

"Wow, she didn't have a life insurance policy on me too, did she?" Jacqueline asked.

"Not that we found, but we'll be looking into it," Tobias said.

It didn't take long for two of the hunters who had come to attack Dane at his house to explain how Wendy, Moose, Felix, and the rest of the gang who were all now labeled rogue hunters had been in on the conspiracy. They would be terminated. The two hunters who had testified against them, were released on probation, but if they got into any more trouble, they could be terminated also.

But Dane and Jacqueline were both so glad they knew who was behind all the crimes against them, that the League was dealing with them in the most terminal way, and now she and Dane were ready to plan their wedding and honeymoon and move on with their life.

25

Besides planning for their wedding that week, Jacqueline and Dane had their second therapy session, only this time Anne had a brand-new pot of coffee for them bubbling away. The meeting room still looked like it was part of an abandoned building, but the fresh coffee brewing sure smelled good. Adonis, Rachael, Michael, Pasha, Danai, and Zachary came too. But what really surprised them was that five more hunters turned showed up besides Anne, Stacey, Dane, and Jacqueline. They were the ones on the list who hadn't shown up at the first meeting. Even the vampires, Reese and his girlfriend, Eleanor, were there.

Adonis got up to speak first and talked about his parents and sister being taken hostage, and his other sister and him being turned.

Danai talked about her and Adonis's ordeal with having to turn Rachael over to the vampire Piaras. Zachary spoke about his issues with fighting the vampire when they were trying to free Adonis and Danai's parents and younger sister. Rachael spoke about becoming a vampire to be able to fight Piaras because he had claimed her for his own.

Then the newcomers to the meeting began talking about their

situations. Stacey mentioned her encounter with the vampire she had hooked up with. There were a couple of chuckles over that. No one expected anyone to be making love to one and being caught off-guard and turned. Fighting one and becoming overwhelmed, yes.

Dane was happy to announce that they had taken down Heskel, Jacqueline's maker, and that he and Jacqueline were now a mated couple—having met at the first therapy session and just hit it off. His words, not Jacqueline's. She remembered it quite a bit differently.

"We came to this meeting," Stuart, one of the newcomers, said, "because we heard how hunters had set up Dane to be terminated by a rogue vampire and how all of you and your families helped to uncover the truth. Also, because you banded together to take down Jacqueline's maker. We were reluctant to just come to a meeting and tell how much we had lost when we were turned. But you showed us that this group is something more. It's a meeting of like-minded individuals who have shared a common experience that has turned our lives inside out. And we knew we needed to be here too, sharing our strengths and weaknesses, and showing how we're dealing with all this on a daily basis."

"And also," Diane, another newcomer, said, "you proved we could visit hunters' clubs and band together. That we could even go to vampire clubs, if we mind our manners."

"And that Tobias and others on the council are trying to change the rules so that those of us who are hunters turned will have the same rules in taking down rogue hunters as hunters do," Xenia said.

"Yes," Anne said. "By meeting together, we can help each other out. I wanted to thank everyone for sharing their stories. We also have two special guests who want to share the age-old rules of vampires—protocols we need to follow while we're among vampires. She welcomed Reese and Eleanor who explained how they had been turned during the Black Death and their rules had been very much different in the early days.

The newly turned vampires gained some appreciation on how much things had improved for vampires since then.

Finally, Anne said, "If anyone is interested, I plan to start painting this building, inside and out and refurbishing it as a safe haven for our kind. I would welcome anyone's help to clean this place up and make it a meeting place that we're proud of."

"I think some family members might benefit from forming their own group to talk about how they feel about us being turned also," Jacqueline said.

"That's an excellent idea," Anne said.

"My brothers will come," Dane said.

"I think my brother will," Jacqueline said.

"Mine might," Stacey said.

Zachary said, "My father and uncles and cousins will come to show their support. They might not do it for every meeting, but just occasionally, to show solidarity."

"Okay, that's sounds good. If someone can oversee that, that will be great. Anyone who wants to paint, I'll be here at eight in the morning to start it," Anne said.

THE NEXT MORNING, everyone was there to paint, including the family members who were eager to have their family support group —even Tobias, who didn't get a lot of painting done, but did a lot of supervising. But after that, they went to sword training—everyone who wanted to—and that meant all the hunters at the building, hunters turned, and even Zeke's little band of Van Helsing hunters showed up. So did Jacqueline's parents to both her and Dane's surprise but they were both grateful to do this with everyone. Dane and Jacqueline had a great time and were creating even greater bonds. Between the hunters turned using their vampire skills to help hunters, and the humans honing their skills, the practice fighting was invaluable. After that, they had a big barbecue at Dane and Jacqueline's house and a pool party for whoever wanted to swim.

Dane pulled Jacqueline onto his lap on one of the loungers as others enjoyed the pool and everyone was eating burgers, french fries, and corn-on-the-cob and enjoying margaritas. "Wow, who would have thought we would have bonded with other hunters and human hunters in such a way after being turned," Dane said, kissing the top of her head.

"Yeah, I thought we would be shunned forever."

Dane's brothers fixed more burgers and margaritas while Jacqueline's brother was making batches of french fries. Zeke and his friends were swimming and had offered them backup anytime they needed it.

Even Danai, Pasha, and Rachael had become Jacqueline's good friends. Van had dumped Lettie and wasn't dating. But no way had they invited him to their training or party afterward.

"We should do this every other week, don't you think?" Dane asked Jacqueline as they watched everyone having such a great time.

"Yeah, and don't be surprised if our training and party afterward doesn't grow."

Dane smiled. "That works for me. Now about selling your house..."

"It's done. So you're stuck with me and Princess."

He laughed. "A situation I'm thrilled with."

"You better be. I sure am. I love you."

"I love you!"

EPILOGUE

Three weeks later, Jacqueline and Dane were at their wedding, attended by hunters, hunters turned, vampires, and even humans. Jacqueline was wearing the beautiful wedding gown she had bought when she was supposed to marry Van. Dane loved Jacqueline in her ice-white mermaid wedding dress, the form-fitting satin and lace fitting her beautiful curves. Dane was wearing his black tux that he had purchased for his wedding that had never happened between him and Wendy.

Even Van was at the wedding, wishing them well.

Jacqueline's father gave her away and her mother and father were thrilled she had married Dane. Robert was too, knowing Dane would always be there for her. And of course his brothers were there enjoying the celebration.

During the wedding reception, everyone enjoyed steak and lobster dinners—a combination of the meals they had planned for their earlier wedding plans with Van and Wendy.

Matt came up to the wedding couple's table that Jacqueline and Dane were sitting at and smiled. "Hell, brother, who would ever have thought you would have so many different kinds of people at your wedding. The Van Helsing hunters who saved Jacqueline's life,

Green, the human/blood bond informant, vampires like Reese and Eleanor, and others you've both befriended, hunters turned, hunters—all of whom admire you both."

Jacqueline and Dane smiled at him. "Who would have ever thought it?" Dane asked.

"None of us." Mathew chuckled. "I'm glad to see your family is supporting you, Jacqueline."

"Yeah, they've turned around completely."

Robert then joined them. He was taking care of Princess while they went on their honeymoon. "What I can't believe is that you're staying at vampire Reese's lakeside cottage in Minnesota for your honeymoon."

"That was so nice because they have a blood bank close by when we need extra supplies," Jacqueline said. "Otherwise, that was something we had to look for—vacation places that had sources we would need during our week there."

Anne and Shelby come over so speak to them then.

Anne said, "We're so proud of you for doing so much good for our kind. Even though Tobias had spearheaded the case of allowing our kind to take down hunter rogues, your situation where the hunters tried to eliminate hunters turned brought it to a head."

"Yeah, not that we wanted that to happen to you or any of us, but you were definitely the reason the rules were changed," Shelby said.

Then it was time for the newly married couple to have their first dance. Dane loved dancing with his wife and in their wedding duds, even nicer. She felt wonderful in his arms, all silky, sexy, and his. He couldn't wait to be with her at the cabin at the lake tonight, making love to her.

∾

After dancing with her real-life hero and though enjoying the camaraderie with everyone at their wedding—it seemed anyone who was anyone was here, except for Wendy and her family—Jacqueline was so ready to be alone with Dane.

But now it was time for her to dance with her father. Dane actually danced with her mother since his own was deceased. Her mother had really embraced him as her son, just like Robert treated Dane like a brother.

"I know I've said a million times how sorry I am that I wasn't the one to take down Heskel for turning you," her father said.

"Dad, I understand. You and Mom were just in shock over the whole business. You were feeling guilty you had let me do so much hunting on my own, but really, I had been fine with that."

"Me not going after Heskel was unforgiveable." Her father was adamant that he had been in the wrong. So had her brother, but he had already apologized so many times that she believed they were both sorry for their actions.

"Well, it's over and I ended up with my dream mate."

"I agree. Dane is perfect for you and great with our family. His brothers too. We couldn't have asked for more."

Then she finished the dance with her father and danced with her brother. She was ready to dance with her mate after that, but this time Dane's brothers wanted their dances with her, and she laughed as Dane smiled at her and them and shook his head. He ended up dancing with Anne and then Shelby. Once they had all danced, Reese danced with Jacqueline, while Dane danced with his girlfriend.

"Enjoy your stay at the cabin," Reese said.

"Thanks so much for allowing us to stay there," Jacqueline said. "We can't thank you enough."

Then she was dancing with Dane again, loving him dearly. "I didn't think I would ever have you in my arms again."

He chuckled. "My brothers figured they were safe dancing with you at our wedding."

She laughed. And then it was time for them to leave for their vacation.

Everyone wished them well, blowing bubbles as they made their way to the limousine that would take them to the airport.

They cuddled with each other in the back seat, their bags in the vehicle. After the flight, they rented the car and drove to the cabin in the woods. They realized as soon as they parked their rental car there, someone was already at the cabin. Dane called Reese and said, putting the call on the speakerphone, "Hey, you did say the cabin was at this location, right?"

"Yeah, what's wrong?"

"Someone's living there."

"That's when you use your vampiric abilities to do what you need to do. If they're human trespassers, I hope they get charged with breaking and entering."

"Will do." Dane glanced at Jacqueline.

"Vampiric persuasion?"

"You bet."

And so that's how they started their honeymoon.

Dane knocked on the door while Jacqueline waited at the side of the cabin. The back of the log cabin was up against the woods. The covered patio on the other side was enclosed with screening. The windows were small around the cabin, except for the ones on the covered patio that had a view of the lake.

No one answered the knock at the door. He looked at Jacqueline. She nodded, and the two of them entered the house in the vampire way.

Three men had been in the living room, talking about what they were going to do about the couple outside their cabin who were now inside the cabin, without opening the front door.

Dane instantly said, "Call the police and tell them you're wanted for breaking and entering the cabin and give the address."

All three men pulled out their cell phones and called the police. They gave their information about having been escaped convicts from Minnesota Correctional Facility in Togo.

That's when Jacqueline began looking through the two bedrooms and said, "There are guns and drugs in both the rooms."

Then several police cars rolled up, sirens going, lights flashing.

"You will tell the officers about all the crimes you've committed, how you broke out of jail, who helped you get here, the whole story," Dane said. "Open the door slowly, call out that you're unarmed and give yourself up."

Dane and Jacqueline appeared next to their car and told one of the officers that they were staying at the cabin but had called the police when they had discovered these men had broken into the place.

The ex-fugitives came out with their hands up and immediately began spilling their guts to the police about all their crimes. The officers looked astounded as they took them into custody.

"Reese owns that cabin," one of the officers said, looking worried that no one on the force had realized the criminals had been staying in the vampire's own place.

"Right," Dane said.

The officer looked a little concerned that Dane and Jacqueline must be friends of Reese and staying there then.

"We'll get this cleaned up as quickly as possible," the officer said.

Once the police took all the guns, drugs, convicts, and anything else that didn't belong in the cabin out of it, Dane and Jacqueline were finally ready to start their honeymoon as two hunters turned vampires in love. Staying at a beautiful, lakeside vampire's cabin for their honeymoon? Who would have thought it would come to this after their rocky beginning!

ACKNOWLEDGMENTS

Thanks so much to Donna Fourier and Darla Taylor for beta reading another vampire romantic suspense! Thanks to Lor Melvin for helping me to brainstorm the story I so appreciate all the time you take to do it! Thanks again for helping me catch my bloopers!

ABOUT THE AUTHOR

Bestselling and award-winning author Terry Spear has written over a hundred romance novels. Her first werewolf romance, *Heart of the Wolf*, was named a 2008 *Publishers Weekly*'s Best Book of the Year, and her subsequent titles have garnered high praise and hit several *USA Today* bestseller lists. A retired officer of the U.S. Army Reserves, Terry lives in Spring, Texas, where she is working on her next wolf, jaguar, cougar, and bear shifter romances, continuing with her Highland medieval romances, and having fun with her young adult novels. When she's not writing, she's photographing everything that catches her eye, making teddy bears, and playing with her Havanese puppies and grandchildren. For more information, please visit www.terryspear.com, or follow her on Twitter, @TerrySpear. She is also on Facebook at http://www.facebook.com/terry.spear. And on Wordpress at: Terry Spear's Shifters http://terryspear.wordpress.com/

ALSO BY TERRY SPEAR

Adult Titles

Romantic Suspense: Deadly Fortunes, In the Dead of the Night, Relative Danger, Bound by Danger

***

The Highlanders Series: His Wild Highland Lass (novella), Vexing the Highlander (novella), Winning the Highlander's Heart, The Accidental Highland Hero, Highland Rake, Taming the Wild Highlander, The Highlander, Her Highland Hero, The Viking's Highland Lass, My Highlander

Other historical romances: Lady Caroline & the Egotistical Earl, A Ghost of a Chance at Love

***

Heart of the Wolf Series: Heart of the Wolf, Destiny of the Wolf, To Tempt the Wolf, Legend of the White Wolf, Seduced by the Wolf, Wolf Fever, Heart of the Highland Wolf, Dreaming of the Wolf, A SEAL in Wolf's Clothing, A Howl for a Highlander, A Highland Werewolf Wedding, A SEAL Wolf Christmas, Silence of the Wolf, Hero of a Highland Wolf, A Highland Wolf Christmas; SEAL Wolf Hunting; A Silver Wolf Christmas, SEAL Wolf in Too Deep, Alpha Wolf Need Not Apply, Between a Wolf and a Hard Place, SEAL Wolf Undercover, Dreaming of a White Wolf Christmas, Flight of the White Wolf, All's Fair in Love and Wolf, A Billionaire Wolf for Christmas, SEAL Wolf Surrender, Silver Town Wolf: Home for the Holidays, Night of the Billionaire Wolf, You Had Me at Wolf, Joy to the Wolves, The Wolf Wore Plaid, Jingle Bell Wolf, The Best of Both Wolves, While the Wolf's Away, Christmas Wolf Surprise, Wolf Takes the

Lead, Wolf on the Wild Side, Her Wolf for the Holidays, A Good Wolf is Hard to Find (2024), Dreaming of a Highland Wolf (2024), Mated for Christmas (2024)

SEAL Wolves: To Tempt the Wolf, A SEAL in Wolf's Clothing, A SEAL Wolf Christmas; SEAL Wolf Hunting, A SEAL Wolf in Too Deep, SEAL Wolf Undercover, SEAL Wolf Surrender

Silver Town Wolves: Destiny of the Wolf, Wolf Fever, Dreaming of the Wolf, Silence of the Wolf; A Silver Wolf Christmas, Between a Wolf and a Hard Place, Home for the Holidays, Jingle Bell Wolf

Wolff Family Lodge Wolves: You Had Me at Wolf, Wolf on the Wild Side, A Good Wolf is Hard to Find

Highland Wolves: Heart of the Highland Wolf, A Howl for a Highlander, A Highland Werewolf Wedding, Hero of a Highland Wolf, A Highland Wolf Christmas, The Wolf Wore Plaid, Her Wolf for the Holidays, Dreaming of a Highland Wolf

Billionaire Wolf Series: A Billionaire in Wolf's Clothing, A Billionaire Wolf for Christmas, Night of the Billionaire Wolf, Wolf Takes the Lead

White Wolf Series: Legend of the White Wolf, Dreaming of a White Wolf Christmas, Flight of the White Wolf, While the Wolf's Away, Mated for Christmas

Red Wolf Series: Seduced by the Wolf, Joy to the Wolves, The Best of Both Wolves, Christmas Wolf Surprise

Wolf Novellas: Day of the Wolf, Seal Wolf Pursuit, Wolf to the Rescue, Night of the Wolf, United Shifter Force

***

Heart of the Jaguar Series: Savage Hunger, Jaguar Fever, Jaguar Hunt, Jaguar Pride, A Very Jaguar Christmas, You Had Me at Jaguar, The Witch and the Jaguar, Dawn of the Jaguar

***

Heart of the Cougar Series: Cougar's Mate, Call of the Cougar, Taming the Wild Cougar, Covert Cougar Christmas, a novella, Double Cougar Trouble, Cougar Undercover, Cougar Magic, Cougar Halloween Mischief, Falling for the Cougar, Cougar Christmas Calamity, Catch the Cougar (Halloween Novella), You Had Me at Cougar, Saving the White Cougar, Big Cat Magic

***

White Bear Series: Loving the White Bear, Claiming the White Bear, Bear of a Halloween

Grizzly Bear Series: Bear in Mind

***

Wolves of Old: Wolf Pack

Heart of the Huntress Series: Killing the Bloodlust, Deadly Liaisons, Huntress for Hire, Forbidden Love, Deadly Liaisons, Vampire Redemption, Primal Desire, Huntress Unleashed

Vampire Novellas: The Siren's Lure, Vampiric Calling, Seducing the Huntress

***

Comedy Romance: Exchanging Grooms, Marriage, Las Vegas Style

***

Science Fiction: Galaxy Warrior

Young Adult Titles

The World of Fae:

The Dark Fae

The Deadly Fae

The Winged Fae

The Ancient Fae

Dragon Fae

Hawk Fae

Phantom Fae

Golden Fae

Falcon Fae

Woodland Fae

Angel Fae

***

The World of Elf:

The Shadow Elf

The Darkland Elf

Warrior Elf

***

Blood Moon Series:

Kiss of the Vampire

Bite of the Vampire

Night of the Vampire

The Vampire Chronicles Series:

The Vampire in My Dreams

Demon Guardian Series:

The Trouble with Demons

Demon Trouble, Too

Demon Hunter

Non-Series for Now:

Ghostly Liaisons

The Beast Within

Courtly Masquerade

Deidre's Secret

The Magic of Inherian:

The Scepter of Salvation

The Mage of Monrovia

Emerald Isle of Mists

www.ingramcontent.com/pod-product-compliance
Lightning Source LLC
Chambersburg PA
CBHW070739180626
46818CB00007B/2914